# Tears
## of the
## Shamrock

# Tears of the Shamrock

An anthology of
contemporary short stories
on the theme of Ireland's
struggle for nationhood

Edited and introduced by
DAVID MARCUS

WOLFE PUBLISHING LIMITED
10 EARLHAM STREET · LONDON WC2

ISBN 0 72340490 9

Printed in Great Britain by
Ebenezer Baylis & Son Ltd.
The Trinity Press, Worcester, and London

# Contents

# Modern Times: Northern Ireland

# Introduction

IRELAND's history—both martial and political—has all the ingredients of the classic, never-ending serial story. The latest instalment—which has held the stage in Northern Ireland for some three years—is the first to have taken place since television came of age, and the consequent world publicity has created a world demand for background information to help the non-Irish man-in-the-street gain some understanding of The Irish Question. That demand has been, and still is being, met with a fast-moving flood of facts, surveys, opinions, assessments, analyses, pamphlets, books, etc., and yet in all this instant history one is not getting down and through to the flesh-and-blood people whose lives and personal dramas are its real source. The explanation is that that sort of story is recorded, not in two-minute interviews, but only in literature—the blood in history's veins. In Ireland's case, the literature that has in modern times consistently sounded the heart-beats of her history is to be found, mainly, in short stories by her greatest writers. This book is a selection of some of the best of these stories.

Broadly, they fall into three periods: the first ended with the establishment of the Irish Free State in 1922; the second was the short period of the Civil War; and the third is the more contemporary period leading to the 1970s. It might be said that in each of these periods the Irish were fighting a different foe—in the first it was the British, then each other, and in the last, themselves; and the stories in these pages illustrate this thesis.

In the first five the British Crown is the foe, and one can gather—particularly from the stories by Daniel Corkery, Mary Lavin and Sean Lucy—to what extent Fenianism/Republicanism was rooted in all sections of the native Irish people. These, naturally, are nationalistic stories but being the work of artists, not propagandists, jingoism never intrudes—except perhaps in Corkery where, in any event, it doesn't obtrude; and this section is climaxed by one of the greatest and most compassionate anti-war stories ever written, Frank O'Connor's classic, *Guests of the Nation*.

Then come three stories of the Civil War—in which the Irish fought each other. O'Flaherty shows what a civil war does to the

7

flesh, O'Faolain what it does to the spirit, and Denis Johnston's comedic interlude is an example of the Dubliner's (but not the countryman's) penchant for self-de-mythicisation (see O'Casey and Flann O'Brien—the latter, though born in Northern Ireland, was surely a Dubliner by mutual adoption).

The final twelve stories cover the period from 1923 to the present day—but the first five refer to conditions south of the Border and the last seven to north of the Border. It is the first group of five that depict the Irish fighting themselves, in that these stories reflect the disillusion and disappointment which many sections felt with the way Southern Ireland developed. Patrick Boyle gives a chilling account of an internal execution in the I.R.A., John McArdle uncovers the plight (economic, social, spiritual) of so many forgotten veterans of the War of Independence, Helen Lucy Burke lifts the stone on political enmities that were a common relic of that War, and Tom MacIntyre, with one searing whip-flick, shows how vividly Ireland's past is her present.

The final seven stories have Northern Ireland and events there as their background, and they combine all three classic Irish foes, the British, each other, and themselves. These stories need no individual introduction or explication. They illustrate cause and effect—as seen from one side only, it is true, but, strange as it may or may not seem, no body of literature has emerged reflecting the views and loyalties of the Northern Ireland Establishment. One may postulate artistic or political reasons for this imbalance but such a fruitless exercise has already been overtaken by events—the kind of event which leaps from the pages of J. J. Coughlan's *Incident*; the kind of event that is, as I write, the common tragedy for all Irishmen.

David Marcus
Dublin, Ireland
February, 1972

# Towards
# The Irish Free State
# 1900-1922

# The Ember

## DANIEL CORKERY

NOT VERY long before the opening of the war I was sent to organise the Volunteers in the north-west corner of County Cork. I made my way to a hamlet called Monera, a windy spot on the lower slope of a mountain—a handful of white-washed walls, sharp-edged, staring, against a background that was rough and dark with heather and rock, hillside and hamlet unrelieved by a single bush or tree. It is a place where everything is hard and black and challenging. For my purpose, it was dead and cold, yet at the same time, strangely enough, still quite proud of the fight it had made for the land in the early 'eighties. Only in few districts in those wild days were such wild deeds done; they tell of them still, but they do not boast of them, the stories are too terrible for that. If you are strange to the ways of the people you will blurt out, 'But which of the brothers shot him?' and you will be answered quietly, almost without surprise, 'Well, now, isn't it a queer thing, the only man could tell you that, he's in America with twenty years.'

It was strange to find such a place apathetic. Doubtless it had carried the rough and overbearing methods of Fenianism into the Land League struggle, and later had carried the methods of the Land League, hardly less terrible, into the politics of a tamer day, only to find them at last discountenanced; whereupon it probably ceased to trouble itself any more with such affairs. The old fight, the Gael against the Sassenach, that was what those windy hillsides were set for. The fragments of Irish verse that even still fall unexpectedly from the lips of the old men, the crafty proverbs they fling at one another when bargaining at a fair, half jocose, wholly earnest, their vague and seemingly fool-simple answers if they cannot fathom the reason of your curiosity—that immemorial fight it was that gave birth to this hard wisdom, this ceaseless alertness, these fierce songs.

I gathered the young men into a lamplit schoolroom, and spoke to them of the Volunteer idea: we must preserve the liberties of Ireland. The fine phrase fell on them as though they were figures of

11

lichened stone, their clothing of stiff, undyed homespun suggesting the image. I soon made an end, weakly and despairingly.

I had a young lad with me, I was breaking him in, he was presently to be sent off organising elsewhere. Well, he then took the matter in hand, and he put the violence of the 'prentice boy into his oratory: he spoke of the impending attack of the Orangemen of the North on us all as soon as ever Home Rule was granted. We must arm against that attack, we must preserve our newly-granted liberty from assault, even with our lives! From his fine voice, the fine attitude he threw—head raised, shoulders stiffened, pillared legs—one would have expected a burst of wild applause—a surging forward as if our rough-built platform must be rushed. No such thing! Only a dull staring and a silence; in which presently a great old figure rose up— I can still see the keen old face, the eagle eye, deep set, the sharp bones—rose up deliberately, faced us a single moment, and then, almost carelessly, threw his right shoulder at us, making for the open door, uttering a vast sigh, 'Home Rule!—Oh wisha! Wisha! Wisha!'

A ripple of laughter went through the men; they were too shy or too unused to such proceedings to make any freer with us. My 'prentice boy was put out. The old eagle's contempt had left him unable to put any thought at all into intelligible words; and I was not anything better. The crowded men below us—the lamps over their heads struck light only on a nose or chin—were shyly turning their heads to one another, and had begun to whisper. I stood up, and at the same moment, in a far corner, a wild-looking figure crouched up against me, fumbling at the air with a great hand, thick and hard from the plough. I saw him making an effort to speak, the light on his working chin. 'Young man,' he gasped, 'that's not the talk old Muirish wants at all—aw!—you're mistaken, you're mistaken entirely.'

The gesture of his open hand downed us for simpletons.

'What is it Muirish wants?' I cried, angrily. I had roused a lion.

'What is it?' he roared at me. 'You know very well what it is.'

His eyes stared, as if they had no power to shift away.

They were now all on their feet, catching his hands, cheering him —and drawing away from us until a gap lay between us. One of them then stepped into that lamp-lit space. 'Go on!' ''Tis all right!' 'Go on, Jack!' a hundred phrases were whispered behind him. He was a splendid bit of manhood; my eyes measured him.

'You mean well,' he said; 'we're not saying otherwise; but Muirish —that man that's gone out—we're all one in these parts—there's no difference—we're all one—we're all one. . . .'

His speech had become incoherent. We were to understand that Muirish had spoken for all. Suddenly there was movement among them, one of them made for the door, just as Muirish had done, and as if rejoiced that someone had discovered what was just the right

12

thing to do, they all at once rose up and crowded eagerly after him into the open air, leaving us there in the empty room with a ripple of laughter in our ears.

I looked at my 'prentice boy—he was so white and rough with passion that I thought it well to keep silent. After some intentional delay on my part, we lit our lamps and cycled away into the dark, that ripple of laughter still in our ears; and I thought how much better it were for an evangelist in Eirinn to leave a place under a hail of turf sods than in such a manner, how he would have more chance of being listened to if ever he returned.

The only comfort I could pluck from the occurrence was the thought that I had at last found the key to somewhat similar occurrences in other places in Munster. In certain baronies we would get a royal welcome, in the very next barony to these we might be treated as in Monera. 'Why,' I now said, with my eyes eating up the stony way, 'there's a Muirish in every one of them!' And then, my mind running on, I saw that every extreme movement in Ireland leaves behind it a remnant of its broken army—an old workman in a factory in a city, a cobbler in a little shop in a village, or, like Muirish, a shepherd in a hut on a mountain-side—great old hearts that preserve to the next generation, even to the second next, the spark of fire that they themselves had received in the self-same manner from those that long since were gone home into the silence. Old embers that seem extinct and grey, Oisins dreaming of the heroic dead they have so long outlived, ineffectual in a thousand cases, except to raise jeers and laughter, but in others, where natural powers of will and mind aid them, not ineffectual in hardening the thoughts of a hillside or the thoughts of a little group of men in a corner of a big town, making of them a rocky soil for newer ideas.

\*  \*  \*

Before I was sent again to Monera the world was far into the great War, and volunteering had become a dangerous propaganda. The 'old fight' was again on. England's difficulty was Ireland's opportunity, and England had plainly never been in such difficulty. Those of us who had learned to read the Irish poets, their well-knit, stone-hard, wolf-fierce songs were ever in our ears; they haunted us, those songs, and indeed the men themselves, they looked at us from the dark with wild eyes; we remembered what they had suffered, we knew what had wrung those songs from them.

> *Life conquereth still; as dust the whirlwinds blow—*
> *Alexander, Caesar, and all their power and due!*
> *Tara is grass, and Troy itself lieth low—*
> *It may be that Death will reach the English too.*

Such lines haunted me. I awoke at night with them flowing from my lips. They were on my tongue as, for the second time, I rode of a nightfall into that death-still, white-walled hamlet—the bearer of a fiery cross.

At the first cry of real war Monera had leaped to arms; witnessing it, Muirish doubtless had thrown a score of years from his back. As fine a company of Volunteers as I had ever drilled awaited me there. Their Captain's name was Felix MacSwiney. Felix is a name common among the MacSwineys. He praised the courage of his men, yet, I could see, he stood afraid of them: he could not hold them in. He had tried to quench that spirit in them by dint of what he called Barrack Square drilling, and now they were growing restive under it. Could I bring variety into their soldiering?

We—he and I—determined on some skirmishing among the rocky hills. We planned a sham attack; that night we would carry it out. He would have his men assembled in a secret place in the hills, I would be guided to it.

It was a moonlight night in August, full of tenderness and breadth, and distance; and this, and the nature of the country—the huge rocks, fallen on their faces, spreading a cloak of shadow, the heathery slopes unresponsive to the moonlight, unlit by it, the leaping streams, flashing and carolling, tireless in both—I will never forget it all—the night, the land, and then the men, the creatures of this land! Young colts were not so touchy, so eager, so highly-strung, so intelligent with spirit: their large eyes flashed at me in fiery earnestness. They would bark their shins against the juts of rocks, rush unthinkingly through streams and boggy hollows, and leap across chasms that frightened me. We surrounded, or rather half-surrounded our objective, and most skilfully took it—a difficult massif that culminated in a huge leaning turret of rock, called the Priest's Tower. Then we rested—where? Between it and the gaping chasm below, on a narrow slope of grass cropped and recropped by those mountainy sheep that our skirmishing had sent, with timid cries, scampering into the dark nooks. Above us, blanched in the moonlight, leaned the towering mass, not unlike an epic priest, indeed; below us, just a mass of shadow, with here and there a flank of rock, bright with moonlight; and far under the shadow a leaping stream whose voice was so constantly in the ear that one forgot it—except in the silences. We looked down into it, this floating, veil-like shadow, and leaning over us that rock-built priest also looked down into it, but with greater intentness, it would seem.

Not long could the lads keep silent. They began to see companies and companies of marching men in these various shadowings. They described their movements, spied out their objectives. Presently they began to drill them—these legions of their restless minds. 'Eyes right! Left turn! Form fours!'—hundred voices (I thought I caught

14

a hint of mimicry here and there in them), a hundred cries, and the rocks, awakened, bravely sent them back. At last I made them a little speech, and Felix MacSwiney dismissed them.

He and I then cut across the defile by a path I had not suspected, crossed the brawling stream, and made up the opposite slope of mountain. I was to sleep in his place. Leisurely we climbed, full of earnest talk, yet not unconscious of the beauty of the night, now so full of calm and silence after the chatter and the ringing cries. We struck at last into a little path. It widened. We came on the traces of a wheel track. Higher up, the mass of a little hut, thatch to the ground it seemed, silhouetted itself suddenly against the sky. A tiny little window, dimly lighted, hid itself in under the thatch. I stepped up.

'That is?' I said.

' 'Tis there he lives,' he answered, 'Muirish.'

'Alone?—Not alone, there?' I asked again quickly.

'Why, yes, except for the dogs—a terrible breed. Whenever he goes into the village for supplies, they walk at his heels. I tell you I wouldn't be the man to take a try out of him and they about; they'd tear you.'

We stepped towards it silently; we were soon within its shadow.

'We'll strike in,' MacSwiney whispered.

'I'd rather not,' I answered. An encounter with Muirish would quite exhaust, I felt, whatever little energy I had left. At the same time, I strained my eye against the little window, there was but one pane in it. I saw a couple of huge dogs, one a greyhound, lying about the hearth flag in the glow of the turves, curled up in sleep. Otherwise the place was empty. As I looked, the hound drew his shoulder-blades up around his ears, slowly and tensely, then suddenly relaxed them and lay still.

'There's no Muirish here,' I whispered, when I was sure of the dog's sleeping.

'But, look! the candle is lighting; he's not in bed.' MacSwiney raised his head; he was wondering where Muirish could be.

'He must be at my place,' he said at last.

The saying was not too welcome to me; but I withdrew my eyes from the glowing and stilly interior, and made forward with him, not speaking a word. We were just about to step from the shadow of the hut into the flood of light when he stopped me.

'There! there!—look at him!'

His back towards us, dark as a pillar-stone, Muirish was standing on a boulder, a long staff in his hand. He was as still as the Priest's Tower itself, which we could see beyond him, standing high and lonely across and above the shadowy defile. The collie dog that stood beside him, its nose in the air, was no less still and alert than its master. The two together, they made a group very like that rocky tower beyond them. That at its own side and these at their side were holding vigil above the tumbled rocks, the waters and the shadows. The old man's attitude was one of listening, listening rather than peering: it was for that reason we held ourselves so still. He slowly raised his head, turned round, and leaning heavily on the staff, descended from his point of vantage. We kept our stillness. He passed close to us, the dog sidling along at his right hand. He lifted the latch and went in, closing the door behind him.

'He was listening to our drilling,' I said softly.

'That's it, surely,' there was relief in my companion's voice. I could not help peeping once again through that dim pane of glass. He was seated on the settle, straight opposite my eyes. He sat rigid, intensely gathered into his thoughts. His sceptre lay beside him; his two fists fiercely clasped his shapeless felt hat against his breast. It was not a restful attitude, yet it would hold him for hours, one felt. He was far removed, whether into the past or future, who could say? Or whether he was making a prayer?

\* \* \*

I will now tell of my third meeting with him. It was late in the summer of 1916—memorable year. I was on the run, or, in the phrase that goes through so many centuries of Irish history, I was on my keeping. I had been in the Post Office in Dublin during the whole of Easter Week. I had seen the ring of fire closing in around us, had gazed, fascinated, at the scared cats walking rather leisurely from the burning houses, had tended a friend whose reason had given way, had taken drugs to preserve my own. Now the police were chivying me and a thousand others, it would seem, from place to place. I had escaped them a hundred times. As an old woman I had walked through a party of them, I cursed them in Irish that they should think a son of mine one of them rebels! I opened the door to them in a country hotel—it was in Claremorris neighbourhood— and helped them to search it, through and through. But one tires of being chivied from place to place in one's own country, and the idea that you will eventually be nabbed grows stronger and stronger, robbing you of the sense of rest; and I firmly believe what I have heard a friend of mine say—one who had led the police a very pretty dance indeed, right round the Five Fifths of Eirinn—that a feeling of voluptuous ease ran through him, as if his whole body smiled, when, after six months of it, a rough hand gripped him one night by the shoulder and held him fast.

It was in the city of Kilkenny—a place where the young men have the voice of history ever in their ears—that the thought came to me, 'I will rise up at midnight and make for Monera in the quiet hills, and there I'll heal me of my grievous wound.' I do not know why or how it is, but when one is living as I was then, acting a part with which so many books of Irish history had made me familiar, a touch of the boy-heroic comes back into one's thoughts, into one's language (at least when alone), and no matter how much one may smile at the quaint phrases, they do bring a certain healing with them, as if one had made a fragment of song. To live dangerously is, I suppose, to live lyrically. My only wound was a deep melancholy that I could not shake off, let me rush as I would from place to place; and no sooner had I spoken the silly words than I really did feel some lightening of the strain of flight. In Monera, at MacSwiney's house, I would lie lost until my nerves were strong again. (And at the back of my mind there was perhaps, at the same time, the sly, malicious thought that I, who had risked all in the burning Post Office, would find out Muirish and fling his scornful 'Wisha! Wisha! Wisha!' back into his teeth.)

I reached Monera, and made my way to MacSwiney's house at Kilsheelan. I walked into it just as his people, his mother and two sisters, were making the place ready for the night. They had had no tidings of me, had thought of me as among the unnamed dead, for they had come to know that I had never been deported to Frongoch with the other prisoners, had never appeared before a court-martial. How their Irish welcome went round my heart! Gaels of the Gael, they received me, spoke to me, welcomed me, slaved for me in the true Gaelic spirit, and quite without knowing it. Their forefathers had been doing as much for the hunted Gaels of four centuries— those shadowy, unnamed warriors, poets, stragglers, kerns, gallow-glasses, tories, rapparees, outlaws, white-boys, fenians—who would crowd on my imagination, unbidden, unlooked for, often in the most listless moments, the name of a bridge or hill, a flash of princely pride in a peasant boy's face, or a verse of vengeful curses from an old bedridden crone summoning them with rude potency from their haphazard graves. My heart opened. 'Yes, I'm tired, God knows it, but . . . let us sit at the door, Felix, the night is too beautiful for sleep.'

We did so, sitting there by each other on two boulders that helped to buttress the gable of his house. We talked quietly, even sadly, for our movement was broken, perhaps finished, yet not dishonoured; and the moon sloped across the Priest's Tower, looking at us with shining, wondering face, as a child might. We sank into silence, as if to let it go by; and I knew the blessedness of a somewhat wistful peacefulness.

Nothing is easier than to overstay your time on the heights; a moment later I had said to my friend: 'And Muirish? There's no change in him? He's the same cross-grained, cranky old fenian? We were only play-actors, he said. . . .' (That malicious thought was uttering itself.)

Felix rose up. He would not answer without a moment's delay.

17

Silently he lifted himself, slowly, in tune with the thought that held him. Then, smiling, he stretched out a hand to the moonlit wall and took hold of a snail that was climbing it obliquely, leaving a silvery track; without looking at it he threw it behind him into the greenery. He wiped his fingers on his trousers. In my mind I was repeating: But Muirish? Muirish? However, Felix making no movement to sit again, I rose up beside him, saying: 'There's a heavy dew, and you'll be rising early in the morning.'

''Tis better go in,' he said.

He slept that night on the settle, surrendering me his bed. He showed me into the little room, placed the candle on the table, and turned to go. He paused then and said: 'As for Muirish—I'm getting frightened about him.' His eyes looked at me. An unpleasant thought swept a shadow across my mind. I dismissed it with a toss of my head.

'Nonsense, I'd trust him; he's too old to change.'

'Oh—not that! Not that! Muirish is true as steel. But he's not himself—that's what I mean. I'm uneasy about him, and he has no one with him.'

I thought a moment.

'We'll go to see him,' I said.

He bent his head. 'I'd like it,' he replied.

'Tomorrow night, then.'

It was delicious rest I had that night. I was too tired to sleep, and indeed I hardly wished for sleep, my nerves were so perceptibly losing the sense of strain that had held them so long. I felt it slipping from me, quietly, quietly. And when I quenched the candle, above my eyes was the rich glow from the turf losing itself in the dark thatch and the dark roof-timbers, very warm and mellow. And sometimes, with a very thrill of delight, I would feel my mind open itself to the vision of the hundred thousand hilltops that were outside those cosy walls—I would feel the moonlight bathing them in peace, and the cold stars above them. 'Monera, Monera, Monera!' I whispered for very love of it, my spirit growing all the time from strength to strength. At last—there was Muirish as I had last seen him, a slab of stone with a skirt of shadow about it! Yet Monera! Monera! was what I still whispered while still beholding in vision the intense old figure watching and waiting above the vale, as if Monera and he were one. I ceased my lyric word. I went into a deep stillness. Then I lifted myself on an elbow, and stared through the little window, on which the turf glow was dancing into the rich blue that lay beyond. But when I settled down again, with firm assurance of sleep, I knew what I should do next day. At breakfast I said:

'Felix, as I came through Duhallow I discovered that the Volunteers were beginning to pull themselves together. . . .'

He caught at my hopefulness:

18

'Do you wish it? Do you wish it?' he blurted out, in the quick way of the southron.

'Why shouldn't I wish it?' I said.

'I was afraid you'd throw cold water on it, you who were in the fight, who saw the surrender.'

That very day Felix went around the valleys, and that same night we had as large a muster as before at the Priest's Tower. My commands rang bravely out; and the lads drilled with a seriousness that had had no place in our previous drillings. I went cold to think suddenly that the next fight, if ever it came, would be fought out to the cry, 'Revenge!' Almost in silence we dismissed the company, and, as before, made for the lonely hut.

A voice suddenly startled us:

'You'll come in, you'll come in?'

Muirish was making down on us, with a nervous swiftness in his plunging forward that frightened me. Felix spoke as quickly in reply:

'We were going up. Be careful, Muirish.'

'Ah—you were drilling, I heard ye, I heard ye. Say it, say it?' He was shaking with excitement.

'We were,' I answered.

'I do be deceiving myself, I do be fancying I hear voices.' His hand went across his brow.

'It was our voices, the lads, you heard.'

'Come in, come in, I want ye.'

We followed him in.

'Felix,' he said; ''tis the same?'

He looked at me, he looked at Felix.

'The same,' Felix answered. 'And he was in the fight in Dublin—he's a hunted man.'

'Ah! Ah!' He was caressing my hand. 'Sit there, my son.' I sat down.

'Felix,' he said, 'maybe you'd leave this young man and myself the freedom of the place for a while?'

Felix sprang up.

'Since you wish it, Muirish.' There was respect and understanding in the voice.

''Tis kind for him to be like that,' the old man said when the door had closed again on us.

The place was not different: there was his staff close to his hand; there were his dogs—the great hound's body taking beautiful curves in his sleep; but the old man was shrunken away a good deal from what he was when last I saw him, and his boldness of address was gone.

'Wait now,' he said, and I could see the concentration it needed before he could say what was in his mind: it was visible in his rapt stillness, in his bent brows. After a long and, for me, nervous pause, my mind running on Felix's fear, he said:

'Ye held out a week.' He was, of course, talking of our fight in Dublin. There followed a deeper silence than before. Then he thrust his head forward into mine, and his fierce old eye held me.

'Cogar,' he said, 'it wasn't any shortage of powder and ball betrayed ye?'

I was glad to be able to answer him:

'Oh, no, not at all—except, except in one place, perhaps, and even there——'

'What's that—what's that you're saying?'

He had clutched my shoulder, I was trembling to his trembling.

'In one place . . . where young Heuston was, they say the ammunition ran out. . . .'

His clutch fell off and he sat back, a figure of stone, before me. For a moment I know that he neither felt nor saw nor thought; I grew afraid.

'But what did that matter?' I rushed out my words. 'In either case he would have had to give in when the general surrender came. No, Muirish, no; it was not want of ammunition——'

'You're sure?'

'I'm sure.'

'You're sure, young man; you're sure of it?'

His clutch was on me again, he would shake the truth from me.

'As sure as I'm sitting here.'

His grip released, but not the force in his voice.

'Then what was it?'

'It was want of, want of . . . everything! Want of men, want of . . . everything!'

'I suppose it was,' he said, very quietly. ''Tis I should know.' His face turned away from me, and I was glad for it. His lips pursed themselves out, and when, after long thought it seemed to me, he spoke again, it was not to me alone he spoke:

'Them big guns of theirs, a mint of money wouldn't buy even one of them.'

'You may sing it,' I said.

He thought again:

'But that's no excuse for me.'

I did not understand him. I said nothing. He rose up.

'If I go into that caboose of mine,' he said, nodding at a little ramshackle room he had made at the gable end away from us, 'you'll maybe wait till I come back to ye?' It was an old man's speech.

'Of course I'll wait,' I returned.

He went slowly across the earthen ground, and I soon heard him searching for something in the little place beyond. . . . He was coming. A little ticken bag it was that he held out to me.

'Take it,' he said.

There were coins in it and notes.

20

'No, no; I couldn't dream of it. Things are so dear, you'll want it; besides——'

'Even if I did want it,' he smiled at me, 'I couldn't touch it; 'tisn't mine to make free with. Them that entrusted it to me—they're cold this thirty years—'twasn't for that they left it with me. Take it, young man, and sorry I am I didn't make it over on ye when ye were here before.'

'That's fenian gold,' I said.

'It is, and for fifty years I have kept my grip on it.'

'It will get to the right quarters, never fear,' I said bravely.

He was smiling to himself. He spoke now in a quiet voice:

' 'Tis queer,' he began, 'but 'tis often I found myself speaking to that little bag of gold the same as if it would be a Christian man. "Ye're useless," I'd say to it; "I may as well throw ye into the river. If I hand ye over to the young men nowadays 'tis on the hounds they'd spend ye, or on the goaling, maybe." That's what I'd say to it; and yet I was wrong; 'tis them very same young lads made the fight in Dublin, so they tell me. But an old man's mind, 'tis a queer contrivance.'

' 'Tis wanted now worse than ever,' I said.

That pleased him.

'Do you tell me so? And it wouldn't have made any difference if I gave it to ye before?'

'Not a bit of difference,' I said.

' 'Tis a great consolation ye're giving me. I was broken with thinking on it. I tell you, a man can be too wise and too careful and too mistrustful. And I was always like that. But 'tis in ease I'll lay my head down in my empty house this night. Good night to ye.'

He had hobbled with me to the door. I paused. I looked up into his face; I suddenly thought of what I would say to him; I would hearten him with those four lines that were ever and always in our thoughts, of how decay would as surely come upon the English as it had come upon Alexander and Caesar:

> *Do threasgair an saol is do shéid an ghaoth mar smál*
> *Alastram, Cæsar is an mhéid do bhí 'na bpáirt;*
> *Tá an Teamhair 'na féar is féach an Traoi mar tá,*
> *'S na Sasanaigh féin, dob' fhéidir go bhfaighdís bás.*

He drank them in, he swallowed them with open mouth.

'Again! Again!' he said; and again I repeated them, I knew he was making them his own. I knew, too, I had given him in perfect form the whole burden and pressure of his thoughts. He turned in, wondering how that could be—wondering, yet comforted, comforted for ever.

21

# The Patriot Son

## MARY LAVIN

IT WAS a couple of years since Sean Mongon had set foot in Conerty's shop, so what did he want now?

From the window in the gable-end Matty saw him swinging down the street, and the next minute he walked in the doorway and up to the counter.

'Will you display this in your window, Matty, like a good chap?' he said casually, and he unrolled a cheaply-printed poster, the paper like a blotter, on which lettering had made a blurred impress.

As far as Matty could see it was a play-bill, with a crude picture of a woman in green in the middle of it, and the wording seemed to be in Gaelic, or in Gaelic letters. He partly guessed what it was, and he glanced uneasily across the shop to the haberdashery, where his mother was serving a customer. She never liked any of the Mongons. And although Matty could remember a time when their own shop was just as small as Mongon's, before the new barracks was built opposite them, yet his mother always referred to the Mongon's shop as poky and smelly, and she wondered how people could eat anything that came out of it.

But the Mongons did a good trade; particularly with the farmers from outside the town. Once when he was a child he had asked his mother why the country people did not tie up their traps and donkey-carts in their yard, like they did in Mongon's.

'Because we live opposite the barracks,' she said promptly, and pulling out the till from under the counter she ran the silver through her fingers like water. 'One R.I.C. man coming into the shop with his shilling in his hand is better than twenty traps tied in the yard and the ledgers swelling with debt! God bless the Constabulary!' she said.

And when, at that moment, through the window, they saw the Head Constable walking down the street, with his stomach out and his arms swinging, she shook her head.

'Isn't it a terrible thing to think a fine man like that would have enemies?' she cried.

23

For a minute he didn't know what she meant.

'Some people never can let bygones be bygones,' she went on. 'It's the Fenian bitterness. It's like a disease that's passed down from father to son. God protect us all!'

He knew then that she was having a dig at the Mongons, because Sean's grandfather had been a Fenian. The Mongons had his uniform in a box on top of the piano. Sean brought him in to see it one day after school. But he had been careful not to tell his mother about it. She was death on the Fenians.

'Oh, you know nothing of what people suffered in those days, son!' she said.

They were in the kitchen at the time of this conversation. He was sitting at the kitchen table doing his homework and she was standing stirring a pot on the range. But she was looking out of the window and after a few minutes she gave a big sigh.

'It would be a terrible thing if it were all to break out again,' she said softly, almost to herself, and the look on her face frightened the wits out of him.

'What do you mean, Mother?' he cried.

She turned to him.

'I'm afraid, son, there is some of the bad old seed still in the ground,' she said. 'The Head Constable was in the shop a while ago and he told me something: there are men drilling in the hills again!' She looked away for a minute, and then she turned and looked steadily at his face. 'Thank God you're only a child still,' she said.

Matty squirmed uncomfortably on his chair; he wasn't such a child at all: the following year he'd be leaving school.

It was just before the end of that year that the Gaelic classes were started. They were to be held at night in the school-house, and Master Cullen was giving his services free as teacher. Needless to say, Sean Mongon was the first to join them.

'Oh, come on, Matty,' he cried. 'Join up! We'll have great sport at them. And afterwards, to warm us up, the Master says he'll push back the benches and have a bit of a dance. It'll be great sport. The Master knows all the old jigs and reels, and the Walls of Limerick, and the Bridge of Athlone. We'll have the best of times!'

For his own part, Matty was inclined to go to the classes, just to be in the swim of things. But he was uneasy about what his mother would say. He knew her views on the Language Revival.

'What next?' she demanded, when she first read about the Gaelic League, and the language classes that were being held in Dublin. 'Do they want to drive the people backward instead of forward?'

He'd never have the face to tell her he was going to the classes.

'I'll have to ask my mother,' he said, shamefacedly.

Sean looked at him, at first incredulous, then contemptuous.

24

'Maybe you ought to ask leave of the R.I.C. as well!' he said. 'It wouldn't do to offend them, they're such good customers!'

Matty felt his face flush all over. And Sean saw it.

'Sorry!' he said, surprisingly, and his smile, that was always so winning, flashed across his face. 'I'm a bit on edge these days,' he said. 'No hard feelings, eh? It's just that we don't want the R.I.C. poking their noses into the classes. The next thing they'd be branding them as illegal organizations! They're terrible eejits in spite of everything.'

Did he fancy it, Matty wondered, or did Sean look at him slyly before he sauntered away. Anyway, he did not go to the classes that winter. And the next winter, although he had left school, he did not go to them either, in spite of the fact that by then the Gaelic League had got itself accepted all over the country, and had established centres in every town and village. As for Master Cullen's classes, they were held openly and boldly. Nearly all the young people in the town went to them, and some of the older people used to go down and stand at the door later in the evenings to look at the dancing. The R.I.C. themselves used to stroll down sometimes and stand in the doorway.

Matty's mother could hardly object to him joining the classes then, but she kept him so late in the shop, and he was so dog-tired when the shutters were put up at last, that by the time he got down to the schoolhouse it wasn't worth while doing anything but hang about the door with the other onlookers. It all seemed very harmless; and he was aware only of the heat and the dust, the sweating faces of the men, the clapping of hands, and the stamping of feet.

But there were other nights when it was too late to go down at all, and then, looking out of the window as he was going to bed, the schoolhouse lights, twinkling across the roofs of the other houses, troubled him, as he used to be troubled when he was a child by tales of faery lights that shone on the darksome bog to lure men to folly and destruction.

It was on those occasions that he was glad his mother had kept him from getting involved in what went on down there. He had begun to wonder if it was all as innocent as it seemed.

And now this play? Was it only what it purported to be; a little entertainment: or was there some undercurrent of intrigue? He looked dubiously at the play-bill he was being asked to display.

But Sean saw his hesitation, and he laughed.

'There are no flies on you, Matty, are there?' he said, and he winked, but affably, and not with any pronounced discretion. Suddenly he leant across the counter. 'It's supposed to be *The Colleen Bawn*,' he said, 'but we've doctored a good few of the lines. Do you get me? It's going a bit further than Irish classes, and jigs and reels, but it's time we showed more guts. Things have changed, haven't they?' he said, and he laughed, and jerked his head in the direction of the barracks across the street. 'We've moved forward since the time we were nervous about the classes at night in the schoolhouse! They know all about them now; or at least they think they do: but they're afraid to take any action in case they might mistake the sheep for the goats. They don't know who to trust, and who to mistrust. And that's the way to have them. I hear they're even beginning to distrust each other. And so well they might. Did you see in the papers where an R.I.C. man down in——'

But at this moment, across the shop Matty caught his mother's baleful eye upon him, and he saw that outside the counter there was a small child with a halfpenny in its hand.

'Excuse me a minute, Sean,' he said awkwardly. 'I'll have to wait on this youngster.'

He hoped he'd go. But instead, Mongon took up the play-bill.

'I'll put this in the window for you. I think that's the best place for it, don't you?' he said, leaning into the window and draping it across the job lot of cups and saucers that were being offered that week at a special price.

When the youngster had gone he turned back to Matty.

'Do you know what I was thinking?' he said, and he chuckled. 'I was thinking that it's a picture of you we ought to have on the poster—a bloody little shopkeeper—and a banner around your arm to say that you were the Ireland of Today!'

Matty stared at him. Was he trying to be funny, he wondered. If so, it was a poor joke, specially when his mother could probably overhear everything that was said.

But Sean didn't seem to be joking, or at least he didn't look very light-hearted.

'Poor ignorant Ireland,' he said suddenly, in a low voice, as if to himself. 'Poor ignorant Ireland that doesn't want to be saved!'

Matty shrugged his shoulders. He must be cracked, he decided. And he wished harder than ever he would go about his business.

But still Sean stayed, leaning against the counter and looking around him.

'It's a long time since I was here, isn't it?' he said. 'But it's the same old place I see. You haven't made any changes, have you?' His eyes strayed idly, it would seem, all over the shop and came to rest on the green baize door at the end. 'That door leads into the house, doesn't it?' he asked, pointing to it. 'Isn't that the way we used to run in and out the yard?'

'I suppose so,' said Matty flatly. He wanted to get rid of him. He could feel his mother's eyes boring holes in his head.

At long last Sean went.

'Well, so long!' he said inconsequentially, and sauntered out.

Partly drawn by the old fascination that the other always exerted on him, and partly to avoid meeting his mother's eyes, Matty went over to the gable window and looked up the street after him, but he could hear his mother crossing the shop and almost immediately she came and stood beside him looking out of the window.

'You ought to be more careful about who you're seen talking to nowadays, Matty,' she said, lowering her voice although they were alone. 'The Sergeant was telling me that several people in this town are under observation. I shouldn't be surprised if Sean Mongon was one of them. I hope he won't make a habit of coming down here. What did he want, anyway?'

Before he had time to tell her, however, she had seen the play-bill draped across the things in the window. Instantly she whipped it out of the window.

'So this is what brought him down here, is it?' she cried, and as she read it her eyes blazed. The next minute she tore it savagely in two bits. Matty was sure she was going to turn on him, but instead she spoke surprisingly gently, almost wheedlingly to him. 'I suppose you were right to let on we'd display it,' she said, 'but wouldn't it be an awful thing if you forgot to take it out of the window and the Head Constable passed and saw it?'

Matty looked at the torn poster. She had made it seem as if he would have torn it up if she hadn't done so.

It might be uncomfortable all right, he thought, to have had it in the window if the Head Constable came into the shop. But it would be ten times more uncomfortable if Sean came back and did not see it displayed anywhere.

What would he do then, he thought miserably? He wished she wouldn't interfere with everything he did. She was an interfering woman if ever there was one. Ever since he was a child. She had dictated to him in everything. Always the same, he thought bitterly. He'd never get a chance to say or do anything while she had her foot on his neck. And he'd never get away from her, because she'd never let him look at a girl, much less marry one, and bring her into the house. There wasn't a girl in the whole town that would have the courage to marry him, and come into the same house as her.

And then, freakishly, there flashed into his mind the image of the girl on the play-bill, and although he had only barely glimpsed her, it seemed as if she had some enormous strength or power that would vanquish any enemy—even his mother.

A paper woman! I must be cracked, he thought, and he set his mind to think of some excuse to make to Sean if he happened to find out they hadn't displayed the poster.

But it was to be three or four weeks before he met Sean again. And the circumstances of the meeting put the poster out of their minds.

One evening Matty had finished up earlier than usual and he had

27

taken it into his head to stroll down to the schoolhouse to watch the dancing. But when he turned into the school-yard to his surprise the schoolhouse windows were dark and the building was empty. He went up to the door and rattled the handle. The door was locked. As he raised his head though, on the sweet spring air he got the faint smell of cigarette smoke, and looking down he saw that the gravel under his feet was marked with fresh footprints and the tyre-marks of bicycles. So they had been here! But why had they gone so early?

Uneasily he moved away from the black shadow of the building into the open moonlit yard. A ridiculous notion passed through his mind: the faery light! Had it lured them away—the gay throng—away from their warm habitations to the cold inhuman hills and the dark glensides?

A shiver ran over him, but he laughed at himself for his foolishness, and he went home to bed.

But he slept badly, disturbed by dreams of faery hosts and lonely glens, and woke when the dawn was coming up the sky. He got to his feet and went to the window.

There was nothing to be seen but the sight that had met his eyes every day since he was born, the ugly concrete walls of the new barracks, and the corrugated roofs of its sheds and out-houses.

Then, just as he was about to get back into bed, between the barracks and the corrugated sheds, he caught a glimpse of the green, dawn-lit fields beyond the town. And as they had never done in full daylight, those green fields called to him; a clear, sweet call. Unquestioningly he answered their call and in a few minutes he was stealing down the stairs so as not to waken his mother. In the street he paused too, and glanced uneasily at the windows of the barracks. The Constabulary, if they happened to see him, might think it odd of him to be out so early. For the rumours of men drilling were no longer so vague. All over the country men were drilling. And people who were not involved were careful to avoid doing anything irregular. But there was no one on foot in the barracks, and he passed unnoticed out of the town.

About two miles outside the town there was an old deserted castle sunk deep in the middle of a lush, waterlogged field. Sometimes in summer he used to cross the field and wander in its dark passages and vaulted arcades, but in winter it was a lonely place, and only served him as a landmark. At this point he usually turned homeward. This morning too, he was about to turn upon coming in sight of it, when his eye was caught by a thin feather of smoke wavering into the air from one of the thick buttressed chimneys. And almost at the same moment, on the other side of the hedge beside the road, he heard a sound of splashing in the little stream that had for some distance run along beneath the hedge.

Impulsively he called out and bent over the hedge.

To his astonishment it was Sean Mongon. For a minute it looked as if he was going to turn tail and run, until he saw it was Matty.

'Oh, it's only you!' he cried.

But Matty was stung to the quick by his tone.

'Who did you think it was?' he cried, nettled. 'Did you think it was the Constabulary?'

Still, he didn't expect Sean to take him up so sharply.

'How much do you know, Conerty?' he said.

Matty stared. There he was—Sean Mongon—whom he had known all his life; there he was—on the other side of the hedge too—a puny figure really, as slight as a girl, and looking—he noted—haggard and worn-out as if for want of sleep, and yet he was in some way a menacing, a dangerous figure.

But it was not fear that surged up in Matty, it was a grudging admiration.

'I don't know anything,' he said truthfully, even sadly. 'I wish I did!' he added with such fervour that Sean stared at him. 'Yes,' he cried recklessly, 'I wish I was in it—whatever it is, that is going on— I always did, but my mother came between me and it—the Movement, I mean,' he said out boldly.

Sean continued to stare at him.

'I wonder do you mean that,' he said soberly. 'I think you do. And I'm glad to hear you say it—at least. But it's too late now, Matty. You'll have to continue to be one of the onlookers.' He was making a reference to the Gaelic classes, thought Matty, and he felt ashamed of how early his caution had taken command of him. 'Go back to your shop, Matty,' said Sean then, gently, but with a tone of authority. 'The shopboys will soon be taking down the shutters and your mother will be wondering why you're not up and about your business. She'll be knocking at your door. Get back as fast as you can. You don't want her asking questions, do you? That wouldn't help us, you know!' He himself glanced to the east where the rapidly rising sun was striking through the trees as through a grille. 'I must be getting along,' he said in his casual way, and he began to stride back in the direction of the old castle, leaving Matty to stare disconsolately after him.

He was in his bare feet, Matty noticed, with his trousers rolled up, and the wet grass had stuck to his ankles, striping his white skin.

It was something that he had been trusted to keep silent, he thought bitterly, as he walked homeward in dejection.

In the town the shutters were still up on the shop-windows, and when he reached his own street he saw that even the barrack door was shut, and there was no smoke from its chimneys. Except for an old man pushing a handcart of straw in front of him, there was no sign of life in the whole street. And even the old man had a grotesque aspect, like a figure out of a dream, with his ragged clothes and his ramshackle handcart, one wheel of which was wobbling about as if at any moment it would roll from under the cart and let it down on the cobbles.

Amused, Matty followed the wobbly movement of the old man and his cart, and then, just as he was about to turn in to his own door, the wheel, with one last wobble, fell flat on the street, and the cart came down on its axle with a clatter, up-ending its load.

As the old fellow let out a loud volley of oaths, Matty laughed heartily. And from the barrack door which opened, one of the constables poked out his head and laughed also, and nodded across at Matty. There seemed no more to the incident, and Matty went into the shop to begin his day's work. Later in the morning, as he was lending a hand in taking down the shutters, he saw the old fellow trying to raise the wheel, but when he put his hand on it, the rotted wood came away from the rim and the whole thing fell flat again. So, after some words with the police, the old fellow shrugged his shoulders and went off up the street, presumably to find some means of putting his vehicle into motion again, or of getting some other conveyance to cart away the straw that, in the crisp breezes of the morning, was beginning to blow about the street. Already it had almost blocked up the mouth of the barracks.

But the police, as they came in and out of the shop during the day for their cigarettes and tobacco, took it in good part. It was his own mother who took it badly.

'A nice thing!' she cried, a score of times, or more, as she went to the window and looked out. 'A nice mess!'

It was when she was looking out on one of these occasions, late in the day, that Matty saw her frown, and looking over her shoulder he saw Sean coming down the street.

'What does this fellow want now?' she cried, and as if unable to endure the sight of him, she left the shop.

As for Matty, the incident of the upset cart in the street had taken his mind off the events of the earlier morning, but now, at the sight of Sean, his heart began to beat violently.

Had Sean come to look for him? He hurried forward to meet him. But Sean was calm and matter-of-fact.

'Hello, Matty,' he said easily, naturally. 'Can you spare me a few cans of paraffin oil?'

It was a bit of an anti-climax, and it made Matty cranky. He had only come on business. Ostentatiously, Sean threw down a pound note on the counter.

For a minute Matty hesitated. There was only a small profit on paraffin oil, and it was a troublesome commodity; it had to be kept outside the shop in the lobby near the yard door, and anyone handling it had to be careful not to contaminate anything else with

30

the smell of it, and so it was usual only to supply it to regular customers.

'I'm sorry to bother you,' said Sean, as if he sensed Matty's reluctance. 'I'm not a customer, I know.' He paused. 'We usually get it in Flynn's, but—well, they didn't have any today,' he finished lamely.

'Oh, that's all right,' said Matty, and he began to take off his shop-coat. 'Have you got a can?' he asked, unable to resist making a compliment of giving it, but he regretted it next minute, as Sean began to make excuses. 'Oh, it doesn't matter, it's all right,' he said hastily. 'This way!' And he went out through the baize door into the little lobby where the big storage tank was kept. There he stooped down, and picked up a can. 'How much will I give you?' he asked.

But Sean was hardly heeding him as he stared around the lobby.

'Oh, fill it up,' he said casually, and going over to the door leading into the yard, he opened it and looked out. 'It's the same old place,' he said. 'I remember it well. I could make my way around here blindfold!' He stepped back and pointed to the other door, the house door, as it was called, that was opposite the baize door. 'That's the way into the front of the house, isn't it?' he asked. 'We used to go out into the street that way.'

But like the last time he heard them, these reminiscences of their boyish friendship sounded empty to Matty. He ignored them.

'It holds a gallon,' he said, putting a cap on the tin, and holding it out to him.

But Sean was peering into a dark corner behind the tank and the wall, and seeing a few old cans thrown together in a heap, he took up two with one hand and three with the other.

'Fill these up too, will you?' he said casually.

Matty was both irritated and surprised.

'Have you a car?' he asked, as he filled the fourth can.

'No,' said Sean shortly, 'but I'll manage them all right.' He took up two of the cans. 'I'll take these with me, and I'll call back for the rest. You can leave them somewhere convenient to the street. Better still, I'll leave them all and I'll get some kind of conveyance for them. But it may be late in the evening; the shop will probably be closed: you'd better leave them in the front hall, if you can manage it. Just inside the hall door would be the best place,' he said. Then he straightened up. 'Have you got that?' he said, in what Matty thought an impudent manner for one who was under a compliment to him. But evidently there was no offence meant, because Sean stooped and lifted two of the cans. 'I'll give you a hand,' he said. 'We may as well leave them out there now so there'll be no mistake.'

'Oh, there's no need,' said Matty.

He was wondering what his mother would say to cluttering up the front hall, but he decided that she seldom went into the hall anyway,

31

and that it was so dark and dingy she might not see them even if she did go into it. He would prefer to put them there himself a little later. 'That'll be all right,' he repeated as he put the lid on the big drum of oil. Without waiting for him, Sean was about to go away, but on an impulse he turned around.

'Is there much left in the drum?' he asked.

Thinking he wanted more, Matty slapped the lid down ostentatiously.

'A few gallons,' he said, 'but I can't give you any more. I can't empty the tank for you. It wouldn't do to let our regular customers go short.'

'Oh, I don't want any more,' said Sean. 'I have more than enough. I just thought it might be no harm if that drum was empty tonight.'

Matty looked up. It was the kind of cryptic remark that lately he seemed to be hearing on all sides, and he was inclined to let it pass, but all at once a thought flashed into his mind—but it was too preposterous.

'You're not—you can't mean——?'

And then he remembered the cart-load of straw that still, at that late hour, stood outside the barracks. And without another word being spoken he knew all.

'You can't do it!' he cried. 'You'd be mad to try it!'

'Don't shout, you fool!' snapped Sean. Then, with less urgency, and speaking in a lower voice, he looked at Matty with something approximating to admiration. 'I didn't think you were so quick on the uptake,' he said, but he had moved nearer, and feeling him uncomfortably close in the small lobby, Matty looked down and saw that from his pocket there protruded the point of a gun. 'I only meant to do you a good turn, Matty,' said Sean, 'but take care you don't turn good into bad.'

Matty swallowed hard.

'I don't know what you mean!'

Immediately Sean stepped back from him.

'That's the right attitude to take!' he cried, slapping his thigh. 'I told you nothing. And you guessed nothing. See!'

Matty kept steady, although he was appalled.

'All right, Sean. You can trust me.'

Visibly, for a moment, the other relaxed.

'I know that,' he said. Then he got tense again. 'It's not only my own trust I'm putting in you,' he said savagely, 'but the trust of twenty or thirty men—perhaps even the trust of the whole Movement——'

Although he had begun to shudder violently, Matty's eyes did not falter.

'I know that,' he said steadily.

'I think you do,' said Sean soberly. Then suddenly he gave a kick

32

to the cans. 'I won't wait to leave them out in the hall,' he said. 'You can do it for me.'

It was only an errand fit for a child, but it carried the implication of an enormous trust. Speechless, Matty nodded his head. His face was deadly white, and seeing that, perhaps, Sean put out a hand and rested it upon his shoulders.

'Look here,' he said, 'I told you nothing—we've agreed upon that —but there's no reason why you shouldn't empty that thing down the drain'—he nodded at the drum—'and as a matter of fact, you might find some reason for being away from here tonight. Not that I think there'll be any danger, but I admit the street is narrow and a lot depends on the way the wind is blowing—you'd never know—— You could take anything valuable with you—money or the like— nothing that would be remarkable, of course—nothing that would attract attention.'

The suggestion was meant to be friendly. Matty knew that. But at the same time he felt there was something belittling in the concession.

'Thanks, Sean,' he said quietly, 'but I think I'll stay here.' Then, with dismay, he remembered his mother. 'Oh, what about my mother?' he cried. 'I suppose she ought to be got out of here?'

Sean only shrugged his shoulders.

'If you can manage it without it appearing odd,' he said, 'to her, I mean.'

'You can leave it to me,' said Matty, wanting to reassure him. 'I won't make a false step.'

Like sunlight in the dingy lobby, Sean's smile broke over him.

'He that is not against me is with me, eh?' he said, and turning back towards the shop, he went out that way.

Picking up the cans in twos, Matty carried them into the hall.

It was dark there all right, and getting darker too, because already the day had begun to fade. With a little feeling of relief he realized that at least there would not be long hours of suspense. Whatever was to happen would be likely to commence soon enough. It was not yet time for the shop to close, but the shutters had already been brought in from the yard and stood against the wall. Once the shop was closed he need not worry if his mother found the tins. It would appear fairly reasonable then that they were left convenient to the hall door.

The shop was over an hour closed when she discovered them.

'Matty, what is all this paraffin doing here?' she cried.

Matty was at the back of the house, afraid that he might give anything away by looking out too often if he were in any of the front rooms. But just as he wondered what answer to give to her, with every nerve thrilling, his strained ears caught a sound in the street. Ignoring all but that sound, he stood transfixed.

His mother too heard something.

'Was that a shout?' she said, coming back from the hall, her face white. 'Listen!' she commanded. 'The Constabulary are challenging someone!'

But there was another sound, fainter than shout or challenge which caught Matty's ear. It was a faint crackling sound, and the next minute he smelled something smouldering. Then his mother too got the smell.

'Oh, good God!' she cried. 'It's a fire—it's the barracks. The barracks is burning!' She made as if to rush out to the street, but he put out his arm. She strained to pass him. 'Will you let me pass?' she cried. 'What's the matter with you?'

It was something in the expression on his face that answered her.

'Oh, God!' she whispered, no longer straining against him. 'It's not malicious, is it?'

Malicious! It was a word out of the civilian life from which, without knowing it until that moment, he had already long since passed. Malicious: more than all the words that one by one had measured the difference between them since he was a child, this one word showed them to be sundered for ever. But he said nothing. Feverishly she was making the Sign of the Cross.

'Oh, God help them!' she whispered. 'Caught like rats in a trap.' Then, suddenly, her thoughts veered. 'Which way is the wind?' she cried. 'Are the sparks flying this way?' She swung around towards the lobby. 'The oil drum,' she exclaimed. 'One spark would be enough——'

But before one thought was completed, another had taken its place.

'Those cans in the hall,' she cried. 'Get them out of there.' And when he didn't move, she darted towards the door. He caught her by the arm.

'Leave them there, Mother,' he said. 'They may be coming for them any minute.'

They? She turned around. And then the full enormity of the truth broke over her.

'Oh, God in Heaven!' she cried. 'It wasn't for that you sold the oil? You don't mean to say you knew all about it and you never told me—we could have warned them—we could have——' She wrung her hands. 'We could have done something,' she groaned. Then all at once she pulled herself together. 'Perhaps it's not too late yet. Those cans in the hall, you say they're coming back for them! I'll spoil their game there, anyway. Never mind about what's done: it can't be helped. Please God they'll never find out you had any hand in it——' She had broken away from him and reached the door, but at the door she couldn't help turning around. 'Oh, how could you do it?' she cried. 'Haven't I been all my life warning you against the like? Do you think a handful of fools are going to get the better of trained men like the R.I.C.? The Constabulary will make bits of them, I tell you. And you along with them if they find out about these—but with God's help they won't find out. Here, give me a hand!'

As she caught up the cans, however, the voices in the street became louder, and there was a sound of running feet followed by a crash against the door behind which they stood, and then heavily, frantically, two fists beat against the panels.

'It's Sean! He wants the cans,' said Matty, 'and he's going to get them too,' he cried, as he tried to drag the cans out of her hand.

But the fists beat against the door again.

'Let me in, for Christ's sake,' said a voice. It was Sean all right. 'Don't mind the bloody cans, but open the door.'

Both together, mother and son, let go the cans, and the oil spilled over the floor. In a second the hall was filled with the acrid smell. But they had both let go from different motives.

'Don't dare to open that door!' screamed the woman, and she threw herself forward.

But Matty had got there before her and the door was open.

Almost falling over them, Sean lurched forward.

'Why the hell didn't you open the door?' he rasped, as he stood panting and trying to get his breath. 'Close it now, you fool,' he cried as, hypnotized, Matty stood looking at him. 'Close it and lock it,' he cried. 'Put on those chains,' he cried, pointing to the rusty old chain that hung down inside it but was never used. 'The whole thing failed,' he said, when he got his breath.

Matty looked up.

'I didn't——' he began.

'I know that,' said Sean, and he gave a bitter laugh. 'You'd be a dead bunny now if you did! No, it was the bloody straw let us down—it got damp, I suppose, out there in the street all evening; it wouldn't catch when we went to set fire to it—it only smouldered, and the beggars smelled the smoke. But we got away,' he cried. 'That's one good thing. And if we failed tonight, we won't fail the next time. Listen!' he said. 'They're searching the street, but I don't suppose they'll think of trying here.' He gave the dry laugh again. 'They'd never suspect you of being a patriot!' he said.

But there were sounds of someone approaching.

'What's that?' cried Sean, alert again.

'They're coming over here,' whispered Matty, the sweat pouring from him. 'Listen!'

Sean listened.

'I was expecting too much,' he said calmly. 'I'll have to get moving,' and he ran into the back lobby. But as he passed the oil vat he stopped. 'I'll throw this thing in here in the dark,' he said, and dragging off the old whitish trench-coat that was a like a second skin to him, it was so constantly on his back, he threw it behind the oil

35

drum. 'I'll travel lighter without it,' he cried, 'and besides, it's too easily seen at night.'

They had forgotten the old woman, but as, at that moment, there was a violent knocking on the door, they became aware of her again. She was dragging at the chain and bolts.

'It's all right, constable,' she was shouting. 'I'm opening it as quick as I can. He's gone out the back way!'

Like a flame from the abortive fire, Matty felt shame run over him. But even in that preposterous moment, Sean put out a hand and laid it for an instant on his shoulder.

'It isn't your fault,' he said, and then as the yard door opened before him he prepared to plunge into the darkness. But on the brink he hesitated, and suddenly he turned back. 'Wait a minute! She may have done me more good than harm,' he cried. 'Prop open this door, like as if it was usually kept open—with that,' he cried, indicating with his foot an old iron weight on the floor. Then, with a last reckless laugh at Matty's stupefaction, he slipped behind the propped door.

It was so simple. Matty stared stupidly. He hardly understood, but it was a chance, he could see that; even if it was only a small one. As long as his mother hadn't seen them! But the oil drum was behind them, and the view from the front hall was broken by the cross-door that had almost closed over after them. It might work out!

A tremendous excitement possessed him. If only there was something he could do! If he could put the police off the scent!

Suddenly, behind the big oil drum, he caught sight of the old trench-coat bundled into a ball. He rushed over and pulled it out.

The next minute he heard the front door crash open and the Constabulary rushed into the hall.

Pulling the old trench-coat over him, Matty ran to the yard door, but on the threshold he waited for an instant till he heard the running feet reach the cross-door. They must catch a glimpse of him. The next minute he was racing across the yard.

What was it Sean planned to do? To get across the sheds and out into the next yard, and from there into the next, and the next?

As kids they used to scramble up on the sheds, but although he made for the lowest of them, the little pig-shed in the corner, he found he wasn't as agile as he used to be. Still, he managed to grasp the ragged edge of the corrugated-iron roof and frantically he began to pull himself up on it. As his head came level with the tin he saw that although the yard was dark, it was dark from being overhung with buildings; above him the sky was brilliant with stars. And all at once, compounded out of the very stars it seemed, a spirit of elation flowed through him, such as he had never before experienced. And it seemed as if something that had eluded him all his life was all at once within his grasp.

Pushing his hands further forward on the rusty iron, and letting go his foothold, he exerted a tremendous pressure and heaved his body upward. But the next moment the house behind him was filled with shouts and then—as loud as if they had rained into his mouth, his eyes, his ears, the air was shattered with shots. And at the same moment he felt a ripping pain run like the jag of a knife down the side of his belly.

They got me, he thought, as he fell forward on his face. But the thought did nothing to dispel his elation which seemed only to grow greater, until in a kind of intoxication of excitement he lay there, feeling the hot blood trickling down inside his torn clothes.

It was a few minutes before it occurred to him that it was odd that they had not come looking for him. From where he lay, by raising his head, he could see the house, and the lighted door through which he had run out. No one had come through it! They were all still inside, the police, and—yes—his mother too. With difficulty he raised his head: they were bending over something. At first it looked like an old sack of potatoes, but as it twitched suddenly he saw it was a body: the body of Sean Mongon.

And at the same moment, the pain that had lacerated him tore again into his guts, and putting down his hand he felt the jagged fang of the rusted iron that had cut into him like a bullet.

Then his mother's voice came clear above the other voices, that now were in the yard below him.

'He's up there on the top of the pig-shed!' she cried, and her voice was wheedling. 'He must have been frightened out of his wits!' she said.

And coming nearer, she called up to him:

'Come down out of that, you gom!'

# The Talker

## SEAN LUCY

CON BRADY was known by the other men in his company as 'the Talker', but the name was a compliment rather than a sneer, because talking was his job.

There would be a meeting in the dark kitchen of a mountainy farm and the plans for the next raid or ambush would be discussed. William Burke, the commandant, thick-set and dark, would listen to the swift speech of the younger men and then, slowly and with certainty, he would shape a complete, trustworthy plan in the active minds of the others. Afterwards he would turn to Con.

'Con, boy, we don't know what that platoon of the Essex is doin' in Ballingeary. They may be wise to us. Will you try an' find out, lad?'

Con had this job because of his college education: his ability to appear the semi-anglicised West Briton. Also, he looked anything but a rebel—a gangling youth with fair hair and a way of looking you straight in the face while he told the most atrocious lies. He would turn up at the danger spot riding a bicycle and wearing a bowler and gloves: the young Cork city clerk out for the day. He also carried an umbrella strapped to his cross-bar. No Englishman will suspect disloyalty in the possessor of gloves and an umbrella.

He would dismount in the village street and walk up to the officer standing uneasily near his men—men who formed little suspicious groups in the silent roadway.

'Nice day, Captain. Your men look a smart lot. Hope this doesn't mean any damned rebels in the area?'

'No, just routine. I don't expect trouble. Still you never know with those bastards. Got to be bloody careful.'

'Well, you men are doing a fine job. It's nice to see you keeping an eye on things. Cigarette? We'll soon have these rebels put down with your help. Only a bunch of hooligans against you. The Irish people disown them really, you know.'

'Still, they get a lot of passive help round the country. It would be easier for us if there weren't so much sympathy.'

'Well, let's hope it will soon be over. I must be off. Got to be in Cork before curfew, you know. I suppose you'll be going to Macroom for the night?'

'Yes, we move in half-an-hour. Nice to meet someone friendly. Good luck.'

'Good luck.'

In summer the mountains, tall around the road, shook in the heat as the straggling villages dropped behind. Dust and warm smells of gorse and heather. In the winter, mud, mist, and thin rain. But always the farm again and Burke's curt: 'Well?'

'Two platoons under a captain, sir. Two lorries. Returning to Macroom. That should make our way to Skibb clear.'

'Fine. We'll go tonight. But I've another job for you, Con, boy. Go up to the City tomorrow. There's a rumour that new troops are arriving, and I don't trust Hegarty to let us know if any are moving west. Stay here tonight, lad.'

It was always like that. It wasn't that Con wanted to fight, but he felt lost and detached. Sometimes the lying talk with the puzzled, angry British troops seemed to infect his soul with the treason he mouthed to them. He acted so wholeheartedly that, as he talked to this officer or that, he *became* the 'loyal' small-minded clerk. He laughed fiercely sometimes, remembering, with bitterness, what he had said to some Englishman under the shadow of his own hills. For there was no doubt in his mind that he was on the right side. Many of the Irish fighters were fools—and worse; some were narrow-minded to an extent that appalled him; but they were all seeking a true thing. Under different forms it was seen by them, but it was a true thing.

And Con stayed on the outskirts in a misty region of words, hating the ambiguity, the dirtiness of his soft talk with the British. He was afraid of fighting, but he would have preferred it.

The summer of the blackest fighting came and in the first week of July the Column moved in on Cork City. Most came in as private individuals, somehow finding friends or relations to stay with in the west and south-west of the town. Headquarters, with most of the arms, was in a big deserted house near the small village of Waterfall, which lies in a hollow below its little chapel, about three miles south-west of the city. Something big had been planned, and Burke's Column was to take part. Only Burke himself had some idea of what was supposed to happen. Whatever it was it was taking a long time. Two weeks and still nothing, with Burke worrying about the discipline of his scattered men.

Con's father had died two months before, and the rent of the rooms in Cockpit Lane had lapsed, so at first Con didn't know where he would stay. He did not wish to ask any of his college friends, partly because he was poor and proud, and partly because he didn't want to mix the two worlds in which he lived: the I.R.A. and the university. Surrounded by the atmosphere of one, the other always seemed as unreal as a dream, the legend of which, though strong in the heart, had nothing to do with living.

Stephanie Forde, the girl he was in love with, belonged to the world of the university. She loved him too and there were times when they seemed perfectly at one in their love. Yet he had not told her where he went when he disappeared from Cork for months on end. Her father, a well-to-do Cork doctor with the conservatism of his class, accepted him rather grudgingly as a possible future son-in-law, and her mother openly liked him. And it was at the Forde's house in the Western Road that he finally stayed, when they discovered that he had nowhere to go.

'I suppose we couldn't let you starve in the street,' shouted Dr. Forde, pompously humorous.

In the evenings, except on Friday when he cycled out to Waterfall by the back road, he helped Stephanie with work for her B.A. exam., which was coming soon. They would sit at the table in the dark Victorian dining-room surrounded by books while the evening grew quiet in the tree-lined Mardyke outside the window and the fading line of the hill above Sunday's Well marked its roads and houses with soft lights.

Stephanie was small and dark and unpredictable, and he loved her more all the time. She would work in great bursts, completely unlike his steady concentrated study. Sometimes he would watch her head bent stiffly over the page or her small hand charging up and down the lines with her green pen held in what seemed a hopelessly cramped position. Occasionally he answered the questions she flung at him. Sometimes he would talk to her of poetry or drama, and forget with his mind everything except the dancing of ideas and images, only his heart always remembering her presence. And often they would do no work at all, but make love and love talk in the summer dusk.

Inevitably, after a week of her company, he told her about his job with the I.R.A. To her it sounded like a brave and clever game, because he unconsciously acted the part of the daring spy to her as he told her. Her approval made him forget the reality of his I.R.A. life, and while he was with her his petty spying seemed to him also a gallant adventure. Only when he reported to Burke at Waterfall on Friday evenings did the degrading reality weigh on him, and in consequence his admiration of his leader gave way to resentment and dislike. The practical details which constantly engaged Burke's attention seemed small and mean now.

'No signs of special activity, Con?'

'No, sir, nothing.'

'O'Malley and Lehane were arrested the other day for being out after curfew. They were drunk. Did you hear that?'

'No, sir.'

'Luckily they weren't carrying guns and they're all right. They swear they gave nothing away. That's all for today, Con; you can go now. Keep your eyes open, lad.'

'Yes, sir. Thanks, sir.'

Stephanie of course wanted to help him.

'Con, couldn't I do something to help? I'm sure I could find out things for you.'

Automatically he smiled the smile of the man who could find out anything by himself—the master spy.

'Ah, I know the ropes pretty well. There isn't anything you could do that I couldn't do just as well myself.'

'But I could go to dances that the British officers were at and get them to tell me things.'

'You could in my foot! Don't let me see or hear of you dancing with any bloody Englishmen.'

Besides his anger and anxiety there was a growing subconscious fear of letting the realities of his two worlds meet. This fear was his nightmare. It was a senseless but powerful terror.

*　　*　　*

It was a dry hot summer evening with an oppressive ceiling of low pearl-grey clouds. The small city was still with the stillness of lethargy. Fine dust lay on the pavements and on the leaves of trees unstirred by wind.

The Doctor was up at the Bon Secours Hospital. Mrs. Forde was out. It was the girl's half-day. After tea Stephanie and Con, with the house to themselves, were trying to do some serious study.

Someone knocked authoritatively on the front door. 'I'll go,' said Con. He kissed her on the forehead and going out into the hall he opened the door. Facing him was the tall Major from whom Con had once extracted information in the course of a casual chat on a road near Kilmurry. Behind him a section of Tans. He looked hard at Con for a very long minute.

'Is Dr. Forde in?'

'No. I'm terribly sorry, he won't be home for about two hours.' Con's voice rang loud and unreal in his own ears. 'Could I give him a message?'

'What is it, Con?' Stephanie came out of the dining-room. She stiffened when she saw the uniforms. Her face became stubborn and hostile. Con noticed with a distant part of his mind that she didn't even look pretty then. Hard and sharp.

'The Major is looking for your father,' said Con. He was conscious that he was smiling diffidently. The old habit.

42

The Major saluted Stephanie awkwardly. 'Miss Forde? I have been instructed to question your father about a man who died while he was attending to him. A wounded man. But, if your father is out, tomorrow will do. It's only routine.'

He talked in a rather dead voice, and as he did his eyes moved again to Con's face, puzzling his memory with familiarity. Con smiled vacantly at him.

'I think you'd better call tomorrow,' said Stephanie flatly.

'Right. Thank you, Miss Forde.' Then, slowly, to Con, 'I've seen you before. Can't place you though.'

'Probably around the city,' suggested Con. He tried to talk lightly, but the words seemed heavy and slow.

'I don't think so,' said the Major. 'I was stationed on Macroom until last week.' He paused, his eyes distant. Then suddenly he turned full on Con, shooting a question.

'Know Waterfall?'

The familiar name shocked Con. But this was his game. The Major was not certain of him. He was trying to snare him.

'Waterfall,' he said thoughtfully, 'yes, I believe I do, Major. A small place four miles or so from here. About south-west I should think. Why?' Push the questioning back at the bastard.

'Oh, nothing much. Just that we heard there were some rebels skulking there. South-west, four miles, you say?'

A poor cover-up, this seeking for information.

'Yes. I think so. One of the turns off the Bandon road if I remember rightly. Sorry to hear that those rascals are so close. I hope you deal with them, Major.'

'If they're there we'll get them all right. Thank you, Miss Forde. I'll call on your father tomorrow. Good evening.'

Con closed the door quietly and stood for a minute looking at nothing, feeling Stephanie's anger in the dark hall.

'Come into the dining-room before you talk,' he said.

Beside the table she turned on him in anger. He was glad it was anger and not scorn with a cold hard face.

'Con, how could you! Sucking up to that man, with a soft voice and your talk of "rebels". And telling where Waterfall was!'

Con felt that she was very, very far away. Out of touch. He fought with this feeling, trying to be aware of her view.

'To answer you categorically,' he said stiffly. 'First, as I've explained before, they've got to be lulled by "loyalty"——'

'Yes,' she said, 'but not like *that!*'

He felt like asking her how it was to be done then, but he knew it would be no good so he went on:

'Second, I had met him before and got information out of him, and he nearly remembered me. Thirdly, he knew where Waterfall

43

was. He was testing me. Our company H.Q. is, or was, there. Somebody split on us.'

'Your headquarters is there?' her voice was high.

'Well, anyway, it was, but I expect the British are either on their way there now or else they raided it last night. It's not far. It's the place I go to report on Fridays.' He sat down heavily.

'But, Con,' said Stephanie, looking at him in angry astonishment, 'surely you're going to do something. Surely you're not just going to sit there!'

A great weariness came over Con. He seemed anchored forever to the hard chair and the soft carpet, in the dark room with her anger and ignorance. But he forced himself to speak.

'Arra, do what, girl?' he said. 'Even if they're not there yet, they'll have the place surrounded and the roads watched. It's no good, I'm telling you.'

'So you're not going to try and warn them?'

'No,' he said, 'I'm not that foolish.'

She gave him a dark look and left the room. He heard her go upstairs and then come down to the hall again. The coat stand rocked on the loose board. He went out uneasily. She was standing in the hall with her coat on.

'Where do you think you're going?' he asked.

'To Waterfall, of course. If you're frightened to go I must then. I know my duty.'

'Ah, for God's sake, Stephanie, don't be stupid,' he said despairingly. 'If there was a dog's chance I'd go myself.' He took hold of her arm, but she jerked it away, flicking her dark hair across her cheek as she did.

'I'm going.'

He stared at her white face and saw she meant it. His hands felt heavy with shame and anger. Suddenly he shrugged.

'Take off your coat, Stephanie, I'll go myself on the bike.'

'You won't just pretend to go?'

'I swear to God I'll go.'

'Ah, I knew you'd see I was right,' she said joyfully. 'We have to try and save them. But you'll be careful won't you, Con? You'll go by the back lanes?'

He choked back bitter words.

'I'll be fine,' he said in a still voice. 'And now don't say any more. I'll go now and it will be dark when I get there.'

She might as well have shot me now, he thought.

Yet there was a certain liberation in action. He went up to his room and put on a raincoat. Into the pocket he pushed his revolver. He tucked his trouser ends in his socks, went to the lavatory, and then came downstairs. Stephanie was waiting in the hall. She was rather pale and she gave him a soft fierce kiss.

He held her shoulders and looked at her. His feelings were a confusion of irritation and despairing sadness.

'I love you,' he said, kissed her between the eyes, and went out the back way to get his bike.

It was a quarter to eight. Curfew began at the hour. That gave him plenty of time to get out of the city if he wasn't stopped. He would go out the Lee Road and come back carefully on Waterfall from the north-west, using the side roads.

By the time the city was behind him he had almost forgotten the risk he was running. On his left the Lee ran softly through quiet evening fields where cattled moved as if in sleep under the grey sky. Beyond the river, beyond the fields, there were low hills half-covered with trees. On the right the wooded slope of Mount Desert rose steeply. It was very quiet.

After a while the road climbed sidling up the hill into the pillared green of a beech wood. Here Con waited for half an hour. He did not want to get to Waterfall before dark. He sat without thought in the stillness of the trees watching the river grow faintly luminous in the gathering twilight of the valley.

Then he moved on, going with more speed and care. It was nearly dark when he came over the top of the little hill opposite the house. He stopped and watched. The house was quiet among its trees; no light in any window; not a sound. After ten minutes he went down the road and left his bicycle in a field. Then he walked up the dark lane to the gate. Still nothing. Either he was in time to warn Burke or else the Commandant had already been given the word and was gone.

In the gloom he saw that the windows of the front room which Burke used were still shuttered and that the front door stood as usual a little ajar. He slipped into the hall. A faint crack of candle-light showed under the door of Burke's room. In time, he thought, and opening the door he walked in.

A British captain was sitting behind the table with the candle-light on his tired young face; behind him two soldiers covered Con with their rifles.

'Put your hands up,' said the Captain quietly.

He obeyed, his mind blank with surprise.

'Search him,' said the Captain.

A big bull of a man moved out of the shadows and frisked Con's pockets with heavy red hands. He grunted as he felt the revolver, pulled it out, broke it and put it on the table.

'I was told that you might come,' said the Captain in a hard voice. 'You are accused of spying for the rebels.' He half turned in his chair and shouted in a petulant voice: 'Mr. Gregg! Mr. Gregg!'

A tall subaltern with a round pale face blundered through the door from the inner room, and obeying a sign from the Captain sat down at the table beside him.

'Well?' said the Captain to Con. 'Have you anything to say?'

Con felt the futility of it; but he fumbled automatically for words. Just as he opened his mouth to speak the Captain said rapidly: 'The rebels who were hiding here got away before we arrived. You probably know where they are. Perhaps you know of others too.' His voice grew slower, wearily emphatic. 'If you give us any information leading to the finding of these men, especially their leaders, I have been instructed to tell you that you stand a good chance of getting off with a prison sentence.' His drawn face looked curiously at Con.

By now Con had got over the shock of being caught, but fear stirred under his surface thoughts. Burke and the men had got away. Someone had talked. He felt deserted. His comrades seemed remote. He became aware of a great useless longing for peace, for Stephanie, for his books. Burke and Ireland could go to hell. He knew enough to get himself free. And not a soul need know. He raised his heavy eyes. What he saw was the Captain's face full of a tired bullying eagerness. Stupid, and confident that he could get what he wanted. A terrible anger came up in Con's chest: anger at this pushing stupidity and bullying confidence in the small tired man at the table.

'You can all go to hell,' he said in a high shaking voice. And then lower and firmer, 'You can all go to hell.'

There was a short silence.

'Very well,' said the Captain in an expressionless voice. 'Gregg, detail a section. You will be in charge, Sergeant-Major.'

The moon-faced Lieutenant went through into the next room. A soft voice in there said, 'Draw cards.'

'You're sure you've nothing to tell us?' said the Captain in the same meaningless voice.

Con said nothing. He stared at the swaying bulk of one of the soldiers behind the table. He should try to pray. He crossed himself quickly and clumsily, his eyes moving to the candle on the table. He tried to think of Stephanie but all he could remember was a rather ugly bracelet that she often wore.

The pale face of the Captain moved near the brown face of the Sergeant-Major with low earnest words. Feet scraped on the floor as six soldiers, indistinct in the shadows, filed into the room.

'Right, Sergeant-Major.'

'Right, sir.'

Their bodies moved around him. He turned with them and walked out into the dark. The door closed.

The young Captain still sat at the table looking at his hands. Voices moved in the next room.

After about three minutes the rifles shattered the night outside. No pistol shot.

The Sergeant-Major came in quietly.

'Sir.'

'We stay here tonight. Post fresh sentries and see that the men get food and perhaps some tea. I don't want any.'

'Yes, sir,' the voice had a note of solicitude which irritated the young Captain. 'Good night, sir.'

The Captain did not answer.

And after the Lieutenant had turned in, he still sat with his elbows on the scratched boards of the table, staring at the white candle flame, on the black twist of the wick. So clear. So bright.

# Ransom

## DAVID MARCUS

---

A s THE car nosed its way past the British sentry on guard outside the barrack gate, Shamus crouched forward in the back seat and kept his gun firmly pointed down towards the figure of the man huddled at his feet. Tensely he stared into the man's eyes, his body stiffening in his anxiety to get beyond the city limits without being discovered by the police or soldiers. Actually, as long as the hostage remained quiet, there was no danger, for from the outside all that could be seen was Shamus, in the back of the car, and D'Arcy Magee, driving, in front. Though Shamus realised this (or, at least, had banked on it before setting out) his inexperience and also his distaste for the job he was now engaged upon made him completely forget it. This sort of work, he felt peevishly, was not in his line.

He knew that to free Ireland of British occupation required patience and the carrying out of many diverse plans, some of which were dull enough chores and difficult to link up, in one's mind, with that burning aim which drew one forward through the seemingly endless months. The ever-present memory of a miraculous Easter day in 1916 when the courage and resistance of his countrymen had fired his imagination made him ache to strike the one mighty blow that would break the chains binding his native land; the day of release, however, never seemed to arrive and already he had learnt four years of hard, fretful patience. It wasn't that he did not realise the necessity of obedience and perseverance, but his idealism made him long for some swift, clean assignment—he would willingly have sprung into action, laying down his life for Ireland, if told to take a bomb and blow up the barracks, or shoot a few soldiers, or sacrifice himself in a bid to assassinate the Lord Lieutenant. But the almost menial task of kidnapping a rich civilian and holding him to ransom, just because Headquarters needed money quickly—this was mere gangsterism, and if it were necessary at all, any strong-arm gunman could surely have handled it.

The more he brooded on it, the more Shamus glowered down at the figure on the floor, transferring his real hatred for what he was doing into a forced and uncomfortable hatred for his victim, and becoming more and more determined to act as if he were indeed only a strong-arm gunman and finish the job off as quickly as possible. His orders were to get the money any way he liked; and in his present mood the way he liked was the curtest, most time-saving way necessary—no matter what it involved.

His thoughts were interrupted by D'Arcy Magee, who half turned his face from the road before him and said, 'We're O.K. now, Shamus. It'll be a clear run to the hide-out. How's your man behaving?'

'Our man is behaving very sensibly, aren't you, Mr. Cohen?' answered Shamus in a mock-pleasant tone, without raising his head.

Mordecai Cohen looked up at the two blue eyes above him, and at the young, intellectual face, and felt puzzled. He sensed that this was not a mere ordinary hold-up and even guessed at the identity of his captors; but if indeed they were members of the underground army who were ambushing British soldiers every second day and pasting slogans up on the walls about a free Ireland, then what could they want with him? He wondered about it, but did not worry himself too much for he realised that whatever it was all about he would soon have to know. He did not even worry a great deal over his wife, Leah—about what she would do when he did not return home for dinner. That, too, was something taken completely out of his control and so it was useless to allow it occupy his mind. What did cause him concern, as being of immediate and pressing importance, was his physical position. He felt bruised and cramped, and the cold floor might bring his neuritis back again, just when he had succeeded in getting rid of it and was beginning to enjoy a good, ache-free summer. And besides, a man could not think properly lying on his back on the floor of a speeding car. He made an effort to raise himself, saying, 'Is it all right if I get up now?'

Shamus roughly pushed him down again, banging his head on the door and knocking off his bowler hat, which was already old and dull enough from use. Mordecai groped around for it and found it sitting on his belly where his gold watch-chain crossed from one side of his waistcoat to the other. He retrieved it and put it back on his head, though in his position he could not get it on properly and had to leave it lying rather low down on his forehead, almost touching his eyebrows.

'At least tell me how long I'll be like this,' he said.

Shamus, still in his determined mood, growled 'Shut up' at him, but simultaneously D'Arcy Magee answered, 'About an hour, I'd say. It shouldn't take us more than that to get where we're going.'

About an hour, thought Mordecai with disgust. *Oi vey*, he moaned to himself—neuritis for the rest of the summer for certain. Well, that

50

too, if it was to be, would be. The next thing in importance was to assess his situation, and not to let the gun waving above his face, or the young man holding it, put him off. It was no use getting worried or frightened; he would have to try and undermine his captors' confidence by an attitude of complete composure. So he tilted his bowler further down until it covered his eyes, linked his hands under his head, and pretended to go asleep.

With Cohen's face now almost blocked from sight, Shamus had nothing left to hold his gaze. He glanced down along Cohen's body, seeing his fat stomach wobble every time the car hit a bump, and the heavy, thickly-soled boots on his stubby legs rap against each other whenever a corner was taken.

Shamus knew that in the eventuality of a struggle he would be more than a match for Mordecai Cohen, so he relaxed and lay back on the seat, allowing the hand that held the revolver to lie idly in his lap. The strong, noonday sun flashed in through the car windows and bathed him in drowsy warmth, glinting on the steel in his hand and often dazzling D'Arcy Magee when he had to drive towards it. Cohen, still lying on the floor, was not high up enough to bask in its rays, but Shamus was in no mind to worry about that. His orders had been to allow the prisoner to see and hear as little as possible, so down on the floor he would have to stay.

For a while his thoughts remained occupied with Cohen and he could not help feeling some mild curiosity about this fat-faced, pleasantly oriental-looking man who had acted, right from the moment the gun had been levelled at him, as calmly as if kidnapping were his awaited destiny. Shamus had to admire his quiet, sensible behaviour and gradually he almost felt the beginnings of pity for Mordecai Cohen's plight. This, however, was soon forgotten as the heat, half-closing his eyes with heaviness, caused his mind to wander. What a wonderful day it was! God's blessing was on it! What a day it would be, he thought, if only one were free—completely free to roam under this sun, in one's own free country, instead of having to make bombs in a cellar or wait in ambush for a squad-car—or be wasted on the tedious job of kidnapping a rich, harmless old Jew.

They drove on, mile after mile of flowering countryside spinning away behind them. Because of their orders there was no conversation between Shamus and D'Arcy, and Cohen had not said another word since pretending to go to sleep. Actually, however, the bowler hat had been shaken to one side a little so that his right eye was uncovered, and every now and again he would open it and look up. From where he was there was little to be seen besides the long range of warm, blue sky dressed here and there with pellets of cotton-wool cloud. Sometimes this expanse would be knifed by black lines that were telegraph-wires and then the almost frightening girth and uprightness of a telegraph-pole would swing into view like a falling club. But by moving his head slightly he could see Shamus's face. And that was something Mordecai Cohen wanted to see, for every time he looked at it he became more certain that the youth above him was no gunman. He noted the fair, well-combed hair, the high and broad forehead, the rather full lips and square chin, and above all, the delicately-curved nostrils and ears. The more he looked the more he convinced himself that this was a mere youth, inexperienced in life, whom he would easily have been able to control were it not for the gun between them.

'Only five minutes more to go,' said D'Arcy suddenly, his voice making Shamus jerk into wakefulness.

'*Gutt sa danken*,' muttered Cohen, pushing the bowler back from his eyes and looking forward to stretching his legs.

Shamus gripped the gun tightly again. The car swung through an open gate and into a field. It continued along a broad pathway that was flanked on one side by a high wall and at the end of this it turned again, out of sight of the roadway, and came into a large clearing where a rambling but prosperous-looking house stood. D'Arcy slowed down and honked four times. A man appeared at the door of the house and waved to them. D'Arcy waved back and drove around behind the house. He got out of the car and opened the back door, then stood while Cohen half-crawled, half-tumbled out onto the gravel, followed by Shamus.

Without a word D'Arcy slammed the car doors shut and turned to walk back to the front of the house.

'This shouldn't take long,' said Shamus to him as he went.

'Give a shout if you need any help,' was D'Arcy's reply.

Cohen stiffly raised himself from the gravel and Shamus turned to see him trying to straighten his back and rubbing it gently with his hands. His bowler was still on the ground but he was too busy with his aching limbs to bother about it or to risk further stabs by bending down to retrieve it. Involuntarily Shamus stepped forward to pick it up for him but just as quickly he remembered himself and stopped, not wishing to show any softness towards one whom he might well have to bully, if not worse, in the next few minutes.

'Come on,' snapped Shamus, motioning with the gun, as Cohen showed no signs of hurrying himself. 'Pick up your hat and move. We've no time to waste.'

Cohen did not look at him but very gingerly bent down for his hat. When he had it firmly placed on his head it seemed to help him forget his pains and face his situation squarely for he arched back his shoulders, letting his big belly lunge forward like a barge butting the waves, and waddled briskly towards a large greenhouse on their right which Shamus had indicated. It was about twelve feet high, and the front facing the two men was all of twenty yards long. From top to bottom it was made of glass set into a framework of narrow, white-painted wood, and at each end was a glass door with a brass handle. From the outside the interior seemed to be an unbroken wall of green leafage.

Cohen stepped towards one of the doors and then turned around.

'Go on,' said Shamus, 'open it and keep straight on.'

Cohen opened the door and made to enter, but he immediately felt himself almost forced back physically by the solid mass of heat that assailed him. It was like walking into a cloud of baked air and momentarily he was gasping for breath. Shamus, however, pushed him forward with the gun and kicked the door shut behind them.

Mordecai found himself standing on a narrow concrete path that seemed to run all around the vast jungle of tomato-plants growing there. A number of other paths, one of them starting at the door through which they had entered, ran down the whole length of the greenhouse and these in turn were traversed by paths from the sides so that the beds were divided into compact, not too large, rectangles, each of the hundreds of plants being easily accessible from a pathway.

Cohen was prodded forward and he commenced to walk between the rows of head-high sprouting tomatoes. After only a few steps he could feel the burning heat of the concrete floor penetrating his boots and even already his face began to perspire. When he had walked about twenty-five yards he reached a point where the ordinary crossing of the pathways had been enlarged into a circular clearing about ten or twelve feet in diameter. At one side of this circle was a wooden box, its empty interior facing them, and next to the box were two plain kitchen chairs. Gratefully, and without thinking of the gun behind him, Cohen flopped into one of the chairs, put his hat on the box, and commenced patting his perspiring face and almost bald head with a large, white handkerchief. Shamus took the other chair, moved it around to face Cohen, and sat on it straddle-wise, leaning his chin and his gun-hand upon its top.

Cohen continued to dab himself with the handkerchief, emitting all the while a succession of exaggerated gasps, and his preoccupation with his physical discomfort, coupled with his apparent indifference to the other (what Shamus would have thought) more important discomforts of his situation, were becoming exasperating. Finally Shamus lost patience, more with his own inability to find a smooth, assured way of opening the proceedings than with Cohen's temporising.

He rapped on the chair with his gun. 'Come on, now. We don't want to waste the whole day. I want five hundred pounds and you'd better just come through with it if you know what's good for you.'

Cohen stopped mopping himself suddenly and gazed in wonderment. Then he put his bowler back on his head and for another few seconds drummed on the wooden box with his fingers.

Shamus felt disconcerted by that long, almost fatherly gaze. He did not know how to treat with this man who, indeed, looked, the thought struck him, old enough to be his father. He rapped on the chair again and waving the gun impatiently, said, 'Come on, come on. How about it?'

Cohen quickly put his hand into the inside pocket of his coat and drew out a bundle of letters and documents and also his wallet. He opened the latter and took from it a pound note and two ten-shilling notes. Then he dug into his right trousers pocket and brought from there a couple of coins which he placed on the notes. Then he looked at Shamus and his round belly began to bounce with laughter.

'What are you laughing at?' asked Shamus with annoyance.

Cohen subsided with an effort and took up his handkerchief to wipe the tears from his eyes.

'Oi, oi,' he said, still happily chuckling, 'why didn't you tell me before we left that you wanted five hundred pounds? I hardly brought five hundred pence,' and his chuckling grew again into more laughter.

His joking, almost contemptuous manner, combined with the thick, furry way he spoke, angered Shamus. 'Shut up,' he shouted. Cohen stopped.

'Don't try to put on an act with me,' continued Shamus. 'You don't think I expected you to have all that money on you? You have your cheque-book there—just write out a cheque for it.'

Cohen put the coins back in his pocket and replaced the notes in his wallet. From the bundle of envelopes and papers he extracted his cheque-book and opened it before him. Shamus watched him anxiously. Cohen looked for some moments at the cheque-book, open at a blank page, and then, after taking his hat off again, he raised his eyes.

'Five hundred pounds is a lot of money for one young man like you, even shared between you and your friend,' he said. 'You must need it badly to go to such trouble for it!'

The implication caught Shamus off his guard, as it was meant to, and he blurted out, 'It isn't for myself at all.' Realising that he had been fooled into giving away more than he had intended, he pulled himself up sharply. But Cohen pretended not to notice anything amiss and asked, 'If it's not for yourself, then who is it for? You can't expect anyone to give you money for another person he's not even told about. Can you?'

Shamus was rattled. He began to feel a vague suspicion that he was being played with but on the other hand he could not deny the fairness and logic of Cohen's question. He decided quickly that if Mordecai Cohen were even half the business man he had the reputation of being, a demand for five hundred pounds on someone else's name might be difficult to enforce without unpleasantness.

'I'm a member of a certain organisation that needs the money,' he said.

'A certain "illegal" organisation?' asked Cohen.

'We're no illegal organisation,' said Shamus heatedly.

Cohen laughed and waved a hand soothingly. 'I know what you mean,' he said. 'You hold that the ones you are fighting are illegal, isn't that it?'

Shamus did not answer. He thought now that things seemed to be moving favourably and he could not help feeling more well-disposed towards Mordecai Cohen. Nor did it any longer appear to be so necessary to preserve his tough exterior, a release which he welcomed, for the intense, cloying heat in the greenhouse was enervating. He pulled open his collar and tie.

'Hurry up now, Mr. Cohen,' he said. 'It's almost one o'clock and we have to cash that cheque today before the banks close. That only leaves us a couple of hours.'

'And whose name shall I put down?' asked Cohen.

'Just leave that blank—I'll fill it in later.'

Cohen took out his pen and wrote on the open cheque. Then he tore it out and handed it across to Shamus. Shamus leant over, half-raised from the chair, took it in his hand and read it. He remained poised in that position as he jerked his head up and said, 'But you haven't signed it.'

Cohen calmly closed his cheque-book and put it back, with his wallet and papers, into his inside pocket. Then he screwed the top onto his pen and clipped that in beside them. He took his hat, placed it on his head, and stood up.

'That's right,' he said, 'I haven't signed it. And I certainly don't intend to. Now let us go home.'

Shamus was furious at being tricked. He rushed at Cohen, digging the gun into his ribs.

'Sit down. Sit down there and sign that cheque,' he commanded, 'or you'll be bloody sorry.'

Cohen looked at him, unmoved. He gave a half-shrug and sniffed indifferently. 'And if I don't?'

Shamus pushed him back into the chair and resumed his own seat. The burst of temper had passed now and he felt he had to regain control of the situation.

'If you don't, I'll just blow your brains out,' he answered. 'And I don't think I'd mind too much doing it at all.'

Cohen smiled.

'If you blow my brains out, you'll have no chance of getting the money.'

'If I don't get the money,' Shamus smiled back, 'I'm likely to want the satisfaction of blowing your brains out.'

55

Cohen took off his hat again and once more dabbed at his face with his handkerchief.

'You might sound bloodthirsty, but you don't look it. Do you know that?' he commented.

'Look, man,' answered Shamus, with some exasperation, 'will you stop your cod-acting? Just sign the cheque like a good fellow. Sure you won't miss the money.'

'Oh, so I won't miss the money! And how do you know? Since when have you counted my money?'

Shamus did not answer. He felt he had made a mistake in his comment for it seemed only to have hardened the opposition, and he was slightly ashamed too, deep in his mind, that his impatience and awkwardness had enticed him into showing that kind of veiled prejudice which he normally despised and shunned.

'And could you tell me,' continued Cohen, 'why should I give you my money? Tell me one good reason why I should give you my money.'

Shamus, disconcerted by the failure of his previous heavy-handed approaches, welcomed the question. It raised the situation to a level which suited him and he felt that by argument and discussion he could acquit himself much better than by fierceness and threats. But just in case his willingness to answer the question should be interpreted as a sign of weakness, he replied, 'The best reason is because if you don't, you won't get up from that chair again. The other good reason is because we need the money—badly.'

Cohen opened his eyes wide in mock surprise and said, 'But don't you know that it is good business when you need anything badly to ask, not to demand. You have a much better chance of getting it that way.'

Shamus, still trying to strengthen his position, waved the gun and replied, 'Not when you ask with this.'

Cohen threw up his hands in disgust and impatience.

'You keep on talking with your gun,' he cried, almost in anger. 'What do you think you have in your hand, Aaron's staff? I'm telling you it is useless to you. Throw it away. It cannot make me change my mind, so if you intend using it, use it now and shoot me. Otherwise you're wasting your time.'

Shamus was taken aback by the show of anger and spirit; and he felt, too, a growing suspicion that Mordecai Cohen meant every word he had said and would prove immovable. He lowered the gun almost unconsciously. Just then a door in the greenhouse opened and they looked around to see D'Arcy Magee come in, carrying a tray with a glass and some bottles of beer. He came up to them and put the tray down beside Shamus.

'By God,' he said, 'this place is like an oven.' Then, suddenly seeing the cheque on the box, he looked at Shamus and asked, 'Have you got it?'

'No,' Shamus snapped back, 'not yet.'

D'Arcy knew from the tone of the reply that his question had not been welcome. He turned without another word and left them.

Both men looked at the bottles and began to realise how thirsty they were. The perspiration was standing out clearly on their foreheads and Shamus felt the gun in his hand moist and slippery. He longed to pour out some beer for himself and to feel it flowing coolly down his throat, but he was again afraid that such easy-going relaxation would make him seem lacking in endurance. It might even things up if Cohen were to drink with him, but Shamus felt that any more *camaraderie* would lessen the gulf between them and make it harder than ever for him to succeed in his task.

Without meaning to, he licked his lips and looked at Cohen. Cohen, as if reading his mind, smiled and said, 'Go ahead, my boy, drink it. You need not worry about me. I don't drink.'

Shamus hesitated, trying to strengthen his failing will.

Cohen leant towards him, for all the world like a confident old doctor worming embarrassing facts out of a shy patient.

'What's wrong? Are you afraid that by giving in to your thirst I'll have a chance of mocking you? So. Here then, you can mock me too,' and Cohen put a hand up to the plant beside him, carefully plucked the reddest-looking tomato and bit into it. Then, with his mouth full and the juice escaping from between his lips, he smiled and said, 'There you are. Now put down your gun and have your drink. Believe me, you need the drink more than the gun——' and, suddenly thinking of something else, he pulled the tomato away from his mouth, saying, 'or better still: shoot me now and you can have your drink in peace. You'll have to shoot me anyway so why not now?' and he resumed eating. Shamus hesitated no longer, but put the gun on the floor with the air of a gambler making his last throw, and poured out a bottle of beer. He took the glass up in his hand and moved his face toward it. Cohen smiled at him benignly and said, '*Lechaim*. That's Hebrew for "long life".'

Shamus was embarrassed by the man's poise and friendliness and also ashamed that he, himself, had not first made the customary toast.

He tilted his drink in Cohen's direction, mumbling 'the same to yourself,' and then took a couple of huge swallows. Sighing with satisfaction he lowered the half-empty glass. Cohen was wiping his mouth dry of tomato juice and mopping his head again. He nodded encouragingly to Shamus.

'Tell me,' he said, 'why did you have to carry someone all the way off here to get your five hundred pounds? Wasn't there anybody you could ask, eh? And if you did have to drag someone here, why did you pick me? Why not an Irishman, one of your own people?'

' 'Twasn't I chose you,' answered Shamus.

'Oh, somebody above you chose me, is that it? Do you know why?'

'How would I know why? I just carry out orders. I suppose it was because you're rich.'

'And because I'd be too afraid to say no? Could that have been why? And tell me, do you agree with the choice?'

Shamus shrugged and took another swallow from his drink. The sun, hotter than ever, caught the rim of the glass and a sparkling circle ran around it, making Cohen blink and feel thirsty again. He plucked another tomato and started to eat it.

'What's the difference?' Shamus answered.

'What's the difference!' echoed Cohen in surprise. 'Don't you think it would be more suitable to ask an Irishman, not a foreigner? It's for Ireland's fight you want the money. What business is that of mine?'

'But you live here the same as the rest of us.'

Cohen swallowed what was left of the tomato and opened his hands out before him as if displaying his answer for inspection.

'I live here, yes,' he said, 'but, tell me, if you were employed in a business run by a family, would that make you one of the family? I work in your country and earn my living in it; and in return I pay my taxes and my rates and I keep the laws. But I am still what I was when I came here,' he ended, as if tying a final knot in his explanation, 'I am still a foreigner.'

'What brought you here so?' asked Shamus.

'What brought me here, you ask. Nothing brought me here. I was driven here. I was driven here as a child from my home in Russia by persecution. My parents were killed by the Czar's soldiers. I was an orphan when I came here and that was not easy. I had to learn a whole new language and work without help all my life. I prospered, yes. But I had to work hard for it all.'

'But why did you come *here*—to Ireland?' asked Shamus.

'In those days we looked to the West for freedom; most of us thought of America. That's where we set out for, but a lot dropped off on the way. I dropped off in Ireland—it made no difference to me as long as it was far way from the Russian soldiers.'

Shamus drained the glass and put it on the box. Cohen took it and held its coolness between his hands.

'But what about the Holy Land?' asked Shamus. 'Don't you Jews look on that as your home? Why didn't you go there?'

'The Holy Land?' said Cohen in surprise, putting down the glass. 'Palestine our home? How can we go there or live there? A desert it is now. And besides, like your land too, it is ruled by the British.'

Shamus raised his eyebrows. 'I always thought the Jews looked on the Holy Land as their home.'

'We do,' said Cohen, 'of course we do. It *is* our spiritual home. As a matter of fact, every year on our Feast of Passover we say a prayer which ends with the words "*Le shonoh aboh b'Roosholoyim*"—and that means "To next year in Jerusalem". But we've been saying that prayer for two thousand years. You know, my boy,' continued Cohen wistfully, 'when you've prayed for the same thing for two thousand years without getting it, you begin to feel that what you are praying for doesn't exist at all. A spiritual home, yes. But you can't live in a spiritual home.'

'What do you mean "spiritual home"?' asked Shamus. 'A country is either your country—your home—or not. Everyone must have a country, usually the place he was born in.'

'Not me,' said Cohen, energetically waving off the thought. 'I was born in Russia but how can I call it my home after what I suffered there?'

'Then if Russia isn't your home and Ireland isn't, what is? It must be the Holy Land.'

Cohen shrugged. 'Yes, good enough then, Palestine is my home. But I still can't live there.'

'Maybe not just now, but surely you Jews are doing something to get it, if you really want it? Look at us—we're fighting for *our* home. Can't you fight too?'

Cohen laughed. 'Fight? Against the British? We would be wasting blood and time. What chance would we have?'

'What chance have we?' retorted Shamus.

'That's what I mean,' said Cohen. 'You have no chance. They could crush you in a day if they wanted. Look how long your country has fought and where are you? No. You'll remain like us—a race with a home they once owned, but now it's a home they can only think about or write about—and pray for.'

Shamus stood up in surprise. 'My God, man,' he expostulated, 'you don't think you can win a country with prayer alone. If you think the place is yours, that your home is there, you must fight for it. Aren't there any Jews who are doing anything to get your home?'

'How can we get it? I told you before, it is ruled by the British just like this country is. They only allow some settlements there. A Jewish society takes care of keeping the settlements going but they are getting smaller instead of bigger. Nobody is interested and there is not enough money to help them spread and grow strong.'

'Not enough money?' Shamus snorted disgustedly. 'Haven't you ever helped them yourself? Wouldn't you like to have your home free, wouldn't you?'

Cohen looked up, his eyes puzzled and surprised. 'Of course I would, if it were possible. But what's the use of doing anything? Believe me, it would all be waste—just waste!'

Shamus gazed down in amazement at Cohen. 'All waste? You

mean it wouldn't be a good investment for you. Is that the way you look at it? Haven't you any real feeling, man, for your own country?'

Cohen refused to get excited. 'Of course I have, my boy, of course I have. But you are young and hot. You don't understand. I have seen how impossible it is to fight against a huge country when you have nothing. I have seen your own country fight with much more than we have, and you are still fighting and spilling your blood after centuries.'

Shamus threw his hands up in despair. Cohen laughed and said, 'All right then, I believe you. You *will* beat them some day—may I live that long. In the meantime what about leaving this place, or do you still intend to shoot me?'

'No,' said Shamus jocularly, 'I wouldn't shoot you now. I'm going to let you live to swallow your words. You'll see, we'll win, and it won't be long before we do.'

Cohen got up from the chair and put his hat on his head. 'Well, my boy, I hope so. And if you do, come back to me again. Perhaps I'll be able to help you then.'

'If I'm still alive, I will. But not for your money—just to make you eat your words. It's when a country is fighting it needs help and without help in its fight it can't win. But it doesn't seem to be any use telling you that. Come on, let's get back.'

Cohen looked hard at Shamus and then silently walked ahead and out to the car. He got into the back and sat in a corner while Shamus honked the horn. D'Arcy Magee came on the run. Seeing Shamus, he asked excitedly, 'Did you get it?'

'I did not,' said Shamus emphatically. 'Come on, D'Arcy, it doesn't matter a bit.'

D'Arcy paused for a moment in puzzlement and then sat into the front seat and drove off. Shamus did not bother to make Cohen lie on the floor and Cohen, seemingly deep in thought, said nothing. They continued in silence all the way back to the city.

On the outskirts D'Arcy turned and asked, 'Are we dropping him here?'

'No,' answered Shamus, 'we'll go on with him. It's safe enough.'

They made their way through the traffic and in a few minutes drew up outside Cohen's business-house.

Shamus opened a door for Cohen, saying as he did so, 'Goodbye now, and don't forget what I told you.'

Cohen got out and turned around. 'Don't go away yet,' he said. 'I won't be long,' and without waiting for an answer he hurried into his premises.

D'Arcy turned to Shamus angrily. 'Why didn't you get the money?' he asked. 'And what the hell are we waiting for? It's dangerous. God knows what he's up to.'

Shamus did not reply but sat still, wondering. Cohen came out and silently thrust a big envelope in the car window. Shamus took it and Cohen disappeared again.

Shamus opened the envelope and a bundle of ten pound notes, wrapped up in some white paper, fell out. D'Arcy grabbed at the notes and started counting. Shamus watched for a moment and then took up the piece of paper. He noticed something written on it.

'There's two hundred and fifty pounds here,' said D'Arcy with excitement. 'I thought you said you weren't getting any money.'

Shamus did not reply but with a smile playing around his lips, read Cohen's message:

> In the long run you're right—a man's home must be worth fighting for. But in that case I have two homes to keep so you can get only half what you asked for.
>
> *P.S.*—'To next year in Jerusalem.'

'Two hundred and fifty quid,' said D'Arcy, in some disgust. 'Trust the old Shylock to get away with as little as possible. I suppose he was too mean to part with the other two hundred and fifty.'

Shamus opened his mouth, as if to explain something, but instead he put the paper and the notes in his pocket and just said, 'Come on, D'Arcy, drive away. We'd better report back with this.'

# Guests of the Nation

## FRANK O'CONNOR

---

A T D U S K the big Englishman, Belcher, would shift his long legs
out of the ashes and say 'Well chums, what about it?' and
Noble and myself would say 'All right, chum' (for we had
picked up some of their curious expressions), and the little Englishman, Hawkins, would light the lamp and bring out the cards. Sometimes Jeremiah Donovan would come up and supervise the game,
and get excited over Hawkins's cards, which he always played badly,
and shout at him as if he was one of our own, 'Ah, you divil, why
didn't you play the tray?'

But ordinarily Jeremiah was a sober and contented poor devil like
the big Englishman, Belcher, and was looked up to only because he
was a fair hand at documents, though he was slow even with them.
He wore a small cloth hat and big gaiters over his long pants, and
you seldom saw him with his hands out of his pockets. He reddened
when you talked to him, tilting from toes to heel and back, and
looking down all the time at his big farmer's feet. Noble and myself
used to make fun of his broad accent, because we were both from
the town.

I could not at the time see the point of myself and Noble guarding
Belcher and Hawkins at all, for it was my belief that you could have
planted that pair down anywhere from this to Claregalway and they'd
have taken root there like a native weed. I never in my short
experience saw two men take to the country as they did.

They were passed on to us by the Second Battalion when the search
for them became too hot, and Noble and myself, being young, took
them over with a natural feeling of responsibility, but Hawkins made
us look like fools when he showed that he knew the country better
than we did.

'You're the bloke they call Bonaparte,' he says to me. 'Mary
Brigid O'Connell told me to ask what you'd done with the pair of
her brother's socks you borrowed.'

For it seemed, as they explained it, that the Second had little
evenings, and some of the girls of the neighbourhood turned up, and,

seeing they were such decent chaps, our fellows could not leave the two Englishmen out. Hawkins learned to dance *The Walls of Limerick*, *The Siege of Ennis* and *The Waves of Tory* as well as any of them, though he could not return the compliment, because our lads at that time did not dance foreign dances on principle.

So whatever privileges Belcher and Hawkins had with the Second they just took naturally with us, and after the first couple of days we gave up all pretence of keeping an eye on them. Not that they could have got far, because they had accents you could cut with a knife, and wore khaki tunics and overcoats with civilian pants and boots, but I believe myself they never had any idea of escaping and were quite content to be where they were.

It was a treat to see how Belcher got off with the old woman in the house where we were staying. She was a great warrant to scold, and cranky even with us, but before ever she had a chance of giving our guests, as I may call them, a lick of her tongue, Belcher had made her his friend for life. She was breaking sticks, and Belcher, who had not been more than ten minutes in the house, jumped up and went over to her.

'Allow me, madam,' he said, smiling his queer little smile. 'Please allow me,' and he took the hatchet from her. She was too surprised to speak, and after that, Belcher would be at her heels, carrying a bucket, a basket or a load of turf. As Noble said, he got into looking before she leapt, and hot water, or any little thing she wanted, Belcher would have ready for her. For such a huge man (and though I am five foot ten myself I had to look up at him) he had an uncommon lack of speech. It took us a little while to get used to him, walking in and out like a ghost, without speaking. Especially because Hawkins talked enough for a platoon, it was strange to hear Belcher with his toes in the ashes come out with a solitary 'Excuse me, chum,' or 'That's right, chum.' His one and only passion was cards, and he was a remarkably good card player. He could have skinned myself and Noble, but whatever we lost to him, Hawkins lost to us, and Hawkins only played with the money Belcher gave him.

Hawkins lost to us because he had too much old gab, and we probably lost to Belcher for the same reason. Hawkins and Noble argued about religion into the early hours of the morning, and Hawkins worried the life out of Noble, who had a brother a priest, with a string of questions that would puzzle a cardinal. Even in treating of holy subjects, Hawkins had a deplorable tongue. I never met a man who could mix such a variety of cursing and bad language into any argument. He was a terrible man, and a fright to argue. He never did a stroke of work, and when he had no one else to argue with, he got stuck in the old woman.

He met his match in her, for when he tried to get her to complain profanely of the drought she gave him a great come-down by blaming it entirely on Jupiter Pluvius (a deity neither Hawkins nor I had ever heard of, though Noble said that among the pagans it was believed that he had something to do with the rain). Another day he was swearing at the capitalists for starting the German war when the old lady laid down her iron, puckered up her little crab's mouth and said: 'Mr. Hawkins, you can say what you like about the war, and think you'll deceive me because I'm only a simple poor country-woman, but I know what started the war. It was the Italian Count that stole the heathen divinity out of the temple of Japan. Believe me, Mr. Hawkins, nothing but sorrow and want can follow people who disturb the hidden powers.'

A queer old girl, all right.

\* \* \*

One evening we had our tea and Hawkins lit the lamp and we all sat into cards. Jeremiah Donovan came in too, and sat and watched us for a while, and it suddenly struck me that he had no great love for the two Englishmen. It came as a surprise to me because I had noticed nothing of it before.

Late in the evening a really terrible argument blew up between Hawkins and Noble about capitalists and priests and love of country.

'The capitalists pay the priests to tell you about the next world so that you won't notice what the bastards are up to in this,' said Hawkins.

'Nonsense, man!' said Noble, losing his temper. 'Before ever a capitalist was thought of people believed in the next world.'

Hawkins stood up as though he was preaching.

'Oh, they did, did they?' he said with a sneer. 'They believed all the things you believe—isn't that what you mean? And you believe God created Adam, and Adam created Shem, and Shem created Jehoshophat. You believe all that silly old fairytale about Eve and Eden and the apple. Well listen to me, chum! If you're entitled to a silly belief like that, I'm entitled to my own silly belief—which is that the first thing your God created was a bleeding capitalist, with morality and Rolls-Royce complete. Am I right, chum?' he says to Belcher.

'You're right, chum,' says Belcher with a smile, and he got up from the table to stretch his long legs into the fire and stroke his moustache. So, seeing that Jeremiah Donovan was going, and that there was no knowing when the argument about religion would be over, I went out with him. We strolled down to the village together, and then he stopped, blushing and mumbling, and said I should be behind, keeping guard. I didn't like the tone he took with me, and anyway I was bored with life in the cottage, so I replied by asking what the hell we wanted to guard them for at all.

He looked at me in surprise and said: 'I thought you knew we were keeping them as hostages.'

'Hostages?' I said.

'The enemy have prisoners belonging to us, and now they're talking of shooting them,' he said. 'If they shoot our prisoners, we'll shoot theirs.'

'Shoot Belcher and Hawkins?' I said.

'What else did you think we were keeping them for?' he said.

'Wasn't it very unforeseen of you not to warn Noble and myself of that in the beginning?' I said.

'How was it?' he said. 'You might have known that much.'

'We could not know it, Jeremiah Donovan,' I said. 'How could we when they were on our hands so long?'

'The enemy have our prisoners as long and longer,' he said.

'That's not the same thing at all,' said I.

'What difference is there?' said he.

I couldn't tell him, because I knew he wouldn't understand. If it was only an old dog that you had to take to the vet's, you'd try and not get too fond of him, but Jeremiah Donovan was not a man who would ever be in danger of that.

'And when is this to be decided?' I said.

'We might hear tonight,' he said. 'Or tomorrow or the next day at latest. So if it's only hanging round that's a trouble to you, you'll be free soon enough.'

It was not the hanging round that was a trouble to me at all by this time. I had worse things to worry about. When I got back to the cottage the argument was still on. Hawkins was holding forth in his best style, maintaining that there was no next world, and Noble saying that there was; but I could see that Hawkins had had the best of it.

'Do you know what, chum?' he was saying with a saucy smile. 'I think you're just as big a bleeding unbeliever as I am. You say you believe in the next world, and you know just as much about the next world as I do, which is sweet damn-all. What's heaven? You don't know. Where's heaven? You don't know. You know sweet damn-all! I ask you again, do they wear wings?'

'Very well, then,' said Noble. 'They do. Is that enough for you? They do wear wings.'

'Where do they get them then? Who makes them? Have they a factory for wings? Have they a sort of store where you hand in your chit and take your bleeding wings?'

'You're an impossible man to argue with,' said Noble. 'Now, listen to me——' And they were off again.

It was long after midnight when we locked up and went to bed. As I blew out the candle I told Noble. He took it very quietly. When we'd been in bed about an hour he asked if I thought we should tell the Englishmen. I didn't, because I doubted if the English would

66

shoot our men. Even if they did, the Brigade officers, who were always up and down to the Second Battalion and knew the Englishmen well, would hardly want to see them plugged. 'I think so too,' said Noble. 'It would be great cruelty to put the wind up them now.'

'It was very unforeseen of Jeremiah Donovan, anyhow,' said I.

It was next morning that we found it so hard to face Belcher and Hawkins. We went about the house all day, scarcely saying a word. Belcher didn't seem to notice; he was stretched into the ashes as usual, with his usual look of waiting in quietness for something unforeseen to happen, but Hawkins noticed it and put it down to Noble's being beaten in the argument of the night before.

'Why can't you take the discussion in the proper spirit?' he said severely. 'You and your Adam and Eve! I'm a Communist, that's what I am. Communist or Anarchist, it all comes to much the same thing.' And he went round the house, muttering when the fit took him: 'Adam and Eve! Adam and Eve! Nothing better to do with their time than pick bleeding apples!'

*   *   *

I don't know how we got through that day, but I was very glad when it was over, the tea things were cleared away, and Belcher said in his peaceable way: 'Well chums, what about it?' We sat round the table and Hawkins took out the cards, and just then I heard Jeremiah Donovan's footsteps on the path and a dark presentiment crossed my mind. I rose from the table and caught him before he reached the door.

'What do you want?' I asked.

'I want those two soldier friends of yours,' he said, getting red.

'Is that the way, Jeremiah Donovan?' I asked.

'That's the way. There were four of our lads shot this morning, one of them a boy of sixteen.'

'That's bad,' I said.

At that moment Noble followed me out, and the three of us walked down the path together, talking in whispers. Feeney, the local intelligence officer, was standing by the gate.

'What are you going to do about it?' I asked Jeremiah Donovan.

'I want you and Noble to get them out; tell them they're being shifted again; that'll be the quietest way.'

'Leave me out of that,' said Noble, under his breath.

Jeremiah Donovan looked at him hard.

'All right,' he says. 'You and Feeney get a few tools from the shed and dig a hole by the far end of the bog. Bonaparte and myself will be after you. Don't let anyone see you with the tools. I wouldn't like it to go beyond ourselves.'

We saw Feeney and Noble go round to the shed and went in ourselves. I left Jeremiah Donovan to do the explanations. He told

67

them that he had orders to send them back to the Second Battalion. Hawkins let out a mouthful of curses, and you could see that though Belcher didn't say anything, he was a bit upset too. The old woman was for having them stay in spite of us, and she didn't stop advising them until Jeremiah Donovan lost his temper and turned on her. He had a nasty temper, I noticed. It was pitch-dark in the cottage by this time, but no one thought of lighting the lamp, and in the darkness the two Englishmen fetched their top-coats and said good-bye to the old woman.

'Just as a man makes a home of a bleeding place, some bastard at headquarters thinks you're too cushy and shunts you off,' said Hawkins, shaking her hand.

'A thousand thanks, madam,' said Belcher. 'A thousand thanks for everything'—as though he'd made it up.

We went round to the back of the house and down towards the bog. It was only then that Jeremiah Donovan told them. He was shaking with excitement.

'There were four of our fellows shot in Cork this morning and now you're to be shot as a reprisal.'

'What are you talking about?' snaps Hawkins. 'It's bad enough being mucked about as we are without having to put up with your funny jokes.'

'It isn't a joke,' says Donovan. 'I'm sorry, Hawkins, but it's true,' and begins on the usual rigmarole about duty and how unpleasant it is. I never noticed that people who talk a lot about duty find it much of a trouble to them.

'Oh, cut it out!' said Hawkins.

'Ask Bonaparte,' said Donovan, seeing that Hawkins wasn't taking him seriously. 'Isn't it true, Bonaparte?'

'It is,' I said, and Hawkins stopped.

'Ah, for Christ's sake, chum!'

'I mean it, chum,' I said.

'You don't sound as if you mean it.'

'If he doesn't mean it, I do,' said Donovan, working himself up.

'What have you against me, Jeremiah Donovan?'

'I never said I had anything against you. But why did your people take out four of your prisoners and shoot them in cold blood?'

He took Hawkins by the arm and dragged him on, but it was impossible to make him understand that we were in earnest. I had the Smith and Wesson in my pocket and I kept fingering it and wondering what I'd do if they put up a fight for it or ran, and wishing to God they'd do one or the other. I knew if they did run for it, that I'd never fire on them. Hawkins wanted to know was Noble in it, and when we said yes, he asked us why Noble wanted to plug him. Why did any of us want to plug him? What had he done to us? Weren't we all chums? Didn't we understand him and didn't he understand us? Did we imagine for an instant that he'd shoot us for all the so-and-so officers in the so-and-so British Army?

By this time we'd reached the bog, and I was so sick I couldn't even answer him. We walked along the edge of it in the darkness, and every now and then Hawkins would call a halt and begin all over again, as if he was wound up, about our being chums, and I knew that nothing but the sight of the grave would convince him that we had to do it. And all the time I was hoping that something would happen; that they'd run for it or that Noble would take over the responsibility from me. I had the feeling that it was worse on Noble than on me.

\* \* \*

At last we saw the lantern in the distance and made towards it. Noble was carrying it, and Feeney was standing somewhere in the darkness behind him, and the picture of them so still and silent in the bogland brought it home to me that we were in earnest, and banished the last bit of hope I had.

Belcher, on recognising Noble, said: 'Hallo, chum,' in his quiet way, but Hawkins flew at him at once, and the argument began all over again, only this time Noble had nothing to say for himself and stood with his head down, holding the lantern between his legs.

It was Jeremiah Donovan who did the answering. For the twentieth time, as though it was haunting his mind, Hawkins asked if anybody thought he'd shoot Noble.

'Yes, you would,' said Jeremiah Donovan.

'No, I wouldn't, damn you!'

'You would, because you'd know you'd be shot for not doing it.'

'I wouldn't, not if I was to be shot twenty times over. I wouldn't shoot a pal. And Belcher wouldn't—isn't that right, Belcher?'

'That's right, chum,' Belcher said, but more by way of answering the question than of joining in the argument. Belcher sounded as though whatever unforeseen thing he'd always been waiting for had come at last.

'Anyway, who says Noble would be shot if I wasn't? What do you think I'd do if I was in his place, out in the middle of a blasted bog?'

'What would you do?' asked Donovan.

'I'd go with him wherever he was going, of course. Share my last bob with him and stick by him through thick and thin. No one can ever say of me that I let down a pal.'

'We've had enough of this,' said Jeremiah Donovan, cocking his revolver. 'Is there any message you want to send?'

'No, there isn't.'

'Do you want to say your prayers?'

Hawkins came out with a cold-blooded remark that even shocked me and turned on Noble again.

'Listen to me, Noble,' he said. 'You and me are chums. You can't come over to my side, so I'll come over to your side. That show you I mean what I say? Give me a rifle and I'll go along with you and the other lads.'

Nobody answered him. We knew that was no way out.

'Hear what I'm saying?' he said. 'I'm through with it. I'm a deserter or anything else you like. I don't believe in your stuff, but it's no worse than mine. That satisfy you?'

Noble raised his head, but Donovan began to speak and he lowered it again without replying.

'For the last time, have you any messages to send?' said Donovan in a cold, excited sort of voice.

'Shut up, Donovan! You don't understand me, but these lads do. They're not the sort to make a pal and kill a pal. They're not the tools of any capitalist.'

I alone of the crowd saw Donovan raise his Webley to the back of Hawkins's neck, and as he did so I shut my eyes and tried to pray. Hawkins had begun to say something else when Donovan fired, and as I opened my eyes at the bang, I saw Hawkins stagger at the knees and lie out flat at Noble's feet, slowly and as quiet as a kid falling asleep, with the lantern-light on his lean legs and bright farmer's boots. We all stood very still, watching him settle out in the last agony.

Then Belcher took out a handkerchief and began to tie it about his own eyes (in our excitement we'd forgotten to do the same for Hawkins), and, seeing it wasn't big enough, turned and asked for the loan of mine. I gave it to him and he knotted the two together and pointed with his foot at Hawkins.

'He's not quite dead,' he said. 'Better give him another.'

Sure enough, Hawkins's left knee was beginning to rise. I bent down and put my gun to his head; then, recollecting myself I got up again. Belcher understood what was in my mind.

'Give him his first,' he said. 'I don't mind. Poor bastard, we don't know what's happening to him now.'

I knelt and fired. By this time I didn't seem to know what I was doing. Belcher, who was fumbling a bit awkwardly with the handkerchiefs, came out with a laugh as he heard the shot. It was the first time I had heard him laugh and it sent a shudder down my back; it sounded so unnatural.

'Poor bugger!' he said quietly. 'And last night he was so curious about it all. It's very queer, chums, I always think. Now he knows as much about it as they'll ever let him know, and last night he was all in the dark.'

Donovan helped him to tie the handkerchiefs about his eyes. 'Thanks, chum,' he said. Donovan asked if there were any messages he wanted sent.

70

'No, chum,' he said. 'Not for me. If any of you would like to write to Hawkins's mother, you'll find a letter from her in his pocket. He and his mother were great chums. But my missus left me eight years ago. Went away with another fellow and took the kid with her. I like the feeling of a home, as you may have noticed, but I couldn't start another again after that.'

It was an extraordinary thing, but in those few minutes Belcher said more than in all the weeks before. It was just as if the sound of the shot had started a flood of talk in him and he could go on the whole night like that, quite happily, talking about himself. We stood around like fools now that he couldn't see us any longer. Donovan looked at Noble, and Noble shook his head. Then Donovan raised his Webley, and at that moment Belcher gave his queer laugh again. He may have thought we were talking about him, or perhaps he noticed the same thing I'd noticed and couldn't understand it.

'Excuse me, chums,' he said. 'I feel I'm talking the hell of a lot, and so silly, about my being so handy about a house and things like that. But this thing came on me suddenly. You'll forgive me, I'm sure.'

'You don't want to say a prayer?' asked Donovan.

'No, chum,' he said. 'I don't think it would help. I'm ready, and you boys want to get it over.'

'You understand that we're only doing our duty?' said Donovan.

Belcher's head was raised like a blind man's, so that you could only see his chin and the top of his nose in the lantern-light.

'I never could make out what duty was myself,' he said. 'I think you're all good lads, if that's what you mean. I'm not complaining.'

Noble, just as if he couldn't bear any more of it, raised his fist at Donovan, and in a flash Donovan raised his gun and fired. The big man went over like a sack of meal, and this time there was no need of a second shot.

I don't remember much about the burying, but that it was worse than all the rest because we had to carry them to the grave. It was all mad lonely with nothing but a patch of lantern-light between ourselves and the dark, and birds hooting and screeching all round, disturbed by the guns. Noble went through Hawkins's belongings to find the letter from his mother, and then joined his hands together. He did the same with Belcher. Then, when we'd filled in the grave, we separated from Jeremiah Donovan and Feeney and took our tools back to the shed. All the way we didn't speak a word. The kitchen was dark and cold as we'd left it, and the old woman was sitting over the hearth, saying her beads. We walked past her into the room, and Noble struck a match to light the lamp. She rose quietly and came to the doorway with all her cantankerousness gone.

'What did ye do with them?' she asked in a whisper, and Noble started so that the match went out in his hand.

'What's that?' he asked without turning round.

'I heard ye,' she said.

'What did you hear?' asked Noble.

'I heard ye. Do ye think I didn't hear ye, putting the spade back in the houseen?'

Noble struck another match and this time the lamp lit for him.

'Was that what ye did to them?' she asked.

Then, by God, in the very doorway, she fell on her knees and began praying, and after looking at her for a minute or two Noble did the same by the fireplace. I pushed my way out past her and left them at it. I stood at the door, watching the stars and listening to the shrieking of the birds dying out over the bogs. It is so strange what you feel at times like that that you can't describe it. Noble says he saw everything ten times the size, as though there were nothing in the whole world but that little patch of bog with the two Englishmen stiffening into it, but with me it was as if the patch of bog where the Englishmen were was a million miles away, and even Noble and the old woman, mumbling behind me, and the birds and the bloody stars were all far away, and I was somehow very small and very lost and lonely like a child astray in the snow. And anything that happened to me afterwards, I never felt the same about again.

# The Civil War
# 1922-23

# The Mountain Tavern

## LIAM O'FLAHERTY

SNOW WAS falling. The bare, flat, fenceless road had long since disappeared. Now the white snow fell continuously on virgin land, all level, all white, all silent, between the surrounding dim peaks of the mountains. Through the falling snow, on every side, squat humps were visible. They were the mountain peaks. And between them, the moorland was as smooth as a ploughed field. And as silent, oh, as silent as an empty church. Here, the very particles of the air entered the lungs seemingly as big as pebbles and with the sweetness of ripe fruit. An outstretched hand could almost feel the air and the silence. There was absolutely nothing, nothing at all, but the falling flakes of white snow, undeflected, falling silently on fallen snow.

Up above was the sky and God perhaps, though it was hard to believe it; hard to believe that there was anything in the whole universe but a flat white stretch of virgin land between squat mountain peaks and a ceaseless shower of falling snowflakes.

There came the smell of human breathing from the east. Then three figures appeared suddenly, dark, although they were covered with snow. They appeared silently, one by one, stooping forward. The leading man carried his overcoat like a shawl about his head, with a rifle, butt upwards, slung on his right shoulder and two cloth ammunition belts slung across his body. He wore black top boots. His grim young eyes gazed wearily into the falling snow and his boots, scarcely lifted, raked the smooth earth, scattering the fallen snowflakes.

The second man wore a belted leather coat, of which one arm hung loose. With the other hand he gripped his chest and staggered forward, with sagging, doddering head. A pistol, pouched in a loose belt, swung back and forth with his gait. There was blood on his coat, on his hand and congealed on his black leggings, along which the melting snow ran in a muddy stream. There was a forlorn look in his eyes, but his teeth were set. Sometimes he bared them and drew in a deep breath with a hissing sound.

The third man walked erect. He wore no overcoat and his head was bare. His hair curled and among the curls the snow lay in little rows like some statue in winter. He had a proud, fearless face, bronzed, showing no emotion nor weariness. Now and again, he shook his great body and the snow fell with a rustling sound off his clothes and off the heavy pack he carried. He also had two rifles wrapped in a cape under his arm; and in his right hand he carried a small wooden box that hung from a leather strap.

They walked in each other's tracks slowly. Rapidly the falling snow filled up the imprints of their feet. And when they passed there was silence again.

The man in front halted and raised his eyes to look ahead. The second man staggered against him, groaned with pain and gripped the other about the body with his loose hand to steady himself. The third man put the wooden box on the ground and shifted his pack.

'Where are we now?' he said.

His voice rang out, hollow, in the stillness; and several puffs of hot air, the words, jerked out, like steam from a starting engine.

'Can't say,' muttered the man in front. 'Steady, Commandant. We can't be far now. We're on the road anyway. It should be there in front. Can't see, though. It's in a hollow. That's why.'

'What's in a hollow, Jack?' muttered the wounded man. 'Let me lie down here. It's bleeding again.'

'Hold on, Commandant,' said the man in front. 'We'll be at the Mountain Tavern in half a minute. Christ!'

'Put him on my back,' said the big man. 'You carry the stuff.'

'Never mind, I'll walk,' said the wounded man. 'I'll get there all right. Any sign of them?'

They peered into the falling snow behind them. There was utter silence. The ghostly white shower made no sound. A falling curtain.

'Lead on then,' said the big man. 'Lean on me, Commandant.'

They moved on. The wounded man was groaning now and his feet began to drag. Shortly he began to rave in a low voice. Then they halted again. Without speaking, the big man hoisted his comrade, crosswise, on his shoulders. The other man carried the kit. They moved on again.

The peak in front became larger. It was no longer a formless mass. Gradually, through the curtain of snow, it seemed to move towards them and upwards. The air became still more thin. As from the summit of a towering cliff, the atmosphere in front became hollow; and soon, through the haze of snow, they caught a glimpse of the distant plains, between two mountain peaks. There below it lay, like the bottom of a sea, in silence. The mountain sides sank down into it, becoming darker; for it did not snow down there. There was something, after all, other than the snow. But the snowless downland earth looked dour and unapproachable.

'It must be here,' the leading man said again. 'Why can't we see it? It's just under the shelter of that mountain. There is a little clump of pine trees and a barn with a red roof. Sure I often had a drink in it. Where in the name of God is it, anyway?'

'Go on. Stop talking,' said the curly-headed man.

'Can't you be easy?' muttered the leading man, moving ahead and peering into the snow that made his eyelids blink and blink. 'Supposing this is the wrong road, after all. They say people go round and round in the snow. Sure ye could see it from the other end, four miles away in clear weather, two storey high and a slate roof with the sun shining on it. It's facing this way too, right on the top of the hill, with a black board, "Licensed to Sell". Man called Galligan owns it. I'd swear by the Cross of Christ we must be upon it.'

'Hurry on,' snapped the curly man. 'There's a gurgle in his throat. Jesus! His blood is going down my neck. Why can't you hurry on, blast it?'

'Hey, what place is that?' cried the leading man, in a frightened voice. 'D'ye see a ruin?'

They halted. A moment ago there had been nothing in front but a curtain of falling snow, beyond which, as in a child's sick dream, the darkening emptiness of the snowless lowland approached, tumbling like a scudding black cloud. Now a crazy blue heap appeared quite close. Suddenly it heaved up out of the snow. It was a ruined house. There was a smell from it too. From its base, irregular tufts of smoke curled up spasmodically; dying almost as soon as they appeared and then appearing again.

The two men watched it. There was no emotion in their faces. They just looked, as if without interest. It was too strange. The Mountain Tavern was a smoking ruin.

'It's gone west,' murmured the leading man.

'Eh?' shouted the curly man. 'Gone did ye say?'

'Aye. Burned to the ground. See?'

'Well?'

'God knows. We're up the pole.'

Suddenly the curly man uttered a cry of rage and staggered forward under his load. The other man opened his mouth wide, drew in an enormous breath and dropped his head wearily on his chest. Trailing his rifle in the snow behind him, he reeled forward, shaking his head from side to side, with his under lip trembling. Then he began to sing foolishly under his breath. There were people around the ruined house. And as the two men, with their dying comrade, came into view, quite close, these people stopped and gaped at them. There was a woman in front of the house, on the road, sitting on an upturned barrel. She was a thin woman with a long pointed nose and thin black hair that hung in disorder on her thin neck, with hair-pins sticking in it. She had a long overcoat buttoned over her dress and a man's overcoat about her shoulders. She held a hat with red feathers on it in her right hand, by the rim. Two children, wrapped in queer clothes, stood beside her, clinging to her, a boy and a girl. They also were thin and they had pointed noses like their mother. One man was pulling something out of a window of the ruined house. Another man, within the window, had his head stuck out. He had been handing out something. Another man was in the act of putting a tin trunk on a cart, to which a horse was harnessed, to the right of the house. All looked, gaping, at the newcomers.

'God save all here,' said the curly man, halting near the woman.

Nobody replied. The other man came up and staggered towards the woman, who was sitting on the upturned barrel. The two children, silent with fear, darted around their mother, away from the man. They clutched at her, muttering something inaudibly.

'Is that you, Mrs. Galligan?'

'It is then,' said the woman in a stupid, cold voice. 'And who might you be?'

'We're Republican soldiers,' said the curly man. 'I have a dying man here.'

He lowered the wounded man gently to the ground. Nobody spoke or moved. The snow fell steadily.

'Mummy, mummy,' cried one of the children, 'there's blood on him. Oh! mummy.'

The two children began to howl. The dying man began to throw his hands about and mutter something. A great rush of blood flowed from him.

'In the name of the Lord God of Heaven,' yelled the curly man, 'are ye savages not to move a foot? Eh? Can't ye go for a doctor? Is there nothing in the house?'

He stooped over the dying man and clutching him in his arms, he cried hoarsely:

'Easy now, Commandant. I'm beside ye. Give us a hand with him, Jack. We'll fix the bandage.'

The two of them, almost in a state of delirium, began to fumble with the dying man. The children wept. The dying man suddenly cried out:

'Stand fast. Stand fast boys. Stand. . . .'

Then he made a violent effort to sit up. He opened his mouth and did not close it again.

The woman looked on dazed, with her forehead wrinkled and her lips set tight. The three men who had been doing something among the ruin began to come up slowly. They also appeared dazed, terrified.

'He's gone,' murmured the curly man, sitting erect on his knees. 'God have mercy on him.'

He laid the corpse flat on the ground. The blood still flowed out.

The other soldier took off his hat and then, just as he was going to cross himself, he burst into tears. The three men came close and looked on. Then they sheepishly took off their hats.

'Is he dead?' said one of them.

The curly man sat back on his heels.

'He's dead,' he said. 'The curse o' God on this country.'

'And what did ye say happened?'

'Ambush back there. Our column got wiped out. Haven't ye got anything in the house?'

The woman laughed shrilly. The children stopped crying.

'Is there nothing in the house, ye daylight robber?' she cried. 'Look at it, curse ye. It's a black ruin. Go in. Take what ye can find, ye robber.'

'Robbers!' cried the soldier who had been weeping. 'Come on, Curly. Stand by me. I'm no robber. God! Give me a drink. Something to eat. Christ! I'm dyin'.'

He got to his feet and took a pace forward like a drunken man. The curly-haired soldier caught him.

'Keep yer hair on, Jack,' he said.

'Look at what ye've done,' cried the woman. 'Ye've blown up the house over me head. Ye've left me homeless and penniless with yer war. Oh! God, why don't ye drop down the dome of Heaven on me?'

'Sure we didn't blow up yer house,' cried the curly soldier. 'An' we lookin' for shelter after trampin' the mountains since morning. Woman, ye might respect the dead that died for ye.'

The woman spat and hissed at him.

'Let them die. They didn't die for me,' she said. 'Amn't I ruined and wrecked for three long years with yer fightin', goin' back and forth, lootin' and turnin' the honest traveller from my door? For three long years have I kept open house for all of ye and now yer turnin' on one another like dogs after a bitch.'

'None o' that now,' cried the hysterical soldier, trying to raise his rifle.

'Hold on, man,' cried one of the other men. 'She has cause. She has cause.'

He grew excited and waved his hands and addressed his own comrades instead of addressing the soldiers.

'The Republicans came to the house this morning,' he cried. 'So Mr. Galligan told me an' he goin' down the road for McGilligan's motor. The Republicans came, he said. And then . . . then the Free Staters came on top of them and the firing began. Women and children out, they said, under a white flag. So Galligan told me. "They damn near shot me," says he to me, "harbourin' Irregulars under the new act". Shot at night, or what's worse, they take ye away on the cars. God knows where. Found in a ditch. None of us, God blast my soul if there is a word of a lie in what I am sayin', none of us here have a

79

hand or part in anything. Three miles I came up in the snow when Mr. Galligan told me. Says he to me, "I'll take herself and the kids to Aunt Julia's in McGilligan's motor".'

'Where did they go?' said the curly soldier.

'I was comin' to that,' said the man, spitting in the snow and turning towards the woman. 'It's with a bomb they did it, Galligan said to me. Something must have fallen in the fire. They stuck it out, he said. There were six men inside. Not a man came out without a wound. So he said. There were two dead. On a door they took 'em away. They took 'em all off in the cars. And they were goin' to take Mr. Galligan too. There you are now. May the Blessed Virgin look down on here. An' many's a man'll go thirsty from this day over the mountain road.'

'Aye,' said the woman. 'For twenty years in that house, since my father moved from the village, after buyin' it from Johnny Reilly. 'Twenty years,' she said again.

'Can't ye give us something to eat?' cried the hysterical man trying to break loose from the curly soldier, who still held him.

'There's nothing here,' muttered a man, 'until Mr. Galligan comes in the motor. He should be well on the way now.'

'They were all taken,' said the curly soldier.

'All taken,' said the three men, all together.

'Sit down, Jack,' said the curly soldier.

He pulled his comrade down with him on to the snow. He dropped his head on his chest. The others looked at the soldiers sitting in the snow. The others had a curious malign look in their eyes. They looked at the dazed, exhausted soldiers and at the corpse with a curious apathy. They looked with hatred. There was no pity in their eyes. They looked steadily without speech or movement, with the serene cruelty of children watching an insect being tortured. They looked patiently, as if calmly watching a monster in its death agony.

The curly-headed soldier suddenly seemed to realize that they were watching him. For he raised his head and peered at them shrewdly through the falling snow. There was utter silence everywhere, except the munching sound made by the horse's jaws as he chewed hay. The snow fell, fell now, in the fading light, mournfully, blotting out the sins of the world.

The soldier's face, that had until then shown neither fear nor weariness, suddenly filled with despair. His lips bulged out. His eyes almost closed. His forehead gathered together and he opened his nostrils wide.

'I'm done,' he said. 'It's no use. Say, men. Send word that we're here. Let them take us. I'm tired fightin'. It's no use.'

No one spoke or stirred. A sound approached. Strange to say, no one paid attention to the sound. And even when a military motor lorry appeared at the brow of the road, nobody moved or spoke.

There were Free State soldiers on the lorry. They had their rifles pointed. They drew near slowly. Then, with a rush, they dismounted and came running up.

The two Republican soldiers put up their hands, but they did not rise to their feet.

'Robbers,' screamed the woman. 'I hate ye all. Robbers.'

Her husband was there with them.

'Mary, we're to go in the lorry,' he said to her. 'They're goin' to look after us they said. Fr. Considine went to the barracks.'

'The bloody robbers,' she muttered, getting off the barrel.

'Who's this?' the officer said, roughly handling the corpse.

He raised the head of the corpse.

'Ha!' he said. 'So we got him at last. Eh? Heave him into the lorry, boys. Hurry up. Chuck 'em all in.'

They took away the corpse and the prisoners. There was a big dark spot where the corpse had lain. Snow began to fall on the dark spot.

They took away everybody, including the horse and cart. Everybody went away, down the steep mountain road, into the dark lowland country, where no snow was falling. All was silent again on the flat top of the mountain.

There was nothing in the whole universe again but the black ruin and the black spot where the corpse had lain. Night fell and snow fell, fell like soft soothing white flower petals on the black ruin and on the black spot where the corpse had lain.

# The Patriot

## SEAN O'FAOLAIN

---

I T WAS doubtless because of the inevitable desire of man to re-
capture the past that they went to Youghal for their honeymoon.
Their friends expected them to go at least to Dublin, if not to
London or Paris, but they both knew in their hearts that they had
spent the gayest days of their lives in this little town, and so, as if
to crown all those early happinesses, to Youghal they went, like true
voluptuaries deliberately creating fresh memories that would torment
them when they were old.

Across there on the little stone promenade, when they were as yet
little more than girl and boy, they had met for the first time. She was
on holiday with her sister; he had come with his aunt for the day. In
the train they had met Edward Bradley, his former teacher, and Mr.
Bradley had walked about with him (in spite of his aunt) for a few
hours, and given them tea. He had been flattered, he remembered,
because old Bradley stayed with them so long, and afterwards he
pretended to Norah that Mr. Bradley was really a great friend of his.
Off there at the end of the promenade they had sat, the three of them,
because his aunt was too old to walk far without a rest, and as they
sat there Norah and her sister came and halted opposite them to lean
on the wall. A liner was passing slowly, almost imperceptibly, along
the horizon and everybody was looking at it, and his aunt was asking
him to tell them—he was young, God bless him, and had the better
sight—was it two funnels or three it had. He had stood up, pretending
to look at the liner, but he was really trying to look at Norah's
black hair and her jet-black eyes without being seen, growing irritated
because he and she could not be there alone, and growing more
irritated still because he saw that she too was trying to look at him
without being observed, turning her back frequently on the sea to
look, as it were, up over their heads at the crowds on the cliffs,
curving herself backwards over the wall and standing on her toes
as if to show herself off to him. In the end her sister drew her away as
the ship became too faint to be seen and Bernard became so dis-
consolate and silent that his aunt plucked at him and said:

83

'What on earth's wrong with you, Bernie? Are you tired, or what is it?'

But Mr. Bradley cocked his eye at him and winked without his aunt seeing. Old Bradley was a cute boyo, he had thought, and flushed because he felt he had been observed. After tea he and his aunt were alone again, and she, who had been so sweet to their companion, was now abusing him roundly for a firebrand who was leading all the young men into wild politics. 'Some day,' Bernie defended, 'that man will be Lord Mayor of Cork and then you'll sing a different song,' but she would have none of it and as he just then caught sight again of his dark girl in the distance and wished to walk on and catch up with her he did not argue further. Alas! His aunt got tired once more, saying that the tea was like a load on her stomach, and they had to sit on another bench. His dark vision passed out of his sight and he felt she had merely floated before him and he would never meet her again.

When he did meet her again it was several years after and she was again on holiday in Youghal, and it was only by degrees they realized they had seen each other before. On this occasion he was an Irregular guerilla—doubly a rebel—seated high up on a lorry, with his rifle across his back and his coat collar turned up, and his cap thrown back and upwards from his forehead to let his curls free to the wind. Seven other lorries were roaring along behind him through the streets and as they tore their way under the old clock archway, there on the pavement, smiling up at them, and waving her green handkerchief to them, was the loveliest dark-haired girl he had ever seen. Their lorry halted just beyond the arch to wait for the troops marching in from the railway, and he alighted and by virtue of being a soldier was able to approach her on the pretence of wanting matches or cigarettes. By the time the troops came into the town they were in a little teashop, and he was flirting away with all the bravado in the world. As the men passed outside, four by four, they sang their rebelly songs, waking, as he said to her, the ghosts of old Raleigh, who had once lived there, and of the stiff Earl of Cork from his tomb in Christ's Church, and the ghost of every Elizabethan sailorman who cast a rope ashore by the crumbled quays they could see through the rear door of the shop, edging with their fallen stones the glittering blue of the bay.

There were descendants of those sea dogs in that town still, she told him, for having come there year after year on her holidays since she was a little child she knew Youghal as if she had been born there. She chanted the names to him, the Merricks, the Gurneys, the Boyles, the Brisketts, and at each name he swaggered his cup on high to curse them, so that it was a profane litany that finished their tea.

'The Yardleys too,' she said, laughing at him.

'God damn them forever!' he swashbuckled.

'Of course the Townshends are Cromwellians,' she smiled.

'Damn them forever!' he cried again.

Her eyes wandered to the bay. A brown-sailed yawl was floating past on the blue water as gracefully as a yacht.

'Isn't she lovely?' she cried, flushing with the delight of it.

'Not as lovely as you,' he bantered.

'Oh! Come and watch her,' she invited, and away they went.

When he found his way to the abandoned military barracks they had taken over, it was late night—discipline was a joke in those days—but he did not sleep for many hours, standing at the window of the deserted messroom watching where the moon poured down across the face of the shimmering ocean, into the little harbour. It lit up as if it were day the shouldering furze-bright hills, and the white edge of motionless surf at the base of the distant cliffs, and every sleeping roof in the town clustered beneath him.

It was curious that it was there in Youghal, too, that same summer, that Norah had first met Edward Bradley. There had been a public meeting in the market place while the guerillas held the town and one of the chief speakers was Bradley. That day he had spoken with a terrible passion against England, and against the Irish traitors who had been cowed by her, and his passionate words caught and flared the temper of the people so that they cheered and cheered until their voices echoed across the smooth surface of the water into the woods beyond. Bernie had cheered like the rest where he stood beside Norah, proud to be that man's friend. After the meeting the three met, and the teacher, flushed with his success, walked between them along the tumble-down quays. He found that he knew Norah's people quite well, though he had not seen them for many years.

'But I'll call on them often now,' he said, looking at Norah, and he began to take her arm, and then he remembered Bernie and he took his arm—like a grandfather, Bernie had said, jokingly, to him, and was angry with himself for saying it, for a deeper blush crept over the face of the older man and, halting, he had said:

'Maybe I am too old to be walking with the like of ye,' and cocking his eye at the girl again he had laughed, half bitterly as Bernie thought, and with a 'God bless ye, my children,' turned and walked away. Wasn't he a very nice man, Norah had said, and stood looking after the teacher so long that Bernie almost thought he was going to be jealous; but he had not thought long of it. It was a warm autumn day, and so clear that they could see across the channel where the hay garnered in for the winter had left white patches on the clovered meadows. Tempted by the fields beyond they had rowed slowly across the bay to spend the afternoon on the other side. The geese had cropped the grass of the foreshore until it was as close and clean as a golf course, except where a few odd straws lost to the granary lay strewn about and, with them, cast up by the tide, bits of reedy sea wrack, and here and there the dark grey droppings of the fowl. The air was so rarefied that as they crossed the low stone walls on their way into the oak woods the stones fell with a gurgling sound like water, and far away the ocean boomed deeply into the crannied rocks. They had gone deep into the woods to lie there while the misty darkness fell, bringing in the night wind a little rain, to lie there in their deep love as still as corpses, as still as fallen leaves. They returned late at night to the town whose yellow windows, bright across the channel, spoke to them of sanded floors in quayside pubs and the first fires before the winter.

But before that week was out the town was abandoned and Norah had to stand under the shelter of the old town walls watching the great barracks smoking against the fading sky and the distant mountains, themselves so faint that in their greyness they blended and were lost in the darkness and the smoke.

It was the way of that guerilla life that for months on end a man never even thought of home or friends, and for months Bernard wandered among those grey mountains to the north of Youghal, as aimlessly as, and, he used to feel, more uselessly than, a lost sheep. Once only did he use his rifle in those seven months of guerilla life and that was when sniping from fifteen hundred yards a village supposed to contain enemy troops. He slept in a different bed each night and never ate twice in succession from the same table so that most of his time was spent in going from place to place in search of food and rest. He did so less from a sense of danger than a sense of pity towards the farmers who had to feed and shelter him and his fellows, never thinking that as all his fellows did as he was doing, it saved nothing to the flour bin lying lightly on the loft, or the tea caddy on the high mantelshelf, emptied almost daily.

The days scarcely existed for him, the weeks flew over his head as unnoticed as birds homing at night, until as a human being he almost ceased to be, enveloped by the countryside as if he were a twig, a stone, an ear of corn. And then, without the slightest warning, as suddenly as the breaking of a thundershower, he remembered how lovely Youghal had been, and Norah, and he hated to look up at the cold and naked mountains. It was late February with the rain falling as by the clock, and for a month they had been hunted through it, day and night. Thinking of that and thinking of the summer his memory began to work on him like a goad. All about him on the night he thought of her, sitting along by the embers of a turf fire after the family had gone to bed, the mountains lay black and silent, wet as if they had been dipped in the sea. Overhead a white path of stars more clear in the washed air than if there were a frost abroad. Out there, too, he felt, was danger; he was listening so intently that he almost leaped when a little cricket chirruped in the dark warmth of the hearth. He feared even to stir, so great a noise did every movement make—almost as great, it seemed, as the resounding *drop-drop* of the leaking thatch beyond the door.

In his pocketbook he had her one letter, reminding him of that little wood where they had loved:

> I went specially to Youghal to see our wood again. The autumn is over it and over all the land. The days are shortening, farmers are threshing, thatching turf-ricks, digging potatoes, culling sheep from their flocks to barter in fair and market, fields are decaying with grief for the loss of their fruits, and grief is a brown and withered hag, nuts are ripening, blackberries are rotting, holly berries are reddening, leaves are dropping yellow. Mists cover the mountains like a hooded cloak, grey rocks ooze tears of desolation, green ferns on the hillside are withering, and purple heather is turning grey. Birds are silent, winds rustling in denuded boughs. In Youghal tourists are departed—no more the hum of the motor, nor the flash of fashionable attire. In my little hotel Mrs. M—— is resting and knitting, K—— turning over stacks of *McCall's Journals* and *Home Gossips*, the serving-girl is considering her return to her mother's home, P—— L—— wearing her shoes 'going aisht and wesht', B—— twinkling with gestating jokes, and R—— counting the takings of the season. Norah is at the moment writing to Bernard; at other moments?—thinking, reading, peering into a dimly lit future. . . .

He smiled at that letter, so full of life as it was. Then he thought of the night outside and went to the door. He could hear the streams swirling down the dark *leaca* and as he listened their roar mingled with the desolation of the silence, and he wished passionately to be away from so lonely and cruel a place.

Three miles across the hills, in a little fishing hotel by a mountain lake, was the headquarters of the division. There, he hoped, he might get money—a few shillings would do—to help him on the road home, and maybe they would give him a clean shirt and collar, and a better hat and trousers than these guerilla rags that, up to now, he had been flaunting as with a deliberate joy in their torn dirt. Above all he might meet Edward Bradley there. For he too had been hiding for several months in the mountains, not daring to stay in the city for fear of arrest. He felt he wanted to talk to somebody like Bradley, someone who would persuade him that this struggle of theirs was not hopeless, that all their humiliation of poverty and hunger was not, as he had long since begun to feel, a useless and wasted offering. Quietly he unbolted the door and stole through the yard into the sodden starlight.

It was midnight when he saw the lake below him and to his surprise every window in the little hotel was lit. He approached warily, alert for a sentry's challenge, an enemy patrol—he might, he knew, be shot as easily by either. But he continued to walk unaccosted past the sleeping farmhouses and the great strewn rocks until he came to the lakeside edge and the lighted windows. Inside the steamed window the room was filled with armed men, smoking, drinking, arguing in groups. He recognized the faces of three or four officers. There was the adjutant with his eyes swollen with too much drink and too little sleep—it was common knowledge that he lived like that. By the fire was Boyle, a great black-faced commandant from Kerry; under the lamp in the largest group he recognized Tom Carroll from East Cork—clearly a meeting of the officers of the division.

He entered unchallenged where a group of men were lounging in the dim candle lit hall. Three officers strode out of the room—it was the dining-room—with empty glasses in each hand, returning gingerly when the glasses had been filled to the brim with black stout or porter. He saw the Quartermaster coming out of the kitchen with a pair of black pint glasses dripping their froth about his wrists. He went over to tell him how dangerous it was to leave the back road unguarded. The Quartermaster only growled:

'Well, what are you doing here then? Go up yourself and sentrify it,' and passed on.

The column Captain came out from the bar with a tray of divers-coloured glasses and to him also Bernie told how the north road was unprotected. But the Captain flew into a rage and glared at him over the tray.

'I've told off six men, there, to go,' he said, jerking his head at the loungers in the hall.

One of them spoke back at him, a fellow with only two walrus teeth above and below in his gums.

'We won't go. Why should we go? Ye're all dhrinking. Why don't we get a dhrink?'

'Go into the kitchen and get it,' said the Captain.

'Where'll we get the money?'

'Ask the Quartermaster.'

'Damn the Quartermaster.'

'I want the Quartermaster,' said Bernie. 'I want a couple of bob to get home.'

The loungers scoffed at him in a loud chorus, and Buckteeth called him Sweet Innocence. Two more joined them, swaggering in their belted and ragged raincoats, out from the glow of the dining-room into the dark hall. As they came they deliberately crushed against the Captain's tray, all but upsetting his yellow and purple argosy. With a curse at them he raced like a waiter balancing his tray

88

into the dining-room, returning to grab Bernard and put him standing in the between passage outside the dining-room door.

'Stand there, you,' he growled. 'And let nobody into this room unless he has business there.'

The loungers cheered.

'Will ye go up, for Christ's sake,' the Captain implored them, 'to the north road and watch it or the whole division will be caught?'

'Oh! It's always deh division, aw!' piped up a little fair-haired sprat of a boy from the foot of the stairs. 'What about deh men, aw? Dere's never any talk about deh men?'

'For God's sake, get us a drink, Jim,' appealed the man with the walrus teeth.

'Go on, Jim,' joined in three or four more. They seemed to have no sense of pride left.

With a sudden air of intimacy the Captain stepped into the middle of them, bending his neck right and left among them like a pecking hen.

'Go in,' he said, 'and take it. Say the Quartermaster will fix it up. They'll never know in the hotel.'

Buckteeth turned away in disgust.

'No! They feed us, and they sleep us,' he said, 'and we're not going to soak drink from them as well.'

'Well, I have no money for you,' complained the Captain.

'Deh Quartermaster have buckets of it,' declared Fair Hair.

'*Buckets* is deh word,' sneered a tall man in spectacles from his dark corner at the door.

They laughed at the word in spite of their anger: it measured the Quartermaster's thirst.

'Well, I can do no more for ye,' said the Captain in a temper, and left them.

Bernie stood where he had been placed by the dining-room door and everybody passed in and out without paying the slightest attention to him. The Quartermaster, already flushed with drink, returned to fill his glasses once more, and timidly Bernie touched him on the shoulder.

'Well? Are you here still?' said the Quartermaster.

Bernie had not the courage to face the refusal of a loan so he asked instead for cigarettes. The Quartermaster thrust a package into his hand.

'Here,' he said. 'You fellows do nothing from morning to night but bum and soak for cigarettes. Why don't ye do something?'

As he passed by, a piece of black and white paper fluttered gently to the ground in his wake. Bernie picked it up. It was a hundred pound note. For a moment he thought of rushing out to his fellows in the hall and waving it in the air before their eyes; for another moment he thought of using it himself to get home. Then he realized he could not steal money like that, and even if he did nobody would change so large a note for them or him. As the Quartermaster returned he tapped his arm once again. A wave of whiskey belched into his face as the fellow turned on him and stuck his potato nose into his face. Bernie held up the note, saw him look stupidly at it, without a word thrust it into his vest pocket and stride into the dining-room with his dripping glasses. What a hopeless sort of army they were, Bernie thought, and he made up his mind that he must at all costs go back into the city out of these mountains where they did nothing for month after month but eat the substance of the people and lounge over the fire like sleepy dogs. Things were still happening occasionally in the city. If he could rest for a while and see Norah, he would become invigorated by her and be of some use again. Suddenly there was a great stirring in the room and the Captain returned to tell him to close and guard the outer door. Bernie did not have the energy to tell him that all this was foolery. Instead he begged a match from him and lit a cigarette and leaned into the corner of the passage to think. He had waited so long he could wait now another couple of hours until the dawn.

By the glow of the lamps in the room beyond the passageway he read Norah's letter again, scarcely hearing the talking and arguing rising hotter and hotter at the meeting, though he faintly gathered as he read the letter by the dim light that they were considering the whole military situation in the south and that some were for laying down their arms at once, and others for fighting on. He was hardly interested. He was thinking only of the summer that was gone and of every little incident of his last meeting with Norah in the woods beyond the bay at Youghal. Gradually the discussion in the room changed to an argument about men and ammunition and money and as the voices fell his thoughts wandered freely to the brown-sailed yawl they saw floating past the frame of the restaurant door, the sun shining on the blue and white sea in its wake and the curling foam at its bows. He remembered how he had whispered an old song to her as they lay among the leaves and to himself he hummed it over again:

*O beloved of my inmost heart,*
*Come some night and soon,*
*When my people are at rest,*
*That we may talk together;*
*My arms shall encircle you*
*While I relate my sad tale*
*That it was your pleasant soft voice*
*That has stolen my heaven.*

*The fire is unraked,*
*The light extinguished,*

*The key is under the door.*
*And do you softly draw it.*
*My mother is asleep,*
*But I am awake.*
*My fortune is in my hand*
*And I am ready.*
*I will go with you. . . .*

He heard Edward Bradley's voice addressing the meeting. Why he should be there he did not know, for he was not an army man. Afterwards he told Bernie that because he was older than anybody there they wanted to hear what the politicians had to say. He was imploring them not to lay down their arms—far better to be defeated, at a blow or by degrees, though that would be slow and terrible for them all. As on that day at Youghal his passion carried the meeting with him and they cheered him loudly when he finished. When he came into the passage he was flushed and trembling, and when he saw Bernie he drew him with him out into the hall and, because the loungers were still there, out into the cool air by the side of the lake. A sedge of broken reeds had been washed ashore by the storms, reminding Bernie of the sedge of sea wrack on the foreshore across Youghal bay, but across the lake the mountain streams made a ceaseless desolate moaning, and a night mist was blowing in their faces so that they had to shelter in the darkness of a gable wall. He told Bernie how terrible things were all over the country and Bernie told him what he knew of the state of the men among those hills, all of them weak and scabby and sore, not a penny in their pockets, not a pipeful to smoke, nothing to do from one week to another but run when danger approached, never together, badly led, beaten all but in name.

'And in this hotel,' said Bradley, 'the officers taking their breakfast at six o'clock in the evening and drinking in the dawn.'

Suddenly Bradley said:

'Do you hear at all from that girl now?'

'What girl?'

'The girl in Youghal.'

'A long time ago. I got a letter.'

He hated to talk of Norah. It was as if she were a secret part of him and he would not bare it.

'She is a very intelligent girl,' said Bradley.

'Yes,' said Bernie as if he were not really interested, but he felt his breath come in heavy waves.

'Oh, yes!' said Bradley. 'I saw a good deal of her before I came out here. I stayed at her house for safety several times before I took to the hills. A very nice girl.'

91

Bernie shivered, his blood turning over in his body, but it was not from the cold.

'Well, I'm leaving in an hour or two,' said Bradley. 'This place won't be safe for twenty miles around after the news of this meeting gets to the military.'

In the hall the candle was guttering out, but the loungers still remained. To say something to them as he passed in Bernie told them what Bradley had said of the conditions about the country and of the officers in the hotel.

'Puh!' taunted the tall bespectacled fellow. 'And what does he do himself but hang over a book in the comfort of the hotel fire from morning to night?'

Bernie returned to his position in the passage. He was sick of these tauntings and tale bearings. He wondered how a man like Bradley could remain out there where he must hear them and notice them day after day. If Bradley chose he could go back to hide in the city any day—there would be many people glad to receive and shelter him, and Bernie wished he had asked for the loan of half a crown and a clean collar and tie. He must see Norah again, and the city, and his people, and friends. The Quartermaster was talking now, in a thick but fierce voice.

' "No surrender" must be our cry,' he was saying. 'I'd rather be shot any day than surrender. Let those that are tired of the fight go into the city and surrender!'

He peeped into the long room. One lamp was guttered low to a smoking circle of red wick. The other glowed like a yellow ball through the skeins of smoke woven in heavy layers from table to ceiling. Beer bottles and empty glasses were everywhere. The men were yawning and stretching themselves, some talking among themselves, paying no heed at all to the speaker, and the chairman was drawing idle circles with a pencil on the table before him.

Somebody silenced the Quartermaster with a question and by degrees the talk fell again to a drone as they discussed men and money and ammunition. He leaned back into a corner of the passage and while he thought of the road home, of every wind and turn in it, of every side road and back road he could take, he fell into a doze where he stood. He awoke to hear Boyle from Kerry cry out in a fury at somebody:

'Let them that want to rat, do it. Myself and John Jo Sheehan will hold Kerry anyway. Won't we, John Jo?'

The meeting seemed to be ending. Sheehan was standing huge against the window with his back to them all; in spite of the lamp, black-shouldered against the pale glimmer of the dawn hanging over the mists on the lake outside. In taunting and utter disbelief he cursed over his shoulder at Boyle.

'Hold Kerry, how are you? You and Kerry may go to hell!'

92

The meeting broke up in laughter, men standing and talking in little groups, edging around their chief to discuss private questions of their own. It seemed as if they would never come out and Bernie sat on the ground to sleep. The first few officers leaving the room poked his stomach with their boots in mockery of their sleeping sentry. He made his way out to the kitchen, where the loungers were strewn asleep on the settle, the table, on chairs or about the floor near the grey embers of the fire. He rolled a porter barrel in from the bar and sat on it and through the sounds of the departing officers, horses stamping, carts trundling out, searchings in the dark for last drinks, calls and farewells, he slept in the corner of the cooling hearth. When he awoke the morning had come and the loungers were, like him, shivering together over the grate, where Buckteeth was blowing the seed of fire into a fresh sod of turf. Seeing him open his eyes they asked him:

'Well? What was deh end of deh meeting, aw? Are we to go home or stay here? Aw?'

'Fight on!' said Bernie.

They looked at him too tired to mock the phrase.

'Stay here, he means,' said Buckteeth. 'Stay bloody well here.'

Bernie shared his cigarettes about and they smoked in silence while the fowl awakened by the echoing crow of the cock began to clatter and suckle in the rain water of the yard, for the rain was now darkening the window, pouring straight down into the dung-filled haggard. Looking out at it Bernie saw again the mist hanging in the woods of Youghal, and Norah running down the slip to the ferry, her black curls swinging as she ran. Their hunger began to stir in them, but they could not find a scrap of food in the house—it had all been eaten by the crowd just departed. In their search they found the Quartermaster snoring on the sofa of the dining-room, a roll of bank notes hanging from his pocket. At once they grabbed them, sharing out the smaller notes, leaving the twenty-fives and the fifties and the hundreds, but as they argued over the division the Quartermaster awoke and in a fury he demanded the money. Buckteeth, who held the fistful of notes, showered them over the furious man's head, and while he clambered under the tables and the chairs to collect them they mocked at him. Beside himself with rage he cursed them for lazy, useless louts and rushing off to tackle his horse and side-car in the yard he left through the blowing rain while in a crowd they cheered him from the door. But money would not buy them food and they went about draining the ebb of porter in every glass, then wandering over the hotel from floor to attic to see what they could find. There was not a soul there but the people of the house sleeping heavily after the long hours of work the day before, so they returned to the kitchen to wait.

At last the girls of the house came down the ladder-like stairs, their legs thrust bare into their dung-covered boots. They sat on the settle by the fire, bowed over their knees until their mother followed.

'A bad morning, Mrs. O'Rourke,' said Bernie to the mother.

She stood by the low window and looked sadly at the rain.

'Isn't it a bad morning, thanks be to God?' she sighed.

Not a word of reproach was said, or of inquiry about the meeting, or of complaint at their long labour. The girls sat looking at the fire or out at the rain. There was nothing for them to eat, and nothing to do on such a wet day. The mother began to scrape the bins and the bags for flour and when the boy of the house came in he milked the cows. The dough was dampened with spring water and fresh milk. It was kneaded and shaped and put into the bastable while they all looked on. Through the open door they could see the rain splashing the causeway outside and a duck poked his eye in by the jamb. Buckteeth spat at the cocked eye and the duck clattered out, but nobody laughed. The bastable was over the fire and they had all turned to it to watch while the cake baked. While they waited six other men came to the house, sodden with rain, arm and thigh and chest, searching for a breakfast and news of the meeting, but when they found the others before them they moved on patiently to the next farmhouse a mile off. They said they must be in Millstreet, twenty miles away, before night. Then they would walk on into Limerick along the Feale. For Limerick, they declared, bare and open though it was, was safer now than Cork. One of them, a Kerry lad, had no socks and his feet were torn by the bare leather of his boots. He had no overcoat, his very shirt clung to his back with wet, and he coughed ceaselessly. The woman of the house took pity on him and asked him to stay, and when he heard the others argue that Limerick was a far more dangerous place than Cork he sat down wearily by the fire and began to cry, telling his companions between his tears that he was afraid to go on with them and would hide here among the mountains. All the while Buckteeth and the others looked awkwardly at him. They offered him cigarettes and tried to cheer him by assuring him that this place was as safe as a house, and while he and they drank the scalding tea and ate soft hot cake the girls searched him out a pair of socks and a dry, if torn, shirt.

But while they ate they were less sure about the safety of the glens and they argued and argued as to what they should do next. The Kerry lad could say nothing but 'We must hide. We must hide in the holes of the mountains,' and the little fair-haired city gamin kept whining plaintively 'But where are our officers? Where are our officers from us now? Aw?' At intervals the boy of the house assured them again and again that it was madness to stay there another day with the valleys filled, as he said, with 'people taking the heels from one another with the news of the meeting to the military in the next village.' So, when the rain lightened they scattered, some going to the north, one declaring that the safest thing was to skirt the village to the east, and Bernie found he had lost courage to attempt the journey home. Tomorrow he would go, he thought, and with Buckteeth and Kerry, as they christened him, he went up among the cliffs in search of a cave to hide in. The boy of the house, though he kept assuring them it was madness to stay there, showed them a dump that had been made in a cleft between the rocks, a grave-like place dug out of the earth and covered with a sheet of corrugated tin and hidden by stones and withered brushwood. There was barely room for the three to lie in this dark, damp tomb, but as Kerry implored them to go into it at once, they lay down there, shoulder to shoulder, peering up and out all day long at the grey spears of the falling rain.

At dark, in spite of their hunger and the cold, they slept. They slept past the rising of the sun, past the late morning, and all the while it rained and the whistling of the rain seemed to lull and keep them asleep in spite of encircling danger. They were awakened by the shattering echoes of machine-gun fire and the impact of hundreds of bullets tearing at the rock above their heads. When the first volley ceased, the echoes carried its *rat-a-tat-tat* across the cliff-top to where another echoing air seized upon it and reduplicated it fainter and fainter into the heart of the mountains before it finally died into silence. There was such a long interval that it seemed as if everybody were listening to that last faint replication so high up and so far away. Then they heard the shouts below them:

'Come out! Come out, ye snipes! Come out or we'll bomb ye out. Come out!'

These cries were echoed, and then a brief silence followed. The next minute the gun seemed to tear the tin roof from over their heads where they crouched helpless, their faces to the clay. They had placed their boots to dry, the night before, on the ledge before their dump and these now shot in on their foreheads torn to pieces by bullets. Again the echoes were reduplicated to the farthest uttermost glen and again the shouts came, mingling with those echoes and their own that followed after.

'Yeer last chance! Ye whores! Come out!'

The Kerry boy began to weep again.

'O God!' he shouted. 'Leave us out. Leave us out.'

'Throw down yeer guns,' cried the echoing voices below.

They did so, and Buckteeth, tearing a sleeve from his shirt, raised it before him as he crawled out into the rain. Below them was a score of sturdy green-clad riflemen and in a minute the three were among them shivering with fear and excitement—broken, timid as children.

They passed through Youghal as prisoners, standing high on a lorry, conspicuous in their rags, and as it roared its way under the old clock archway, there across the wind-blown bay Bernie glimpsed his woods shrouded in mist, growing, as it seemed, out of the grey-green bay. Never did anything seem so definitely past to him as his

95

summer flirting under those trees. It might have happened to him in another life, it might have been something he read of in a novel, so distant did it seem.

They drove him to Cork that night and there he remained in prison until the winter was passed and another winter had come again. Norah wrote to him many times while he was in jail—at first briefly but kindly, sending him gifts as she might to any other prisoner, later on long letters at greater length, as to a special friend. After a while she brought herself to reproach him for his long silence of that lonely winter, a winter in which she had tried hard, and vainly, to be, as he had been, forgetful of the sweetness of their summer and autumn love. It was Christmas when he received a letter from her confessing how miserable and unhappy those months had been, and he was glad of the confession though it was a torment to him to be reminded, in the place where he was, of his foolishness when he had been free. When she wrote that Edward Bradley often stayed with them, and spoke kindly of him, it was a double torment —that worst torment of all prisoners—to think what lovely things life could have given him, too, if he were out in the world and part of it. When he was freed he was very ill and weak and the doctor ordered him to the sea and he went, as a matter of course, to Youghal. It was February again, just a year since he had passed through it as a prisoner, and the woods and the bay were again shrouded in haze, but because Norah came to see him, and walked with him there, and showed him the rain in the cobwebs among the branches, and—it was so mild there by the sea—an early celandine hiding under a root, he thought those woods even more beautiful than they had been almost two years before when they watched the red globe of the autumn sun sinking behind its black branches.


Small wonder then that they should come back to the little seaside town for their honeymoon. It was Easter and late in the spring—the fifteenth of April had been Easter Sunday—so that the catkins' furry paws were already raised to the sun, and the long tails and the tiny wet noses of the lambs protruded from the red and blue creels rumbling in to the lamb fair. The yellow furze was ranged high against the blue sky along the slopes of the hills, and over the surface of the sea beneath there was a cold layer of air that made the waves break with a brittle noise such as one never hears in the soft, dead heat of summer. They went about that first day, their wedding day, noticing everything with new delight—the spears of green grass shooting through the dead fields, the primroses and the violets clustered near the grey stones in the ditches, the beech buds swollen red, the patches of hawthorn green lighting the withered hedges.

The long country lanes were empty; they had the ocean to themselves. The summer visitors had not yet even thought of coming and all the length of the old stone promenade was bare. They even felt a delight in the shuttered windows and the bathing boxes nailed up since last autumn. On the sands stretching for miles in front of them, lost in the end in the spume of the incoming waves far off in the distance, they saw only a sandpiper or two strutting by the skirts of the spreading sea, or peewits in their swoop turning as if to command on their white bellies, then turning again on dark wings, low over the thunderous waves. When they lay under an early blossoming blackthorn high above that singing sea and in the long silences of love gazed over the empty horizon, or back at the clustered smoking chimneys on the farther shore, Bernard felt, and knew that his young wife felt, that if another gull should wheel through the blue air, another distant lamb call out to its dam, their cups of ecstasy must overflow and roll upon the ground. They crossed back then, as of old, to the points of light that marked the town through an early sea haze and sought out that little restaurant where so long ago they had cursed the Elizabethans and the Cromwellians, and there they had their tea, watching back through the open door at the rear of the shop the channel darkening with the fall of night. As they ate they suddenly saw beside them a little green poster bearing that day's name and date. They read it with interest:

SINN FEIN ABU
A Public Meeting
will be addressed
in the Town Hall
at 7 p.m.
by
EDWARD BRADLEY

'Shall we go?' asked Bernard.

It was almost the hour as they made their way down the wandering side lanes that led to the wharves and the town hall. There, hidden deep in the crowd, they stood by an open window through which they could see the ever-present channel and the waters of the bay. The gas lights in the hall hummed like flies, huge green luminous flies that had floated in from the half night outside, so blue and lovely where it sank down, darker and darker, over the masts and the brown sails of the fishing smacks in the harbour, and far in the distance the peaked mountains that Bernard knew so well. It was so lovely to watch the hollow night fall outside, and through it now and again a green light climbing up a mast, and to turn from it to the pale pink-washed green-lit room within, that they paid but little heed to the speakers until their friend the teacher rose.

The years between that night and the day in the market square had not dulled his eloquence, and though his temples were gone quite white now—premature for his years—the terrible passion of the man blazed like the fire of burning youth. Yet as he talked the lovers did not join in the cheers of the audience. The night had fallen now and nothing showed beyond but the eyes of green or red on mast and poop. The mountains had vanished. The far woods were gone. They barely heard the lapping of the bay. As by one thought they moved quietly out through the cheering crowd into the darkness. But, shyly, they did not go back directly to their hotel. Wrapped in their own silence and the silence of the night they wandered about the quays or in and out among the lanes as if prolonging the night to the very last moment. The meeting was over before they returned to their hotel, and the lights of the houses in that street, and doubtless of every street in the town, were gone up to the second storey. When they entered their room they saw that the pale light of the gas lamp outside the window fell on the high old-fashioned ceiling and from there glimmered down on the wide, carved bridal-bed, and needing no other light they used none. Across the street was another row of sleeping houses, and beyond that the bay, widening to the ocean, and when they stood without stirring they could hear the low boom of the waves on the cliffs and across the bar. As they undressed, the faint hum of a motor rose in the distance and approached along the street.

'Bernard,' she whispered.

Over his shoulder he could see her pale body in the dim light, but where he stood by the window with one hand raised to draw down the blind his eyes fell on the passing car. He saw the white hair of their orator friend, the old bachelor, the patriot, driving out of the town into the country and the dark night. The hedges would race past him; the rabbits skip before his headlights on the road; the moths in the cool wind would fly round his flushed face and his trembling hands. But that wind would not for many miles cool the passion in him to which he had given his life.

'Bernard,' she whispered again, and her voice trembled a little.

He drew the blind down slowly. The lamp shadowed the framework of the window on it. Slowly he turned to her where she gleamed even in the dark.

# The Call to Arms

## DENIS JOHNSTON

THIS STORY was told to me one evening by a friend of mine across the counter of a pub in Lower Abbey Street in the City of Dublin. I believe that it's largely true because my friend Barnie would never lie to me, unless of course it paid him to do so. Barnie draws the beer and serves the spirits every night to all of us men of action and men of business who have the time to drop in, and of course, the talk often runs high about the old days and all the things we did too long ago to bear contradiction.

I am usually more impressed than I should be by big talk. Whenever I'm with geographical liars I feel that I have really been nowhere, and as for personal reminiscences about celebrities—well, they just make me feel like a leper. But perhaps most of all I feel out of it whenever tales of wars and battles are going the rounds. You know the kind. Although now I come to think of it, I have lived through a war or two and a couple of rebellions not to mention a mixed selection of minor civil commotions. Yet, though I have tried to get into most of them, I never have succeeded in firing a shot in anger in any cause, however praiseworthy. I think, perhaps, that is why Barnie's experiences appealed to me so much.

Anyhow, they were all at it this night—rugby small talk with a leaven of limericks, and of course the inevitable well-worn war news (though goodness knows 'news' is a sad misnomer), when I caught Barnie's eye across the counter as he swilled the glasses in the sink. It seemed to me that his expression of scepticism was too marked to be boredom. So I moved along thinking I'd try him.

'Barnie,' I said, 'have you ever been in a war?'

I knew from the curl of his lip that I was on to something, but his vehemence surprised me.

'No,' he said, 'I have not. An' if there was another tomorra I wouldn't join it. War's all my eye.'

I looked at Barnie with a new interest. From my knowledge of him I found it hard to believe that he had any intellectual objection to the use of physical force. From time to time I had seen him carrying out his more vigorous duties in the pub with a relish that would have been no credit to a pacifist. It was a matter that called for further investigation, so I asked him what he would have and this is what he told me:

'Them craw thumpers, who would mind them? To hear them blidderin' their old guff about this war an' that war, sure you'd take them all for ragin' yeomen. Wars is all cod. The only medal I ever got or gave was a black eye, thank God. Mind you I didn't always think that way. Ah no. Onct I had a notion to be in one o' them flyin' columns. Ah but them jackeens, they'd give you the sick. Sure it was all swank and jobbery gettin' into them things unless you knew someone. It doesn't signify. D'ye know.'

For a moment his words took me aback. I had never contemplated the social side of revolution in that light before. Yet after a moment's consideration I saw how reasonable it was. It was natural that they should not admit Barnie into a flying column without some knowledge of his respectability. And it was just as natural that the system should lay itself open to charges of nepotism and snobbery no less than in Aldershot or Cowes. He went on:

'Then I remember in the summer o' 'twenty-two when it was all made official an' they started batterin' the Four Courts—one lot inside holdin' Ceilidhes in the Central Hall and the other lot outside lettin' off old bombs at them from a big gun onct every half-hour as fast as they could load it—I thought to meself, well maybe it'll be different now. This is big stuff and aren't we payin' for it all ourselves? An' sure enough in a day or two didn't all the papers come out with blazing placards askin' us to join in. "The Call to Arms" it was. An' they give us a list to' Recruitin' Stations, d'ye know, where if you went they'd let you into the war an' no questions asked. Oh I remember it well. First there was Brunswick Street Police Barracks an' then there was Amiens Street Railway Station. There was the City Hall an' Portobello an' Beggarsbush. An' somewheres out in Howth too I think. Aw, when I think of it I have to laugh. Sufferin' Job. "The Call to Arms", moryah! There was me believin' every word of it an' hoppin mad to get in on one side or the other. D'ye know.

'You see, there was this fellow Doyle out o' Cassidy's the Chemists an' the O'Connor girl we were both mottin'. Aw, that fellow was a mean little bowsey an' there's no blottin' it out. An' the motor bike on the instalment plan sittin' outside her door all evenin' while he spread himself on the old settee airin' his medical knowledge like a windy Professor out o' the Royal College o' Surgeons. Medical knowledge me foot! The only medical knowledge that chancer had was what he'd maybe read off an old bottle an' he delivering them on his bike or maybe an odd time selling a toothbrush when the boss was out. I declare to God there was many a time I could have found it in my heart to take a runnin' lep at that gazebo when I'd had enough of his blowin' for the day.

'It was the O'Connor girl, of course, that wanted us in the war. You know the way it is with them strips. Dead nuts on politics. If it wasn't a protest it was a funeral. And when it wasn't a funeral it would be a flag day. She'd have had us in and out o' cemeteries from crack of dawn to rosy fall o' night if she couldn't have use anchored in gaol which'd be better still. D'ye know. Ah it's the way with all them motts. Trouble an' nothin' but trouble. An' what they can't be up to themselves some fella has to do it for them. Looka, I often wonder what them ones will do when the country's free an' there's no gaols or cemeteries at all! They have no regard for a man that's not blidderin' with a Glasnevin wheeze, worn to a livin' corpse with route marching and hunger striking or lookin' into the clay face o' death itself.

'An' when she saw "The Call to Arms"—well I knew it was now or never for yours truly an' I'd better get down to it at onct without any argufyin'. Well, when I said I was goin' for to be a militiaman I saw well enough that motor bikes or no motor bikes I'd taken a long lead on His Lordship. There come a look in her eyes, an' I could see she was laying me out in my shroud already with the brave smile of one that would gladly give all for the old country. I suppose His Nibs saw it too, because before the evenin' was over he was goin' to join the war as well. An' that put us back on the level so to speak. Though mind you, it was no ordinary infantryman or bombadier the like o' meself that Doyle was going to be. Aw no! None o' that for Doyle. He was going to be something special, you may be sure, with all his learnin' from washin' bottles. I declare to God I had to go home before the venem in me heart rose up an' I landed a quick one on his gob.

'Well, next morning off I goes like a gamecock in me brown boots an' leggins an' me haversack an' the old water-bottle I borreyed from the Church Lads' Brigade an' me ration o' tea an' me pocket knife or slasher an' a map of the district like they tell you in all the books. Oh, I had everything. I was fit for the Dardanelles. An' I got out an' read "The Call to Arms", and went off to Brunswick Street to join the war.

'When I got there I don't mind sayin' I was a bit put out to find it all shut up, an' after I'd knocked an' rung a bit an old fella sticks his kisser out of the winda next door an' tells me to move on an' not be disturbin' the neighbours. "Is this bell workin'?" says I, givin' another tug at the string. "It is not," says he. "An' even if it was, much good it would do you, for they're gone away out of that this t'ree weeks," says he. "Well," says I, "there must be some mistake." An' I got out me paper and I crossed off the Barracks an' I went on to Amiens Street.

'Well, there on the Howth platform, breaking open the slot machines, didn't I find a high officer in a uniform all complete, an' I thought to myself I'm right this time. "Come here," says he, when he saw me. "Have you ere a knife on you?" says he. "I have indeed," says I, gettin' out my slasher. "I have the whole boilin'," says I. "I'm ready for action." "Thanks," says he, twistin' back the lock with the blade. "Will you have a throat pastille or a jujube?"

'Well what with the throat pastilles an' all it wasn't long before we was as thick as thieves an' I was askin' him who he was and all that. "Colonel Commandant Foley," says he. "I'm the officer in charge of this district."

' "Begob that's good," says I. "Because I've come to join your army."

' "Ah, don't be a fool," says he. "Sure there's nothin' doin' here."

' "There's enough for me," says I. "I'm not lookin' for trouble."

' "Nor am I," says he. "An' that's why I'm not havin' any more of you gutties in my Brigade."

' "Oh is that so?" says I sarcastic like. "Well let me tell ya there's no call for you to be so familiar with me. Isn't this an official recruitin' station?"

' "If it is, it's the first I heard of it," says Foley. So I got out me Call to Arms, an' I showed it to him. "There," says I. "Now call me a liar."

'He was a bit shuk by that, an' I could see I had him down-faced. But even so he wouldn't falter. Oh, he was a hard nut was Foley.

' "Well I tell you what," says he. "Come back again tomorrow an' I'll see what I can do for you."

' "Oh yes," says I. "And find myself shut out. I know you."

' "Well," says Foley, "that's the best I can do for you. An' it's my belief you're top-heavy with barley."

' "Give me back me slasher," says I, "for I'll not come back again tomorrow. I'm going off to the City Hall," says I, "and when I've joined the Army, it's you I'm going to report to Headquarters Staff for insultin' behaviour an' misdemeanours in the conductin' of an official recruitin' station."

'An' with that I crossed Amiens Street Station off me list an' I left him in a lather of sweat wonderin' whether I meant what I said. And mind ya I did at the time, I was gettin' that nettled.

'So I went up to the City Hall then an' I had a goster with the sentry on duty. There was a bit o' pluggin' going on down in Dame Street at the time, I remember, but nobody was taking much notice of it, an' sure it was doing no harm anyways. But the sentry might as well have been Foley, though mind ya, lookin' back on it now I can see he meant well by me. If it hadn't been for the porter being out an' no one to lock up the place he'd have brought me somewheres himself. But it was Staff Captain Savage I'd have to see, he said and

102

he was away at his tea. "Would you try the Café Belge," says he. "He often goes there of an afternoon."

' "May your buck teeth choke ya," says I. "What do you take me for, going to the Café Belge, an' I leggin' it up the back stairs to glory?" An' I went down to Trinity College an' I waved me Call to Arms at the Guard and said, "Will ya tell me how the blazes ya get into this fiddlin' war?" But they only laughed in me face, an' sent me on to Beggarsbush. An' there they didn't even come out to see me. A scrawny little fella looks out through the grille in the door and tells me to skip off outa that before they have me run in for trespassin'.

'Well, with that I knew I was bet. Mind ya I daresay I could still 'a' walked eight miles out to Howth and thried them there, but me spirit was broke an' I went round to try an' explain me difficulties to the O'Connor girl feelin' pretty low in meself. The motor bike was at the door sure enough an' there was me brave Doyle inside spreadin' himself worse than ever an' as pleased as Punch.

' "Well," says he, "I'm off tomorra." I wouldn't give him the satisfaction of askin' him where, but I needn't 'a bothered for he went on just the same. "To the Curragh I'm goin', no less," says he. "To take up me official duties at Headquarters. I'm to be on parade at Wellington Barracks at eight o'clock in the mornin",' says he. "I suppose I won't see you there?"

'Ah, what with the fat laugh of him an' the smug airs he was puttin' on it was more than a man could stand, so I got up and come away before I sent him in his carcase box to Bully's Acre. It was goodbye to the O'Connor girl for yours truly, an' as I went out I heard him still gassin' away about himself, an' the whole family sittin' round respectful, hanging' on to the precious words of wisdom like they was at a Sodality.

' "They were leppin' to have me," says Doyle. "They're mad to get specialists. There's many good enough to tote a gun, but when I told them about me medical knowledge they said I was just the fella they wanted. I'm to be some class of an officer, an' it's straight to the Curragh they're drafting me." '

My friend Barnie paused in his story, and a strange look came over his face.

'And so you lost the O'Connor girl?' I asked.

'Well I did and I didn't,' he continued. 'That wasn't quite the end of it. The next day me bold Specialist sets off for the wars an' the O'Connor girl an' the whole family out wavin' goodbye down the street. It was a brave sight. A thunderin' fine send off. An' he was to write every other day an' tell them all about the war. I don't mind sayin' I kep' out of sight when I saw him go. Yes, an' for some time afterwards, I felt bad about it all. Me only consolation was to get douched in malt.

'But not for long I'm glad to say. We heard nothin' for a while, but by an' by we used to get word from the fellas comin' back that Doyle was tryin' to get out o' the Army. It seems that he was some class of an officer all right, thanks to all his great medical knowledge. Yes, says the boys, he's what they call a Sanitary Officer.

'Well, I won't go into what it was that Doyle was put to at the Curragh, except to say that for six weeks they kep' him at it until his mother managed to get into Government Buildings by the grace o' the parish priest an' a couple of T.D.'s an' got him home at last.

'Well, I laughed till the tears streamed down me face. "Take him," says I to the O'Connor girl. "An' if he comes out from this war with a medal," I says, "you'll know where to hang it," says I, for there was great bitterness in me heart, God forgive me. An' with that I left her, an' I haven't seen her from that day to this excep' maybe an odd time to nod to coming out o' Mass. Nor more she him either for the matter o' that, for that's the way with women, an' a man only trying to do what they asked him. As for meself I made up me mind then, an' God grant I never change it, that them that tries to show off by joining wars deserve all they get.'

# Modern Times—
# Southern Ireland

# The Lake

## PATRICK BOYLE

'WELL!' Mac says, 'This is the place!'
He sounds pleased with himself.
'What d'ye think of it, Jim?' he asks.

We are standing on the edge of a huge crater hollowed out of the mountain ridge we have just climbed. Below us, a thousand feet or more, is a dark rock-strewn valley walled in by towering slopes. Massive boulders are scattered around higgledy-piggledy—a crazy pavement of grey rock that runs round a small lake, fans out and piles itself up in a jagged barrier choking the gap that is the only entrance. The crater has a raw lacerated look as though some great beast had flung itself on the mountain slashing and tearing gobbets of rock from its flanks in savage fury. The tiny pin-points of white that are grazing sheep might be maggots crawling on an open wound: the lake, brown and still, a smear of clotted blood. Gigantic shadows roll across the valley, dashing themselves in a smother of sunlight against the slopes facing us.

'You certainly picked a choice spot,' I say.

'Bloody apt I did. Yer man'll stay roosting down there till the crack of doom and damn the one'll be a bit the wiser.'

He grins delightedly.

I try to place the bare-gummed smile. A glass-tank. The green-glow of scummy water. A long grey shadow, dull-eyed jutty-lipped, nuzzling at the glass.

'And what's the layout like?' I ask.

He squats down, rummages round in his pockets and flings across a packet of fags.

'It's like this. There's an old sheep-track runs up from the road and in the butt of yon pass. A bare mile of easy going. We could be in and out of here with the job done in under two hours. And mark ye, not a sinner lives within five solid miles of where ye stand. Sure, man alive, it was created for the job.'

A pike, that's what he is. An amiable dull-witted black-murdering pike.

'There's forty foot of water if there's an inch in yon lake. Forty foot of ould bog-water that ye couldn't see a stymy through. And I've got tucked away under a heap of stones a ten foot length of anchor chain and a bloody great iron bar as thick as yer arm. Enough to sink an elephant, let alone a Christian. Man, he'll never rise till the Day of Judgment, that's certain sure. Now what d'ye think, Jim?'

'I think you're a cold-blooded sod,' I say.

He gapes up at me.

'What's bitin' ye anyway?' he asks.

I drop down beside him on the broad of my back, hands locked behind my head. I have to close my eyes against the glare of the sun.

'I don't like this job,' I say. 'It's a dirty business.'

'It stinks,' I say.

He lets out a great neigh of a laugh.

'Oh, lovely jazus,' he says. 'Would ye for Christ's sake look what's talkin'? The hard man himself. Listen to this, will yez. . . .'

I hear him clear his throat.

'It stinks! It stinks!' he says in a high nasal voice.

He whinnies again. I feel his hand grip my knee.

'Is it coddin' me ye are? Puttin' on a bloody act or what?'

'It's a dirty business,' I say. 'Riddling a man and sinking his body underwater as though it were the carcase of a mangy dog. One of our own crowd, too.'

'But what would ye have us do? Give him a blank wall and a firing squad?'

'It might not be a bad idea.'

'Well, I like that. Of all the girning, contrary . . .'

He spits noisily.

'Listen here, Jim. It's the bloody Government makes the rules of this game. Not us. Aren't the jails of this country stuffed with prisoners whose only crime is being good honest Republicans? Aren't they tryin' to smash the Movement with every kind of black-guardism? Couldn't ye hunger-strike till the walls of yer belly met each other and not a one know ye were even in jail? I tell ye we're bloody outlaws—that's what we are. This is the only way the fight can go on.'

The sun beats down on my face and seeps through my eyelids. I feel too lazy and contented to reply. What is there to say anyhow? Mac has all the answers—match force against force, cunning against cunning, secrecy against secrecy. No use telling him that it is merely evil vindicated by evil. And that it will go on and on until nothing is left but a hard core of bitter hatred.

A cloud passes across the sun, stroking my face with a cold hand. Perhaps we have already reached the stage where growth ceases and all chance of broadening out into something massive and urgent has gone for ever.

I fling away my cigarette and sniff at my fingers savouring the rich tang of smoke-scorched flesh.

'You're wrong, Mac,' I say. 'As well might you piss against the wind and start calling down Heaven to witness the spatters.'

'So ye'd have us sit down on our backsides and never so much as stir a hip to stop an ould skin-the-goat from rattin' on us? Oh, there's only the one cure for them boys—the bloody lead. That's the medicine for them.'

'But are you sure he *is* an informer?'

'Wasn't the hoor court-martialled? Isn't that a fair enough crack of the whip for any man?'

I open my eyes. A gull floats belly up on the surface of the sky. I wait till it glides past the sun with only the tip of a wing scorched. I say:

'Can't you for once in your life form an opinion of your own? You know the man's record as well as I do. Through the whole racket from 'sixteen on. Not a labour dispute or a bit of land agitation but he'd have to be in it up to the neck. In and out of jail as often as fingers and toes. And when he wasn't in the Joy or the Glass House or in Arbour Hill he was being kicked out of one job after another because of his activities. This is the man you're so sure is an informer. Why, if they couldn't batter information out of him each time he was arrested, is it likely he'll slobber up anything now for a few lousy bob?'

'But the court-martial. . . .'

'It be damned. Sitting in smug judgment with us to do its dirty work.'

'What's the use of talkin' that way, Jim? Aren't we only doin' our duty as soldiers of the Republic? You're not meanin' to forsake yer principles because the goin' gets rough. Sure a man's life is a small thing when . . .'

'Bullshit,' I say.

I roll over on to my stomach and wriggle forward to the lip of the crater.

The gun in my pocket presses against my groin.

Queer how much the lake seems to resemble an eye—a grotesque disembodied eye like the Cyclopean all-seeing eye of God that used to stare down at me from a holy picture in my bedroom—at night cold and antagonistic; in the morning with a knowing, malicious, I-told-you-so sneer.

I say to myself:

Hump you, I'll bloody soon wipe that look off your dial. And I raise myself on my elbows, slip out the gun and let drive. The bullet drills a neat hole in the smooth water, the delayed sound of the impact coming up to me with a startled phut. Like a grunt of annoyance. I'll swear on the Book that the sleek tawny surface gave a startled blink.

Mac jumps up.

'God blast yer maggoty sowl, are ye gone mad?' he shouts. 'D'ye want to have the whole countryside in on top of us?'

'What d'ye think ye're doin', anyway?' he asks.

'Oh, just a bit of target practice for tonight,' I say.

And I let fly again. I don't let up until I've emptied the revolver into the lake. Each time I fire I seem to reach down effortlessly and tease the water with a flicking fingertip. A feeling of power and immensity grips me. The giant shadow sprawled out across the crater is my own. I have but to crouch down for sunlight to come foaming back, or stand erect for my shadow to darken the land.

I get to my feet.

'Would you believe it, Mac,' I say. 'I've got an arm as long as ever reached down out of the sky.'

'We'll go,' I say.

Mac scratches his head.

'Christ, y're the odd bloody fowl,' he says.

*   *   *

We trudge along in silence—the prisoner in front, Mac and I a few paces behind. At first we walked abreast but when the path commenced to narrow, winding in and out amongst the rocks, the two of us dropped back. There was no danger of the prisoner getting away—a full moon and a clear sky took care of that—but to be certain I knotted one end of a length of rope to his bound wrists, holding the other end myself in my left hand, the other gripping the gun in my pocket. It was a mistake. If the rope goes slack for an instant he pulls up, frozen into the tense attitude of a pointer. He remains like that, his whole body clenched in expectation, until I give a chuck at the rope and shout:

'Get going, blast you.'

Then he throws back his shoulders defiantly and moves off again.

I try keeping the rope taut. Immediately he quickens his stride. It is as though the steady drag of the rope, twisting his bound arms back from his shoulders, is at once a menace urging him forward and a temporary guarantee of safety. He steps it out bravely with an insolent swagger to his shoulders.

Everything assumes the fantastic logic of a dream. One moment I am trying to check a wild Gadarene rush towards destruction: the next it is myself who is being dragged along bewildered and protesting.

I try to concentrate. I tell myself:

'You've got to plug this bowzie. A 0·45 bullet in the back of the

110

poll and the job is done. Quick and clean. That's all there is to it.'

But my thoughts keep coming back to the rope. It sets up a curious intimacy between myself and the man I am to kill. It is an umbilical cord linking us together, fusing our separate thoughts and feelings into a single consciousness.

I feel my blood pounding through his veins. There is a gnawing pain at the back of my skull as though the casing of bone is stripped away exposing a palpitating web of shrinking tissue. My arms are tearing at their sockets; my wrists numb; my neck stiff from the effort of not looking back. I keep my gaze fixed on the path ahead but I cannot escape the casual beauty of the night—a star swinging below the moon, the sweep of the mountain black against the sky, the delicate moon-shadow of a leafless tree. Alert for the click of a cocked hammer, I catch the furtive scamperings and rustlings, the tiny comings and goings of the mountain. I am intensely aware of my own body. It brushes against my clothes like a kitten, neglected and importunate. I should like to press my cheek against the warm skin of my shoulder or run the palms of my hands down my flanks or grip a scruff of plump belly-flesh and feel the taut muscles beneath.

A snipe gets up with a screech and a rush of wings. I jerk back on the rope.

'Sorry,' I say.

Then:

'Come on! Keep going!'

We move off again towards the gap, the prisoner striding along with the same jaunty swagger.

I find myself keeping in step. Even placing my foot down where he has just trodden.

I shorten my stride and half-close my eyes, allowing myself to be led along like a blind man. I count a hundred paces and look up. I am back in step again.

I pick out a rock a long way ahead and guess the distance. Now, I decide, I shall not look up until I am level with it. I commence to count. Before I reach five hundred my gaze drifts up. The barrier of rock is only a few minutes distant.

The muscles of my legs go slack and the increasing tension settles in a warm lump in the pit of my stomach. I wonder if he feels the same way. Probably does. Kidneys loosening up too. Probably wetting himself by now.

At this I become aware of my own urgent physical need. The gnawing discomfort helps to steady me. There is even something funny in the thought of the three of us, lined up, shoulder to shoulder, as we pumpship against a rock. You could hardly shoot a man after that.

A hundred yards more.

A dark cloud slides across the moon. Mac flashes on his torch, cutting down the beam with a cupped hand. It lights up the shabby coat, the frayed trouser-ends, the patched shoes. A hole gapes in one sock. At every step the ill-fitting shoe slides up and down emphasizing the stained unlovely flesh.

I won't do it, I swear. So help me God, I won't do it.

The torch flicks off. Ahead lies the lake—a smooth sheet of polished steel rimmed with moon-bleached rock.

An elbow is dug into my ribs. I can barely hear the whisper: 'Now!'

At the same moment the man swings round and faces me, whipping the rope out of my hand.

'Ye cowardly bastard,' he says.

I don't even know that I've drawn the gun till I feel it leap in my hand. The bullet must have grazed a bone for it whines away across the lake with the sound of ripping calico.

He remains facing me, standing stiffly erect, feet sprawled apart, his face white and featureless against the dark background of the mountain, the lake draped across his shoulders like a billowing silver cloak.

'Ye cowardly little rat,' he says.

I let him have it. The bullet goes home with a crunching kind of thump—like you drove your boot into a bag of meal. His mouth gapes open in a black soundless scream. His arms and shoulders jerk violently. You would swear for all the world that he is a great bird flapping pinioned wings in an effort to get off the ground.

All at once the knees buckle under him and he slithers to the ground. He starts to scream—a thin wisp of sound like the whining of a peevish child. He drums his heels in the ground.

Mac is shouting:

'Do something! For Christ's sake do something!'

I see and hear all this, but it means nothing to me. Inside me is a cool, spacious emptiness. I am strong and light and spare—gutted clean of emotion. I am only aware of one thing—the limp, yielding beauty of the lake. It stirs up something inside me that I cannot control. I want to strip off my clothes and wade in, very, very slowly, letting it creep up my thighs, my belly, my chest. Up over my closed mouth and wide-open eyes until I am silvered from head to feet. I want to slip down into the womb of the lake where there exists no impulse to feel or think or act; where there is nothing but a dim swaying silence.

The twisting grotesque is still screaming: the other is down on his benders. Praying.

Home—airy—mur—gaw—pray—frus—inner—noun—tower—death—men.

Gabble and whimper become one unbearable irrelevancy.

I go over to the writhing figure, I pour shot after shot into it. I

112

keep jerking the trigger even after the revolver is empty. And all the time I keep shouting:

'Shut up, you bloody slob!'

Not knowing which of the two I mean until at last there is nothing left but the night and the black jaws of the mountain—and the lake. The kneeling man looks up at me. In the moonlight I can see his eyes flickering rapidly from side to side as though they are loose in their sockets.

I fling down the gun and start running towards the lake.

I run as in a dream—flying with gigantic strides on sluggish leaden feet. Drawn irresistibly forward and just as powerfully held back. Dreamways the ground keeps pace with me. I seem to make no headway. As well might I be ploughing through a snow-drift or a bank of cloud.

I feel tired. All the strength and certainty has left me.

I lean against a boulder, my head whirling dizzily.

My left arm is numb. Aching abominably. I stare down stupidly. It is held out stiffly in front of me, the fist clenched, the thumb still pressing down on a non-existent rope.

The emptiness fills up inside me with a sickening rush. I press my forehead against the cool surface of the rock, teeth gritted, eyes squeezed tight, fighting down the choking waves of loathing and nausea. I hate myself and every living creature. I hate the loyalties and prejudices that bring us buzzing together like dung-flies. I hate the night and the mountain and the pale-faced bitch of a lake. All that has happened tonight will mean no more to her than a splash and a few fugitive ripples—the merest shadow of a frown of disgust on the lovely ageless face.

My knees are shaking, my eyes scalded, I keep gulping down mouthfuls of bile.

Mac is beside me. He says:

'Ye're a hard man all right, Jim. Ye made a proper butcher's job of him.'

'Well,' he says. 'We'd better be startin' if we're to have his nibs dumped before mornin'.'

My stomach gives a final heave and I retch up the griping bitterness inside me.

I feel his arm firm across my shoulders. I hear him murmuring to himself.

'Ho-ly God! Oh, Ho-ly God!'

He starts slapping my back vigorously.

'Spit it up, lad. It's better out than chokin' ye.'

He stops. His fingers drum a tattoo on the back of my neck.

'Bejazus, ye're an odd duck surely,' he says.

# The Light's Edge

## JOHN McARDLE

J EM GATHERED a wet thread from his overcoat sleeve around his hand and cut it with his teeth. Better be rid of that. The sleeve was well-ravelled, threads going every way and him breaking off a bit every couple of days. He'd have to get someone to sew it— some neighbour woman. Three years only he had this coat and it starting to wear already. Long ago a coat used to last him and last him for years and when it was finished it lasted him for a few more years for frosty mornings outside. Bad stuff in coats nowadays.

He reached through its torn pockets, loosened his belt one notch, and back-handed, pushed his shirt down over a cold spot, gave it a rub of his hand to warm it and tightened his belt again. He stood, maybe to rest himself, maybe to look around at the cold hills turning khaki with the withering grass and ripened potato stalks. 'Thirty days have September, April, June and November,' twenty-nine days to Christmas—no wonder the grass was beginning to wither—ripening and withering, 'much the same, aren't they.' He turned his back to the icy wind to look back at his own brown hill with six pits of potatoes—two straight rows of three. They looked longer in the thin light—six big pits ten foot long every one of them, except the wee one, and it took him only a week to dig them. 'Begod they'll be starting to grow again before Pete gets finished,' he laughed to himself as he turned into the wind and faced Pete's hill. Look at the way he dug them—a wee patch here and another there as if he thought he was getting on better that way, and he took a cup of tay between every few stalks to give himself an excuse for a rest—a bit lazy, Peter was, maybe. But all right. Pete was all right. All the same he should fix that footstick and put a railing along it to catch on to—and he should have taken in that spade and not leave it out all night. 'Them's the spuds that'll take a long time to dig. In the end he'll wind up giving good money to Deery or some big farmer with a digger and two big horses.'

He rubbed something clammy from his moustache and followed the winding path between the white-topped rushes. The path was well worn with him going over to Pete and Pete coming over to him and it was already getting hard with the night's frost. Jem put his hand round to his back and rubbed a painful spot. His legs were getting sore too, now that he was getting cold. It was hard work digging and gathering. Some men had women to gather and it left it easier. When he was young and strong he'd have dug that field in three days and danced on the third night. No pains then. Not much sense either. But you didn't need sense if you were a wild devil because if you were a wild devil people took you like that and made allowances. That was when he was young. Young and wiry. In the middle of his young strong days.

\*    \*    \*

The accordion-player struck up a creaking waltz. Jem kicked a loose stick into the bonfire, cheered, and swaggered over to Mary McCabe. Pete just got there as he reached her so he cheered again, hit him a shoulder and landed him among the shawled women leaning against the earthen ditch. Pete picked himself up, lifted his cap from Mrs. McBennett's lap and with three sharp strides vaulted through the flames into the bunch of lassies on the other side. He picked one out and whisked her to the centre of the crossroads where he bumped into Jem again.

'Did I see you somewhere before?'

'Get outa my road.'

'Here, Pete, surely you can squeeze her tighter than that,' and he pushed them closer together.

'Were you not listening to Father O'Kelly on Sunday, were you not, you heathen you? I always say there's one thing about Father O'Kelly, you can't play poker on the chapel steps and listen to him at the same time.'

'Put in your shirt-tail.'

'And give me back that shirt tomorrow morning. I don't mind lending them but I like to get them back. And mind that woman for me. I'll want her back too when you're finished with her. Yahoooo,' and he buck-leaped into the middle of a bunch of girls.

Jem watched him over Mary's shoulder. Pete turned round, now surrounded by girls as he liked to be and shouted something which Jem couldn't catch in the swaying rhythmic kicking of pebbles and chattering voices rising above the creaky notes of the huddled musician. Jem laid his elbow on Mary's shoulder to loosen the second button of his shirt, and he felt how soft her shoulder was and how three strands of auburn hair tickled his forearm and caught his throat.

'Hello,' he said as if he hadn't noticed her before.

'Hello. You're back?'

'Back.'

'Maybe it'll soon be over.'

'Hope so.'

'Where next?'

'I'm not supposed to tell.'

'Do you not be afraid?'

'Wicked sometimes, when you're waiting for them to come along. Too much time to think.'

'It might be soon over.'

'It might.'

He eased her into a shadow where the flickering fire lit her face with a red orange glow. 'It might. I hope it does.' He looked back through the eerie haze between the flames where he could see Pete lift two girls by the waist, and stole a soft kiss. What odds if she was Pete's girl; she'd never marry him anyway. In better times she'd marry a solid farmer with fifty acres or a braggart like himself who'd gallivant green townlands in summer sun. 'We'll sit down I think,' and he laughed. Languidly she sat on the dusty grass at the road's edge and laid her back against his shoulder for support. He looked at her white neck, and put the thought from his head.

'Hi, Pete,' he shouted, but Pete didn't hear him. 'Pete,' louder, and the noise faded in expectation.

'Give us a sword-dance.'

'No sword.'

'Use a stick.'

'No stick.'

Jem pulled one from the bushes and flung it to him.

'Right, me flower. Pat, wind her up,' and he whipped off his cap and whisked it through the flames and Jem caught it with his outstretched left hand. Mary was tapping her feet like the rest, tapping her feet and clapping her hands as Pete swayed and jumped around the stick moving with imperfect rhythm to imperfect music. Clapping, tapping, cheering, lilting, dancing, and the armpits of Pete's faded blue shirt were turning green. It was under his armpits that Jem noticed the jiggering light on top of the brae. Everybody else had seen it too for the clapping stopped, the music faded, young men froze where they were and old women gathered their shawls around their breasts to hide imaginary infants. Over the crackling noise of the fire he heard the lorry.

'Tans,' someone whispered.

'For Jesus' sake play on,' Jem shouted the whisper as he reached into the roots of the bushes for his gun, pulled it out and vaulted the ditch with one movement, and ran in wild panic through knee-deep dewy hay. He tripped on a stone and got up again. The music and dancing started again as he reached the river. He jumped it and landed in the soft ground on the other side. He felt a twitch in his ankle as he hit a stone under the muddy surface but he pulled his feet clear from the clinging earth and hurried through the rushes towards where a bushy ditch divided two hills black with whins. He jumped the ditch and almost collapsed as a sharp pain knifed his ankle. He limped on, dragging his right foot up the hill, till at the top he sank into a hollow in the earth, rolled over and landed on his back in damp grass. Lying on his back with his gun between his legs, its barrel facing towards his head, he tried to mute the sound of his heavy breathing. He sat up with his head between his knees and the gun over his shoulder. He lifted his head and looked through the bushes. The music had stopped again and shadowy forms moved between him and the firelight. After a while he heard the faint purr of the engine, saw the lights illuminate small bent figures heading homewards. The lorry moved off and he lay under a starry sky till the dew soaked through his shirt. He sat up to feel his already-swollen ankle. What was this? Pete's cap still clutched tightly in his fist. Pete was probably seeing her home now. Lucky for Pete. Buck him, he had nothing to fear from the Tans. 'He'll enjoy his freedom like the rest of us all the same.'

\* \* \*

'Pete.'

'Hello, Jem.'

'Cool.'

'Aye, cool is right.'

'I wish it was your turn tonight but sure you came to me last night.'

Pete was hanging the kettle on the crook and didn't answer.

'I saw a rat eating haws off a bush today. Looks like a bad winter. That's always a sure sign of a bad winter.'

He edged between a barrel of wet meal and a table covered with pieces of bread, tin dishes and brown delph, and threw the cat from the top of the settle-bed to make room for himself.

'You got finished the digging I see.'

'Aye, just got it finished there before dark. Ah now, it's tough work digging. It's the stooping that gets you. In the back you know. I see you have rats.'

'They come in for the winter. The cat's clean useless—got a sort of used to them.'

'You should get Dak.'

'I got some one time and the cat got caught in it. I got her the next morning and freed her but she only lived a few days—strained herself or something.'

There was silence for a few minutes. It went on too long so Pete said 'Aye. I'd say she strained herself,' to fill the gap.

After another silence 'That kettle's not boiling. Give the bellows a blast and I'll make the tea.'

Jem moved into the corner at the end of the settle to turn the wheel.

'You should do something with them bellows. They're loose in the ground.'

'I was looking for blue clay at the edge of the bog there this evening. There was a great seam of blue clay there but I must have used it all.'

'It's bad for the bellows jigging about like that. It loosens all the screws in them and the next thing you'll find they won't blow at all.'

'I might buy cement the next day I'm in town.'

'Aye, mix it with a bit of sand and lime and it should do your job.'

Pete shook tea from the bag into the kettle and Jem blew the bellows again. Pete buttered the bread, sugared the cups, poured the tea and handed the cup to Jem with two thick slices of bread on top. Jem hated that. The steam from the tea always wet the bread and he couldn't stand wet bread. There were brown streamers down the side of the mug so he rubbed them with his sleeve till they became a bigger patch of lighter brown, and started to drink.

'Great strong tay, Pete.'

'Nothing like it. Good tay and a good fire is all a man wants.'

'Begod that's a powerful fire all right. You'd make a great divil, Pete.'

'Aye, or a purgatory.'

They smiled and went solemn again.

'Purgatory wouldn't be too bad, Pete.'

'I suppose not.'

'But I wouldn't like Hell. Purgatory would only last for a wee while.'

'A man told me once that you might have to spend a brave while in it.'

'I don't know. I suppose so. You heard Mary Deery died today.'

'God be good to her.'

'Died about twelve, I think. It was the creamery man that was telling me.'

'She was failed now this last few years.'

'Got very grey and pale.'

'Shockin' grey. She used to have lovely auburn hair.'

'A brave woman.'

'Ah God, aye. A lovely woman. She shoulda never married Deery.'

'Not at all.'

'God be good to her.'

It ended at that. For a moment they were left alone with their thoughts. Separate. Pete coughed and said 'I see you got finished the digging.'

'Aye, just got it finished before nightfall. It's hard work digging—on the back, you know—with the stooping.'

'A good crop you had.'

'Six big pits. That's a great field, Pete. I mind selling seven tons off that field one time. Seven tons of Aran Banners that'd melt in your mouth.'

'I'd rather Kerr's Pinks myself. They're a better yielding spud.'

'Ach, they're a weak sort of spud. Not much body to them. Them Aran Banners had a flouriness. Boil them and you had half an inch of flour before you came to the heart.'

'But they're a rough spud. A rough skin on them. A Kerr's Pink—did you ever see the way you could peel a Kerr's Pink with your nail or even a rub of your thumb and you had the skin off it.'

'They're a bad spud, Pete.'

'No, now Jem, there's nothing like them.'

'A bad spud.'

'No.'

'Aran Banners from the Aran Islands. Give me them any time.'

'But they're a rough spud.'

'Give me Aran Banners from the Aran Islands. Them other ones is a British spud and you'd know it.'

'They're a good fine spud.'

'They're watery.'

'They're not watery.'

'They're watery—like the British.'

'I wasn't trying to start politics.'

'Doesn't matter. They're a watery spud. Dead watery.'

'I wasn't——'

'Doesn't matter.' And Pete didn't answer.

Jem knew he shouldn't have bothered. Pete was all right. He shouldn't have argued with him. Dammit all there wasn't much use in fighting at this stage of their lives because Pete wasn't a bad fellow. He got on your nerves betimes, but you'd be lonesome without him. Like in the snow when he couldn't cross the footstick for fear of slipping and you had to spend the long dark night on your own. No, begod, fair play to him. Pete was all right. A bit thick, but all right. He'd say he was sorry. He'd swallow his pride and say he was sorry. He stretched out his legs and drew in a big breath to prepare himself, and said 'That's a powerful fire,' but Pete didn't answer.

Pete didn't answer. No use saying any more. But he should have answered. If you said something to somebody they should answer. No use talking if they didn't answer. But he'd sit it out because if he left now Pete mightn't come over the next night and then the next night he wouldn't go to Pete and it could go on like that into the long winter—winter nights with a candle and a cat, one after another till spring—if you ever saw spring. You could go to McCabe's or

Lennon's but you didn't know whether they wanted you or not, they'd maybe turn the wireless on and you were afraid to talk. No. Pete'd come round in a wee while.

A clock hurried across the floor. Jem hit it with his stick and smashed it and threw it into the fire. It disappeared in the flames. A clock. There was an English fella one time home in Lennon's that used to call them cockroaches. A tweedy wee fella with riding breeches and a moustache. A bit of a cockroach himself. No sign of it now. No sign of the clock. Gone into the flames, the leaping flames climbing up the black bricks to escape the white heat in the heart of the fire, jumping up to catch the crooks. A lovely white heart, a wee world in an empty space with the sun shining. Shining bright and warm, taking away the pains from his legs and shoulders —digging without effort, no pain from digging—bend down, give the spade a twist, shake them away from the stalks, lift them into the bucket. No trouble. Ten drills dug already but you'd have to watch the spuds so they'd stay in the pit. That little beggar was escaping, get back, batter it back, back, back, there now you little brat. A Kerr's Pink—you'd know it you wee watery brat. Back to the digging and stay there you, stay there. Damn your soul you wee watery brat with your moustache and riding breeches—'Ha, Pete, he used to call them cockroaches.' Pete didn't answer. He looked over at him but he was sitting there with his eyes closed looking into the fire. He couldn't leave now. He'd have to sit it out. Sit it out on this cold hill with the rain beating down on him soaking his uniform. Where the hell did the other lads go to? He was afraid himself but he wouldn't leave one man to fight them on his own. God knows who it was waiting for him—maybe his own trying to surround him, closing in on him. There he was. That one coming through the whins. Come on. Come on. Come on me boy and you'll get what you're looking for. Come on. He felt someone else behind him and he turned with his gun ready but the man took off his cap and floated it through the shimmering haze where sun shone on golden leaves and Jem caught it with his outstretched left hand and with the force of it he fell back into the pink rose petals of apple blossoms with Aran Banners from the Aran Islands falling lazily like autumn leaves into ethereal pits covered with shimmering web on either side of him and he sank deep so that the petals flowed over him immersing him in a wrapping encircling warmth—warm, safe from the starry night skies—safe and cosy, safe from the cold dew and angry wind, cosy, safe and warm, warm and cosy and safe. Something scurried across his foot and he sat up in the chair.

He was cold. He shivered and drew the coat across his chest and tightened the cord round the middle. He poked the ashes with his stick and one spark rose and died. The lamp was gone out—a good job because it saved oil—but the chimney corner was beginning to brighten. The clock in the window said a quarter to six and behind it the sky was brightening. Another cold day. He knew from the breeze that came under the door and the white frost on the small window-panes. A rat was scratching in the low corner—rats used a slower, heavier stroke than mice. He rubbed his legs to get a bit of heat into them. Very quiet it was at this time of the morning— nothing only a rat scratching and Pete's heavy breathing. Pete'd have a sore neck when he wakened, the way he was sleeping with his head back and sideways on his shoulder. He made to move him but stopped. He'd only waken and it wouldn't be fair—he'd only be mad with him again. He turned as quietly as he could, took two turf from beside the fire, put them on the ashes and poked the ashes with his stick. He went over and lifted the top of the settle-bed, shoved in his arm and pulled out the first thing he met—a grey army coat—and laid it on Pete's chest and let it fall down over his knees. He got a queer feeling that Pete was looking at him because Pete always slept with one eye open—some disease he had when he was a gasun Pete always said. At the end of the jamb he stopped to look back. Pete was snoring now and beside him a small flame was feeling the bottom of one of the turf. It'd be a good fire when Pete'd waken.

He gathered his coat collar round his neck and up to his chin, lifted the latch and went into the dirty street with dirty white-washed outhouses and a lone bush growing in the middle of it. A cool morning with hens beginning to cluck on the roost. A frosty morning. Pete'd be warm enough in a wee while when the fire got lit up. It'd likely light up nice and red. Pete'd be all right—nice and warm. A funny man, Pete. Terrible thick. But all right.

122

# The Scoop

## JAMES PLUNKETT

A DISCREET glance to right and left assured Murphy that no undesirable interest was being taken in his movements. He tilted his umbrella, turned expertly into the alleyway and entered the Poolebeg by the side door. He shook the January snow from his clothes before mounting the narrow stairs, and once inside the lounge called for the hot whiskey he had been promising himself all morning. He then looked around to see who was present.

There was the usual lunch break crowd; some actors from the nearby theatre, a producer, a sprinkling of civil servants who, like himself, worked in the nearby Ministry for Exports. His friend Casey was in deep conversation with a group which included three of the actors. There was a stranger among them, who seemed to be the focus of their attention.

Murphy's head was not in the best of health. He found the friendly buzz and the artificial brightness a relief after the drabness of the streets. He curled his fingers about his glass and sighed deeply. It was comfortably warm to the touch. As he lowered it from his lips his eye met Casey's and he nodded. Casey in return winked broadly. At first Murphy interpreted the wink as a wry reference to their mutual drinking bout of the previous evening, an acknowledgment of suffering shared. But Casey followed the wink by indicating the stranger with his thumb.

So that was it. The stranger had fallen into the clutches of the actors and there was some joke going on at his expense. Strangers who entered the Poolebeg had to run that risk. The actors were adept practical jokers who had given the other regulars many a memorable laugh at some casual's expense. They were good fellows, whose companionship Casey and Murphy relished. Murphy, eyeing the group with added interest, smiled with fellow feeling. In matters of this kind, he was one of the initiates.

He had called for his second whiskey and was wondering who the stranger could be, when Casey stood up and came across to him.

'What goes on?' Murphy asked.

'It's priceless,' Casey said in an undertone. 'Come on over and join us.'

'Who's his nibs?'

'An English journalist. Name of Smith.'

Murphy, preparing to relish the fun, asked, 'What's extraordinary about a journalist?'

'Do you know what he wants?' Casey said. 'A photograph of the I.R.A. drilling and an interview with one of the leaders.'

'He doesn't want much,' Murphy said, his eyes widening.

'Someone told him the Poolebeg was an I.R.A. hangout. The actors are playing up to him. Come on over for God's sake. It's gas.'

'Wait a minute,' Murphy said. 'I'll call another drink first.'

He did so. This was one of the things that distinguished the Poolebeg from other houses. There was colour and life in it, the regulars were a cut above the ordinary. One could discuss philosophy and religion with them. They knew what they were talking about. Or poetry. Or, if the mood prevailed, horse racing and dogs. And there was always the chance of some well-manœuvred joke, the telling of which would enliven the dull hours in the office of the Ministry for Exports.

Murphy got his drink and followed Casey. He was introduced as Sean O'Murchu. The use of the Irish form of his name puzzled him but after a while he concluded that it must be part of the joke. The journalist took an immediate interest in him. He spoke of several recent raids on Northern Ireland by the illegal army and of the interest which his paper took in them. The editor wanted photographs and an interview. Since his arrival in Dublin he had been trying to make contact. Murphy hid his amusement behind an unsmiling mask. Then the journalist said:

'When I got the tip-off about this place I wasn't inclined to believe it, Mr. O'Murchew. I don't easily despair, but I'd got several false leads already. But the moment I heard the Erse I knew you boys were straight.'

One of the actors affected a guilty start.

'We were speaking Irish and he overheard us,' he explained.

He said it directly to Murphy, in a tone of embarrassed apology, as though to forestall a possible reprimand.

'That's right,' another added, 'Mr. Smith here took us completely by surprise.'

The first, fawning on Murphy, said:

'Oh—completely, sir.'

The word 'sir' alarmed Murphy. He began to see what they were up to.

'What the hell do you mean by "Sir"?' he demanded.

'Sorry—it slipped out,' the actor said. To Murphy's horrified eyes the actor appeared to blush.

124

He decided to take control of the situation at once. It was one thing to enjoy their leg-pull of an English journalist who was fool enough to think he could collect photographs of an illegal organisation such as the Irish Republican Army by walking into a public house and making a simple request. It was another thing if Murphy himself was to be pushed forward as an officer of that organisation and find God knows what dangerous reference to himself appearing in the English papers. Apart from the law, he was a civil servant and supposed to keep a mile clear of such things. It wouldn't do at all.

'Look here,' Murphy said, with a show of tolerance, 'I don't know what yarns these fellows have been spinning for you, Mr. Smith, but I know nothing whatever about the I.R.A.'

'I appreciate your reticence, Mr. O'Murchew,' the journalist assured him. 'Don't think I'd betray anything. Or that our paper is going to be unsympathetic. We know the wrongs of the Irish. We've carried articles on the Irish question that have rattled the Tories. That's why we want these pictures.'

'After all, think of the publicity,' one of the actors suggested.

'That's right. The organisation needs it,' said the other.

'A sympathetic review of Aims,' the first urged.

It took Murphy some time to collect his thoughts. The combined attack petrified him. The journalist, interpreting his silence for indecision, looked on hopefully.

'Look here,' Murphy said loudly, 'I know nothing about the bloody I.R.A. I'm a peaceable man with twenty years' service in the Ministry for Exports. I came here to have a quiet, contemplative drink. . . .'

Casey suddenly gripped his sleeve.

'Keep your voice down, for God's sake.'

This Judas touch from his closest friend made Murphy almost shoot out of his chair.

'Are you going to side with them too? Holy God. . . .'

'No, no, no,' Casey interrupted. 'Look who's just come in.'

Murphy looked up and immediately subsided.

A newcomer had taken his place at the counter and was ordering a drink with a grim inclination. He was tall, spare and hatchet-faced. He acknowledged those nearest to him with a curt nod of the head and immediately excluded them again by studying his newspaper. Hempenstall was Murphy's immediate superior in the office. He seldom appeared in the Poolebeg. If he drank it was for a strict medicinal purpose. A sneeze in the course of the morning had caused him a moment of apprehension. Or a spasm of stomach cramp. Or a touch of 'flu. His world was essentially humourless and, since his wife's tragic death, a deliberately joyless one. His only release was the study of Regulations—all kinds of Regulations, which he applied rigorously. They were his only scruples. He spoke little, and that little only in the way of business.

'Do you think he heard?' Murphy asked in an undertone.

'If he didn't it wasn't *your* fault,' Casey answered sourly.

Hempenstall was Casey's superior too. The journalist leaned forward avidly. 'Who is he?'

'My superior,' Murphy whispered, using only the side of his mouth.

One of the actors said, 'The Wig.'

'I beg your pardon?'

'No one must know his real name,' the actor explained, 'so we call him The Wig.'

'Ah!' the journalist said, with complete understanding.

This was too much for Murphy. He tried to speak quietly, but emotion amplified what he had to say.

'Lookit here. This has got to stop. When I said it was my superior I meant my superior. I'm not going to sit here . . .'

Hempenstall was seen to lower his paper.

'Keep your goddam voice quiet,' Casey appealed. 'He's looking straight over.'

The journalist, who had formed his own conclusions, said:

'I suppose there's no use me making a direct approach to the . . . eh . . . Wig?'

The sudden change in Murphy's face gave him his answer. He added almost immediately: 'Sorry, Mr. O'Murchew. I know how these things are. Forget it.'

He lowered his voice further and asked for what he termed a tip-off. A photograph of a contingent drilling would complete his assignment. It would be used in a manner which would reflect nothing but credit on a brave and resourceful organisation.

'You might as well tell him,' said one of the actors. 'He's a sympathiser. I've read his articles before.'

But the journalist was meticulous. It was the effect of four hot whiskies.

'Not a sympathiser—quite,' he corrected. 'My rule is—Understand one another first. Then judge. Present the case. I mean—fair hunt. What my colleagues and I are proud to call British Impartiality.'

'British Impartiality,' the actor approved, with the hearty air of being man enough to give the enemy his due.

Impulsively his colleague said, 'Shake.'

The journalist looked at the outstretched hand in surprise, then gripped it with genuine emotion

'Now tell him,' the first actor said to Murphy.

Two matters troubled Murphy simultaneously. The first was the continuing presence of Hempenstall, who was uncomfortably within earshot. The second concerned the journalist and the actors. He found it impossible to decide which of them he would annihilate first—given the ability and the opportunity. He thought the journalist. He glanced around at the windows on his left and saw the snow dissolving in endless blobs against them. It tempted him with an idea for revenge. There was a mountain valley about seventeen miles distant, a lost, isolated spot which boasted a crossroads, a good fishing river and a public house. In summer Casey and he sometimes journeyed there by 'bus, for a little air and plenty of drink. In winter it was a godforsaken wilderness, frequently cut off from the outside world by deep drifts.

'Keep it very quiet,' Murphy whispered. They all leaned forward.

'There's a valley about seventeen miles out to the south, Slievefada,' he continued. 'Go there tomorrow and visit John Joe Flynn's public house.'

'How do I get there?' the journalist asked.

'Any of the car-hire firms will fix you up. Just tell them you want to go to Slievefada.'

'And what do I say to Flynn?'

One of the actors took over.

'When you walk in just say *Dia Dhuit.*'

'I get it—a password.'

This was better than the actor intended.

'Exactly. If Flynn answers *Dia's Muire Dhuit*, everything's O.K.'

'Do I mention Mr. O'Murchew sent me?'

'No. If he asks you that, just say—The Mask.'

'The Mask.'

'Now you've got it.'

They spent some time teaching the journalist how to pronounce the simple Irish greeting which he had concluded to be a password and they wrote down the customary response phonetically so that he could study and recognise it. While they were talking Hempenstall left. Then the journalist found it was time to go too. His leave-taking was the occasion of a series of warm handshakes. As his bulk disappeared through the door, Casey felt the need of emotional release.

'Well . . . I declare to God,' he began. But having got that far, words failed him. He looked at the rest and they began to laugh, the actors helplessly, Murphy uneasily. He was already apprehensive and inclined to regret his surrender to temptation.

His regret grew as the afternoon wore on. The office of the Ministry for Exports was an oppressive warren of corridors and offices, lit by hanging bulbs under ancient cowls. The whiskey had left an unpleasant after-taste. He felt depressed. Life, from no tangible cause, bristled with vague but threatening uncertainties. On afternoons such as this the thought often suggested itself to Murphy that he was growing too old for the joking and the drinking, a thought he now and then discussed with Casey. They referred to the feeling mutually as a touch of Anno Domini. Sometimes they wondered if it would have been better to marry, even on the salary their modest abilities commanded. There was troublesome correspondence on his desk too. A Lady Blunton-Gough had started a campaign against the export of live horses to France for use as food. She had founded a 'Save-the-Horses' Committee. The trades unions had also made representation to the Minister because the horses were being exported. Lady Blunton-Gough had publicly praised the humanity of the working class. As it happened, prematurely. The trades unions had soon made it clear that they had no objection to the French getting their horse meat. They simply wanted to export the meat in cans, in order to provide employment for the butchering trade and the factory hands. As a result Lady Blunton-Gough and the trades unions were now at daggers drawn. It was part of Murphy's job to make a first draft of a letter to Lady Blunton-Gough advising her that her representations were being closely considered, and one to the Trade Union Congress to the effect that in view of the heavy unemployment figures their suggestion was receiving the sympathetic attention of the Minister. Both organisations would publicise the respective replies. He was struggling for the fifth successive afternoon with this unwelcome problem when the buzzer indicated that he was wanted in Hempenstall's office.

He found his superior sitting in an aroma of disinfectant, sucking throat lozenges from a box on his desk.

'What I have to say is not official,' Hempenstall opened, waving him to a chair.

Murphy made signs which conveyed that anything Mr. Hempenstall cared to address to him would be avidly received.

'I speak in your own interest and that of the Department.'

'I understand, sir.'

'At lunch break today I visited the Poolebeg. I had a premonition of 'flu and felt the need of a preventative. You may have seen me?'

'Now that you mention it, I believe I did.'

'I happen to overhear a remark of yours, a reference to an illegal organisation. I have no doubt that it arose in the course of conversation. . . .'

'I assure you it did.'

'Still, I think it my duty to remind you that even during his free time a civil servant remains a civil servant. Prudence requires him to avoid discussions of a political nature. Especially conversations involving the activities of an illegal army which operates in defiance of the Government he serves. I don't think I need labour the point.

In mentioning it I have your career in mind. You are a long time with us.'

'Twenty years.'

'I thought even longer.'

'I'd like to explain that the subject of the I.R.A. . . .'

'Quite. I trust it won't be necessary to refer to it again.'

'It arose, Mr. Hempenstall. . . .'

'Excellent. I won't keep you any longer from your desk.'

Frustrated and upset, Murphy returned to his desk. He found it more difficult than ever to concentrate on the question of horse meat. The evening dragged on; against the darkened windows he could sense the silent melting of snowflakes. After some nervous reflection he 'phoned Casey, who seemed to be in remarkably good form, and said to him:

'That was desperate carry on.'

'What was?'

'What-you-know.'

'Lord, yes. Priceless.'

'He seemed a bit of an ass.'

'Who?'

'Who-you-know.'

'It was good fun.'

'Do you think he'll really go?'

'Where?'

'Where-you-know.'

'It wouldn't surprise me.'

'Look. Meet me after the office.'

'The usual?'

'No. I think the other place.'

'Dammit. I can't. I've an appointment.'

'That's a pity. Oh well. See you tomorrow. Lunch-time.'

'In the other place?'

'No. Better make it the usual.'

'Righto. By the way, I thought it very funny.'

'What?'

'Calling you The Mask.'

Murphy shuddered and replaced the 'phone.

Two days later nothing had happened and Murphy was beginning to see the bright side of the incident. The story of his sending the journalist on a wild goose chase to Slievefada had gone the rounds of the bars. In three different haunts he found himself invited to give the story to the *habitués*. It was received with tremendous hilarity. Here, their inner fantasies had been translated into reality. A man with a camera, armed with a harmless Irish greeting as a password, had gone off into the snow-bound wilderness for a glimpse of the

I.R.A. It was as though Murphy had sent him hunting a unicorn. Someone said it was typical of the English and showed that they lacked imagination. Another said it didn't. On the contrary, it showed they had too much imagination. Somebody else said imagination had nothing to do with it. It showed that the English had what the Irish always lacked, faith in themselves. Another said not at all; if it demonstrated anything it was that the English had faith in the Irish. Murphy, when asked for his opinion, modestly owned himself at a loss. It was dangerous to generalise. It was a matter of judging the individual character he said, weighing him up carefully and deciding how best to exploit his weak points. Of course, it was all easier said than done.

'And you were the man to do it,' someone enthused. 'I take off my hat to you.'

Then they all took off their hats to him, even those who were not wearing them. Murphy found the experience pleasant. To be well thought of in such company was the only taint of ambition in his make-up.

Life had taught Murphy to believe in Fate. It had also taught him not to trust it, a fact of which he was reminded the following day when Hempenstall again called him to his office.

'You will remember our recent interview?' Hempenstall began.

'Of course, sir.'

'Have you seen the *Daily Echo*?'

'No, sir, I don't get the English dailies.'

'I have this morning's issue here. There is a photograph in it.'

Hempenstall unfolded a paper and laid it before Murphy who bent down to examine it. His heart missed a beat. The photograph showed about twelve men, spread out in wide formation, advancing up a snowy clearing which was flanked by pine trees. The men were armed with rifles. The top caption read, *I.R.A. Manœuvres*, and underneath, *Our Special Reporter scooped this candid shot of warlike preparations in the Irish mountains* (see below).

The accompanying article began:

*Within twelve hours of his arrival in Dublin, enquiries sent our special reporter battling through snow and ice to a little known village less than seventeen miles from the heart of the Capital. The village— Slievefada, the mission. . . .*

'Slievefada,' Murphy echoed involuntarily.

'You know the place?' Hempenstall said.

'Vaguely,' Murphy confessed.

'You are hardly being frank, Mr. Murphy,' Hempenstall accused. 'You spent your vacation there two years in succession. We have it on your file. You will remember that during the recent war the regulations required everyone of this staff to furnish information as to his whereabout when going on leave.'

'Now I remember,' Murphy said. 'I was there for the fishing. Funny I should forget.'

Hempenstall looked at him closely. He had the lowest possible opinion of Murphy's intelligence, yet this new sample of its level surprised him.

'I show you the photograph because you may feel I was over-severe the other day. I realise, of course, that your choice of Slievefada as a holiday resort and the present picture have no connection. But I trust it will help to drive home my point about careless talk in public places.'

'Very forcibly, sir.'

'These English reporters are everywhere. Think of your situation as a civil servant if one of them were to overhear you and approach you.'

'You make it very clear, sir.'

'Good. I want no action of any officer under my control to reflect discredit on my Section. You may go back to your desk.'

'Thank you, Mr. Hempenstall.'


Murphy's appointment with Casey that evening was in none of their usual haunts. He was thankful for the darkness of the snow-bound streets, thankful for the swarming tea-time crowds. He felt he might already be a hunted man. Now and again the picture flashed into his mind of a middle-aged body spreadeagled and lifeless among the shadows of some courtyard, the word 'Informer' pinned to its shabby coat. The body was his. Casey was already waiting for him in the restaurant. It was a cheap and noisy basement with a multi-coloured juke box around which a group of teenagers wagged assorted bottoms. They drank two bowls of indescribable soup while Murphy urged the wisdom of going at once to Slievefada to question John Joe Flynn. Casey was disinclined.

'I don't see any sense in it,' he objected.

'Maybe you don't. But I do. It's the talk of every bar that I sent the reporter out there. If the I.R.A. get to hear it God knows what will happen. They might even shoot me.'

'That's what I mean,' Casey said, making his point clearly. 'If we go to Slievefada they might shoot both of us.'

'John Joe's a friend of ours,' Murphy pleaded, 'he'll advise us for the best and let us know how we stand.'

'The roads are too bad,' Casey resisted, changing ground.

'There's no harm trying.'

'And look at the expense. Even if we persuade some driver to chance it, he's bound to charge us through the nose.'

'Not if we hire a self-drive.'

'And who'll drive it?'

131

'I will.'

'You!' Casey protested. 'Not bloody likely. I'd rather give myself up to the I.R.A. and be done with it.'

'All right,' Murphy said at last, with a look of pitiable resignation. 'I'll go by myself.'


Two hours later Casey bitterly regretted the sense of loyalty which had made him yield to the unspoken challenge. He looked sideways at Murphy and wondered what strange love it was which induced him to stand by this thin, miserable, unprepossessing piece of humanity. He had a half bottle of whiskey in his lap which they had brought with them in case of emergency, but the potential comfort it contained failed to cheer him. The hired car slithered from ditch to ditch when they went downhill and slipped alarmingly when they climbed. Murphy crouched inexpertly over the wheel, his chin out, the rest of his face pinched and small with concentration and the cold.

'If I ever get back home alive,' Casey said finally, 'I'm going straight in to have myself certified.'

The car swung wildly but righted itself. Murphy's nerves were in a bad way. He snapped at him:

'There you go—distracting my attention.'

He crouched over the wheel once more. For some miles the headlights lit up a snowy wilderness. Soon it narrowed to a few yards. Slanting streamers of white surrounded and enclosed them. It was snowing again. The pine trees which marched up steep slopes on either side of the road disappeared. Once the near wheel slithered into the ditch and Casey got his shoes full of snow as he pushed and strained to lift it out. After less than a mile his feet were wet and cold. He stretched out his hand for the whiskey bottle. He began to grope about, calmly at first, then wildly.

'Holy God—it's gone,' he said at last.

'What's gone?'

'The whiskey.'

Murphy reacted automatically by pressing his foot on the brake. They careered from side to side, straightened, swung in a slow circle and, straightening once more, came to rest.

'How could it be gone?'

'It must have fallen when I got out to push you out of the ditch.'

'What'll we do?'

'What the hell *can* we do?'

'Nothing, I suppose. We'd never find it now.'

'You'd better drive on,' Casey said.

As they drove his feet got colder and colder. He no longer gave a damn about the I.R.A. because he felt convinced he was going to die of pneumonia anyway. Once or twice he sneezed. After another half hour, during which they both thought more or less continuously of the whiskey bottle gradually disappearing under the falling snow, a view of the matter occurred to Murphy which he voiced for Casey's consolation.

'Ah well,' he said, 'thanks be to God it wasn't a full bottle.'


At last they crossed the hump-backed bridge on the floor of the valley and swung left to the parking area in front of John Joe Flynn's. The two petrol pumps stood like snowmen, the blinds were down behind the windows, the door shut fast. John Joe could hardly believe his eyes. He dragged them in to the bar and over to the blazing log fire which reflected on the bronze and glass of the bar. Three or four times he repeated:

'Glory be to the Man Above Us, Mr. Casey and Mr. Murphy, well I declare to me daddy.'

But he wouldn't let them talk to him until he had poured out a welcome, which he brought over in two well-filled tumblers.

'Get that inside the pair of you now,' he said, 'and take off the shoes and stockings. Youse must be soaked to the bone.' He had a glass in his own hand too, which he raised.

'*Sláinte,*' he said.

'*Sláinte Mhór,*' they replied.

'You still keep a good drop,' Casey approved.

'Hold on there now,' John Joe said, 'till I get you something to go with it.'

He went down into the kitchen and they were alone for a while. Their shoes had left a trail of footprints on the flagged floor, their coats dropped wetly on the hanger. There was a smell of groceries, of drink, of woodsmoke. The oil lamp slung from the centre of the ceiling cast a yellow circle which was edged with black. It made a faint buzzing noise which they found comforting. John Joe returned with a pot of tea and a plate of meat which they dispatched ravenously. They talked of the weather, of mutual friends, of this and that. Then Murphy pushed aside his empty plate and said, deliberately:

'We had a purpose in coming, John Joe.'

John Joe smiled and said:

'It occurred to me that it wasn't just to admire the scenery.'

They acknowledged the joke. Murphy took the *Daily Echo* from his pocket and spread it on the table.

'As a matter of fact, John Joe, it was this.'

'The photograph,' he added, when John Joe looked puzzled.

John Joe put on his spectacles and studied the photograph gravely. 'Well, I declare to me daddy,' he said at last, 'that fella was in earnest, after all.'

'What fellow?' Murphy asked.

John Joe put his spectacles back in his pocket. They hindered conversation.

'This fellow the other day. He blows in here from nowhere with a bloody big camera and an English accent. He knew me too. "Are you Mr. John Joe Flynn," says he. "That's what the priest called me when he poured on the water anyway," says I, "what's your pleasure?" He looked around once or twice as though he felt someone might be listening. "*Dia Dhuit*," says he. "*Dia's Muire Dhuit*," says I, surprised to hear an Englishman using the Irish. The next thing was he leaned over and whispered in me ear, "The Mowsk sent me".'

'The Mowsk?' Murphy echoed.

'I think that's what it was,' John Joe corrected, 'but I couldn't be sure. You know the funny bloody way the English has of talking. Anyway I left it at that and your man stayed the night. The next morning after breakfast he told me he was here to get a picture of the I.R.A. drilling.'

'What did you say?'

'What would you say to that class of lunatic? I humoured him. I told him it was a bloody serious thing to direct anyone to I.R.A. manœuvres and asked for time to think it over.'

'What did he say to that?'

'What he said before. The Mowsk sent him. He had this Mowsk stuff on the brain. Anyway, half an hour later, just to get shut of him, I told him there might be something stirring if he went down to Fisher's Point at twelve o'clock or thereabouts. And for the love of God, says I to him, don't on any account let yourself be seen. Dammit, but I clean forgot about the boys.'

'The boys?' Casey repeated.

'An arrangement the boys had made here a few nights before.'

John Joe cocked his ear at the sound of a heavy engine which sent the windows rattling before it churned to a stop. 'This'll be Lar Holohan and his helper. Hold on for a minute.'

He went over to unlock the door and Murphy exchanged glances with Casey. Both had the feeling of being in the centre of a hotbed of illegal activity.

'He means "The Mask",' Casey whispered. It was quite unnecessary.

'I know,' Murphy answered. If anything, the whiskey had made his nerves worse.

The lorry driver and his helper sat down near them while John Joe got tea and bread and meat. It was a fierce night, the lorry driver told them, with a blizzard almost certain. When were they going back?

'Tonight,' Murphy said.

The lorry driver addressed his helper.

134

'They won't get back tonight, will they, Harmless?'

'Not unless they has an airyplane,' Harmless confirmed.

'We got ditched twice coming through the pass,' the lorry driver said, 'it's closed by now.'

'Will it be right in the morning?'

'With the class of a night that's in it now, I wouldn't think so. Not for two days at least.'

'Three,' Harmless corrected.

The food was brought and they attacked it with gusto. When they had finished, John Joe asked Murphy for the *Echo* and spread it in front of the lorry driver.

'Have a look at that, Lar,' he invited.

His eyes shone with expectation. Lar examined it thoroughly.

'Can you guess what it is?' John Joe asked after a while.

The lorry driver stroked his chin.

'It's not the I.R.A. anyway,' he said at last. 'I recognise Tim Moore and John Feeney.'

'So do I,' Harmless added. 'I wouldn't accuse either of them of ambitions to shed their heart's blood for Ireland. Or anything else.'

'I'll tell you,' John Joe announced triumphantly, 'it's the dog hunt.'

The lorry driver guffawed.

'I declare to God,' he said, 'that's what it is.'

'Dog hunt?' Murphy said with a look of enquiry.

'You may remember Matt Kerrigan that lived by himself up the mountain,' John Joe began.

Murphy and Casey both remembered him, an old man who was something of a hermit.

'He died a few months ago,' John Joe said, 'but nothing would induce the bloody oul mongrel he kept to quit the house.'

'A ferocious-looking blackguard of a brute it was too,' Harmless assured them. 'Not a Christian class of a dog at all.'

'That's not a word of a lie,' said the lorry driver.

'It stayed on at the house,' John Joe continued, 'and of course after a while it went wild.'

'It was never what you'd call tame,' Harmless said. He had a grievance against the dog which had once bitten him.

'It did terrible damage to poultry, and latterly it began to attack the sheep. So when the bad weather came and the boys got together to help bring the flocks down to the lower slopes they thought they'd kill two birds with the one stone and shoot the oul dog if they could round him up as well. That's why they brought the guns.'

'They got it too,' Harmless said with relish, 'shot it above at Eagle Rock. They said it was mad as well as wild.'

'And that's the photograph the journalist got?' Casey asked.

'That's the photograph you see in front of you,' John Joe said. 'The boys setting off to get the bowler.'

'And he thought it was the I.R.A.,' the lorry driver commented, looking at the photograph with renewed relish.

John Joe proceeded to tell the lorry driver why. He described the visit of the journalist and about sending him down to Fisher's Point to get shut of him. Three or four times the lorry driver nearly fell off his stool.

Murphy looked over at Casey. They found it impossible to join in the general laughter. Outside it was snowing hard. A wind had risen which made a deep, rumbling noise in the wide chimney. They thought of the pass filling moment by moment with its barrier of snow.

'We may as well have a drink anyway,' Murphy said; 'we'll have whiskey all round, John Joe.'

The lorry driver stopped laughing in order to hold up his hand and ask him to make his beer, explaining that both he and his helper had had a skinful of whiskey already.

'It was when we were struggling with the lorry the second time we got ditched,' Harmless explained. 'Suddenly my foot kicked something. It was a half bottle of whiskey.'

'Someone must have let it fall,' said the driver.

'So we polished it off,' Harmless concluded and then cocked an ear to the night. He considered carefully.

'At least three days,' he added at last, meaning the Pass.


Harmless turned out to be right. Murphy and Casey stayed in John Joe Flynn's. There was nothing else they could do. They telephoned the post office and had a telegram sent on to Hempenstall, explaining that they were weather bound. On the same call John Joe sent a request to the post office to order a dozen copies of the *Daily Echo* and hold them. Every one involved in the dog hunt would want one for himself, he said.

On the third day, while Murphy was gazing out of the window the thought occurred to him that the telegram they had sent to Hempenstall would bear the name of Slievefada Post Office as its point of origination. This was a fresh complication. It would be difficult to explain to Hempenstall. As he thought about it he grew pale. Even Casey noticed.

'What are you thinking about?' he asked.

Murphy's eyes dwelt in silence for a while on the snow-covered desolation outside. His pallor remained.

'Siberia,' he said eventually.

# Battles Long Ago

## HELEN LUCY BURKE

THE 'BUS stopped at the corner of the road with a great screeching of brakes. It took several minutes to persuade the Hero out of the bellicose trance which had dropped on him. Shoulders hunched high and eyes slitted, he glared at the two Englishmen on the bench seat opposite. In light nasal voices they talked about Manchester United.

Cahal said, 'Let you come on with yourself, Tom. Sure the like of them is beneath notice.'

The braver of the Englishmen, the one who had argued earlier, tittered.

Waving a fist the Hero lurched to his feet. The 'bus conductor and Cahal seized him by each wrist and hurried him off the 'bus. As Paddy jumped off the platform after them the conductor shouted: 'And you can stay off my 'bus in future, you and your Commandant.'

The Commandant was lying on the ground with Cahal kneeling beside him. In the light of the street-lamp frost glittered on the pavement and grass verge like white icing. Paddy wondered it if was true that alcohol acted as an anti-freeze on the blood. He hoped so, for getting Tom up off the ground was a lengthy business. Every time they got a grip on him he pivoted on his backside the way a seal does, and tried to pull them down beside him. At first he roared with laughter and did it as a joke, and then his mood changed and he did it out of peevishness.

Twice, going up the road, he fell, and once he and Cahal stopped to be sick. They took a long time about it, hanging in over a neighbour's wall.

Paddy looked delicately into the distance. To see a man puking up his guts reduced him to mortal quality: and Paddy had fought under the Commandant and had wonderful respect for him. He breathed deeply: and at each breath the air rushed into his lungs with the cutting edge of a knife. It made the blood sing in his head almost as if he were drunk himself.

Overhead the stars made hissing noises as they fizzed and sparkled.

It was the kind of night which made you want a gun in your hand, and an enemy in front of you to shoot, and the youth with which to do it.

When they moved on Paddy said, 'This reminds me of the night at Cloonbawn.' It was what he always said, no matter what the weather was like, if Tom got depressed. Also it reminded people that he, too, had played his part and had got a mention in the *Ballad of Cloonbawn*.

He started to hum it under his breath. The others joined in, bawling it out.

'There were five of us that fought and three of us that died, And two and twenty Tans that met their doom.'

When they came to the bit mentioning Tom O'Neill and Paddy Duff they all linked arms.

Cahal said, 'Well, all ye got out of it was the song.'

The Commandant stumbled, swore, and veered around the slippy path in search of his balance.

'Minister for Defence, that was what I was promised. And I'd have taken care of ye all, I would. Ye know that.'

'Sure of course we do. We know that indeed,' said Cahal soothingly.

Paddy thought cynically: 'So well he can be soothing after dropping the bit of poison. Cahal had never got a mention in a song. A great man with a rifle but a bit windy for grenade work.' They turned in the front path of Tom's house.

He had become lachrymose. In a low voice he sobbed that he should be coming home in a black Government Mercedes instead of a sixpenny 'bus-ride. As he was unable to find his key they knocked three times on the door, twice very loudly to show that they were heroes, and the third time softly because they were rather afraid of Mrs. O'Neill.

When she opened the door they could not see what humour she was in as her back was to the light. Without saying a word she turned and walked back into the sitting-room, leaving the hall door ajar.

'Come in and never mind herself,' said Tom. He stumbled truculently and noisily across the threshold. They followed him with less parade.

The hall was narrow, furnished with worn black linoleum and red scatter mats. On the right-hand side was a little table holding the telephone. It was lost from sight behind twenty or thirty dolls in the dresses of various countries. The hall stand was of fancy ironwork covered with coloured knobs.

The men hung up their coats and filed into the sitting-room. Cahal lost his footing to a scatter-mat at the entrance and fell in headlong. The others helped him up and then pushed him into a chair.

Tom had come out of his stupor for the moment. The challenge of a battle with his wife cleared his wits.

She had resumed her seat in the blue upright chair opposite the television set. There were other more comfortable chairs but she never sat in them. This was her protest against her husband's roistering ways. Nights when he was very drunk indeed she did not even sit down but stood against the wall. On these occasions she did not eat either. Days, sometimes, went by without her putting a bit in her mouth. Then she would faint at Mass, a neighbour would bring her home, and the parish priest would come up to reprimand Tom.

In the neighbourhood she was considered a saint. Her husband hated the living sight of her.

'Ye'll all have another drink?'

Out of politeness they shook their heads.

'Ah, and something to eat. Go to God, it's no trouble to herself.'

She went out and came back in with a brass tray. In silent amazement the men inspected a plate of cream crackers. In the centre of each an anchovy lay coiled in sophisticated state. Another dish contained something red and oily. There was a pot of tea, three-quarters of a bottle of lime juice, and some lemonade.

'It's smoked salmon,' Mrs. O'Neill said proudly, pointing at the oily red stuff.

'In the holy name of Christ get us something fit to eat and leave your shalmon ... your shmoked ...' Lowering his head to his knees he muttered the rest of what he had to say to the carpet.

'It's for my daughter,' said Mrs. O'Neill. 'She's coming home tonight with her fiancé.'

'In England, isn't she?' said Paddy, contorting his mouth over an anchovy. 'Are these brown things all right, ma'am? They taste a bit funny.'

'Aye, in London. That's the way they're meant to taste, I think.'

There was silence in the room, except for the wordless tone poem which Tom was still droning downwards. Paddy put a bit of the salmon in his mouth and at once wished he had not. Being the only sober man in the room put a terrible strain on a fellow. Cahal had sunk into a torpor, disturbed now and then by frantic twitchings like a dog having nightmares.

'Her fiancé, ma'am, you said. A local boy, would he be?'

'It's my first time meeting him. You'll have another of these. Or some lime juice.'

'Plenty, plenty.'

She got up and turned on the television set with the air of one offering the final rite of hospitality. A man with a smooth fat face limned himself on the screen and began to talk.

Three more minutes, said Paddy to himself, and then if I can get legs under this fellow we'll go.

'Bloody spies,' bellowed Tom suddenly, raising his head. He glared bull-like at the television screen on which another man with a vinegary look had joined the fat man.

With eyes closed Cahal come in antiphonally, 'Sound man, Commandant. True for you.'

Tom lifted his fist into the air and brought it down towards the table. Just before it struck the dishes he halted its course, drew it in towards him, and spread the fingers open on his knees as if they were battle trophies distinct from his own body. The fingers were splayed and broken. With his other hand he fondled them. He said pathetically, 'For Ireland. And now they send me home in a sixpenny 'bus.'

'When you come home at all,' said Mrs. O'Neill.

'He's not himself,' said Paddy.

'He's his usual self,' said Mrs. O'Neill.

'Bloody spies and traitors,' said Tom, in a low quiet voice. 'Ye deserved what ye got. Wouldn't ye have done the same to me?'

His little red eyes were straining towards the men on the television screen who were talking earnestly about the problems of world over-population. Their lack of response infuriated him. He started to shout.

'Didn't I hear that you had turned? Didn't I know that you were only waiting to put the gun to my own back? That's what they told me anyway. . . . Don't look at me like that, for Jesus' sake. . . .'

Paddy felt cold all over. He felt the hair lift and move on the nape of his neck, as if there were someone bad behind him breathing on him. So it was true that Tom had shot the Maguires in the back.

He looked quickly at Mrs. O'Neill. She was standing against the wall, her broad smooth face contorted with an expression of sick loathing. Paddy remembered suddenly that she had been a Maguire before her marriage and some sort of cousin to the two boys.

When she saw him looking at her she hurriedly refilled his teacup and spilled the rest of the salmon onto his plate.

'For my daughter and her fiancé I got it but there's plenty more outside.'

Paddy nodded. ' 'Tis grand weather we're having, I hope it will stay dry for them.' Merciful God, he thought, I'd better get out before I hear anything worse. He glanced furtively at Tom who seemed to be listening intently to what the two men on the screen were saying.

'Well now, I think we'd better be getting along,' he said in formal tones. 'Would you like me to give you a hand with himself before I go?'

Mrs. O'Neill shook her head. 'I wouldn't like to be the one that would try.'

'In that case I'll just waken up Cahal here.'

It was easier said than done. Cahal had sunk deep into the armchair and was snoring there, an immovable hulk. His mouth hung open; a trail of spit ran down towards his chin out of the corner of his mouth. Paddy felt deeply ashamed for him in front of Mrs. O'Neill: and at the same time he felt that in her heart she despised him for his sobriety. He tried not to listen to what Tom was saying behind him, but in spite of himself he caught terrifying snatches. There was a lengthy account of what the Tans had done to him, the time they caught him at Ballinleck: and heaving with nausea, Paddy caught sight of a little look of triumph on Mrs. O'Neill's face.

'Sure don't you know I had no choice? I couldn't face that again if ye had turned me in.' He waited, head cocked, to hear the reply.

'Improved agricultural methods is only a short-term answer,' said the fat man on the screen.

'But they told me you had gone over. What choice had I?'

The vinegary man shook his head. 'Only if you consider them in relation to existing farmlands.'

'I couldn't take the chance. And I gave it to ye quick and easy, and both together.'

A third man, the chairman of the programme, came onto the screen. As he opened his smiling mouth to talk the Commandant struggled to his feet, swaying, yelling, gesturing. 'Oh, there he is. Oh, that's the bastard himself. Grinning there at ye.'

Mrs. O'Neill murmured: 'He told me to do it.'

'He told me to do it,' her husband groaned. ''Twas he who made me.'

Paddy got his shoulder under Cahal's armpit and gave a powerful heave. Wavering, they stood together on the rug in the position of a couple about to waltz. There was still the problem of getting his coat on. Mrs. O'Neill led the way into the hall. She made no attempt to help. Eyes downcast she straightened the scatter mats with the tip of her shoe.

Outside there was the sound of a car drawing up. Voices drifted in cheerfully over the sharp air. The car moved off and there was a knock at the door.

Without any hurry Mrs. O'Neill opened the door and drew in the couple, linked and laughing. The girl was plump and pink-cheeked, the man tall, very blonde, healthy looking in a brutal sort of way, and unmistakably English even before he opened his wide pale lips.

As Paddy went down the road, hurrying as best he could with the dead weight of Cahal on his arm, he said over and over to himself in a low voice 'Oh merciful God this night.'

And as he said it and hurried away he strained his ears with avid pleasure for the fight.

# An Aspect of the Rising

## TOM MacINTYRE

OPPOSITE Adam and Eve's, the up-river east wind that would frizzle a mermaid's fins a zephyr tickle the second I sighted her. Plump chiaroscuro: black bobbed hair, white cheeks, black coat, white calves, black shoes, high-heeling along the far footpath. She looked recklessly like herself, in her wisdom gazed neither to the left nor to the right but let the plastic bag winking on her rump com'ither me through the scooting traffic and urgent to her side.

'We're in business'—I matched her step, leaned towards her, eager as a guitar.

'Fast from the trap, aren't you'—she spoke from the lips out, never slackened pace—'wonder you weren't made ointment of crossing the street.'

'You're beautiful'—pursuing, I ladled compliments into her small skin tight ear, and now she coy'd. The black pencilled line above her visible eye, the right, took my admiration. Oblique but eloquent of the horizontal, a masterpiece. Still we hurried—

'Where'are we going?'

'You have a car?'

Had a car.

'I have to have a cup of coffee'—her mauve mouth belonged to the first woman, the destined rib—'You can get the car. And wait for me up here outside The Last Post.'

She went. Captive, I watched her buttocks acclaim a royal leaving. Her scent stayed. A firm scent. And ready. Appled. That was it. Apples and muscles. Taffeta flashing above her bright-bare calves, the door of The Last Post opened before her.

Philomena, she introduced herself. And my instinct, I decided, had been sound. Anything with ears on it bar a pot is the rule along the river most nights but here was a real professional, her every motion *credo*—

143

'How're they hanging?' she enquired as we drove off towards Kingsbridge and The Park beyond.

'Two eggs in a hanky.'

Chuckling, she produced cigarettes, lit two, and passed one to me. They were Polish and smuggled—a sailor from Riga.

'Poles, I say to him,' she reminisced, settling back in the seat—knees sudden and vocal as the skirt rose, 'poles is right.'

Sure of your wares is sure of your stares. Philomena, slowly, fingered open her coat, and—I glanced across—the wares, big unbiddable breasts, trim belly, and roomy thighs, began to move and converse under blouse and skirt as if equally sure of themselves. To the silencer in these excitements I bowed. She reading me with black eyes, understood, and, leaning over, petted my abundant crotch. Jesus, I thought—giddy—I'll have to be dug out of her. The last 'buses were being shunted home, on the roof of the Brewery a bouncy moon. Apples and the contraband of the Baltic odorous about us, we took the hill, sped through the gates and into The Park.

'Here, Philomena?'

A few hundred yards in, and impetuous, I was steering for a convenient nest under the adjacent and glooming trees.

'No, keep going. Right. Keep going. There's a little spot I know. I'll show you the way—'

Venue. Between friends, I asked, what was the difference, here or there? No good. We drove. Insistent, she directed me, her neat coaxing hand slipping in and out of the light—'It's a special spot I have. Not far—'

On reflection, I yielded. She was right. Not any hole in the wall but a sanctified lair. What a woman! We passed the zoo. A lion raged within, and down to our right flamingoes fluttered and gossiped in the pink insomnia of their watery beds.

'The zoo's grand,' she voiced dreamily, 'Keep going.'

Open spaces, right, left, this fork now, trees, silver choppy in the branches, no trees, silver seamless along the grass. Delay's a randy foreman. I glimpsed the dank remains of turfstacks which had warmed Dublin winters ago, I glimpsed the long-legged ghosts of slaughtered deer but I thought neither of the huddled fire nor the red jittery stag. She sat there, relaxed, substantial in the run of shadows, now and then nibbling my neck.

'Nearly there.'

'Christ,' I grouched, 'we'll be at the Boyne before we know it.'

Next moment—'Here,' she pointed, 'left—'

And (it wasn't just the voice, curiously level) I felt—alteration. On the turn, I inspected her. Sure enough, she was tight in the seat, tight as Christy's britches. Suspicion cranked me. No, I calmed myself. The cramp of an instant. It means nothing. We were driving towards a stand of fir and pine a hundred yards away, a large building visible in fragmented outline beyond. Deep into the trees, I pulled up. Philomena, my new Philomena, was out of the car, wordless, before I'd switched off the ignition. Worried, I followed.

Smell of the trees. And the place's seasoned privacy. And the midnight dusk. There she was—a stranger and grim—her back to a young fir a few yards off. What was she at? Climbing the palisade of her remove, I advanced. Rhinestones flickered but didn't beckon. I was beside her, whispering. Weep for my whispers. She was wood against that tree. My fingers implored. Colder than wood—

'What's wrong?'

Two bleak eyes, she stood there. I made a rude remark. It passed lightly through her—your hand through a ghost.

'What is it?' I tried again, 'What's wrong?'

Useless, I scanned her face, a hunter's face, stalking what? Wind skidded on the branches. Philomena and I waited. For five stinging seconds, and then the spurs of a mean anger raked me. Let me omit the vituperation I flung upon her. It shames my balls, and it balls my shame. Tranced black and white in a shaft of the moon, she paid, thank God, no heed. I wheeled to depart, and not three steps had I taken when the woman, cat-spitting, was soaring to her singular and sainted glory—

'You crawthumpin' get of a Spaniard that never was seen'— incredulous, I stopped: the wood rang—'with your long features and your long memory and your two and twenty-two strings to your bow, what crooked eggs without yolks are you hatching between Rosaries tonight?'

Birds racketing. The Spaniard? To a skelp of joy, I connected. The building beyond—Arus an Uachtarian, de Valera himself under sharp and sharpening fire—

'Diagrams,' I heard, 'diagrams'—and a sneer bisected the word as it flew—'more of them you're amusing yourself with maybe, proving that A is B and B is C and a Republic is Jazus knows what until Euclid himself'd be cracked in Dundrum trying to make y'out. But Professor Isosceles'—she drew harsh breath, raced on, discovering the beat of her scorn—'it was damn all diagrams or anything else we got from you above in Boland's Mills when Simon Donnelly had to take over the command, you sitting there with your heart in your gob and your arse in a sling—'

Listen to me. There are sights you never forget. Her face wild, throat wilder, hands two kicking lanterns, knees ivory below— immobile and smooth. Philomena roasted The Long Fellow. Practice graced her, rancours unnameable and a fury of the bones powered her—she left nothing out, there was nothing she didn't fit in: The Treaty, The Civil War, The Oath, The Hangings of the 'forties, Emigration, Inflation, Taxation, the Language, the lot. An eighth of a mile away, brooding or at his prayers, His Excellency heard not

145

a word but, chosen by the gods, I heard, the ground heard and the wind and the sky's cupped ear. We listened to that alto scurrility leap the air, listened in ecstasy and heard—reaches distant—back-lane and gutter answer, stir, shift, and jig maddened to an old, a blithe, a bitter tune—

'You,' she cried aloud and aloft, 'you long spear in the side of a Christian people. May God drop a clog on you. May the Divil make a knot of you. May coals scorch you and may cinders choke you. May smoke annoy you and may soot destroy you. May the day peel your skins and the night screech your sins. May . . .'

Don't ask me how long it lasted but bring back Moses and I'll say it to his teeth: she finished that diatribe a creature of flame. You'd kneel to her—

'You there,' says she—there was barely a pause—into the shriven quiet, 'Are you comin' or goin'?'

I was dazzled but comin'. Gaily she murmured me in. Zips purred. The undergrowth lured. To it we went, and at it we stayed.

Birds settled again on the branches. In the great house beyond the trees—lights burning here and there, in the city below, and all over Ireland, medals were being dusted, ribbons spruced, orations polished and artillery oiled for The Fiftieth Anniversary of The Insurrection.

# Modern Times
# Northern Ireland:

# Miss Gillespie and the Micks

## ARNOLD HILL

---

W E CALLED her old Miss Gillespie, although I do not suppose she was more than forty-five or fifty. She was a big stout woman with rosy cheeks and red hair and an enormous bosom. She always seemed to wear far too many clothes and always appeared to be very warm and out of breath. She had practised midwifery until her fondness for drink caused people to lose faith in her. They pitied her, but would not have her attend them in childbirth. Still the brass plate remained on the door-frame of her house: Miss Gillespie, Certified Midwife.

She lived with her brother, a retired sea-captain, in a little house on the outskirts of the village. Her brother was a short, stocky man with a red face and a sailor's roll. He was very quiet and spent most of his time working about the garden, but occasionally he would come down to Johnston's pub and sit in a corner drinking beer and telling yarns about his sea-faring days. He had served his apprenticeship under sail, and always spoke with contempt of the steamship, maintaining that any landlubber could be a sailor nowadays. 'It was a sad day,' he used to say, 'the day they traded a clean spread of canvas for a splutterin', stinkin' donkey-engine.'

Our favourite prank used to be letting down the back tyre of her bicycle. She always cycled down to Johnston's on Saturday night and left the bicycle outside while she got drunk in the bar parlour. It was a strange thing, but she always seemed to ride much better when she came out of Johnston's. At other times her method of riding was slow and wobbly and uncertain, as if she were on a bicycle for the first time. But on leaving the pub on Saturday nights she would heave her huge body on to the saddle and go pedalling furiously up the narrow street, weaving in and out among carts and dogs and herds of cattle, narrowly missing other cyclists and shouting at anyone who got in the way.

If, however, we had previously removed the valve from the back tyre, she would pull up before she had gone more than a few yards, hop clumsily off the saddle and begin to shout at the top of her voice, standing in the middle of the street with one foot on the ground and the other supported on the pedal. The anger and the shouting made her very red in the face, and we who crouched giggling in some nearby doorway could almost have sworn that her hair became redder, too.

Some of the men who always stood about Johnston's would come over to her and ask her what was the trouble. 'Och, it's them children again,' she would shout. 'Sure they'd break a body's heart. They haven't left me what air in me back tyre would blow out a candle. Bad cess to them! Of all the meddlin', interferin' wee brats that ever were let into this world, them in this place takes the cake! I'll put the polis on them. Declare to God I will; I'll put the polis on them and have them banished from the country. A pack of common thieves and rogues and liars, that's what they are. A decent, respectable body doesn't get a chance with the likes of them around, so they don't.'

Then she would begin to cry and would have to be taken back into Johnston's for consolation while someone repaired her flattened tyre.

Half an hour later they would bring her out, blear-eyed and breathing heavily through her nose, help her on her bicycle and send up a ragged cheer as she shot off up the street, stiff and solid as a rock, her mouth grim with determination.

Never slackening her pace for a moment, she would push up the hill, past the post office and the Orange Hall, round the corner and along the straight, wide road to the church. Turning to the right, where the houses of the village began to thin out and to be separated by little plots and patches of meadow, she would come to the home of the O'Hagans, sitting back from the roadway, with dirty children playing around the door, the washing on the hedge and peat-smoke filtering from the slanting chimney.

Invariably, she would ride past the house, looking neither right nor left; then, as though some thought had suddenly occurred to her, she would pull up, leaning to one side and gripping savagely at the inefficient brake, and slowly circle round in the roadway.

The O'Hagans were the largest, and perhaps the poorest, family in the district. The father was a tall, quiet man, who seemed to spend all his time working with a few chickens and a meagre plot behind the house. He was very shy and was rarely seen in the village. The mother was a little harassed, anxious woman, who only appeared outside the house to draw water from the nearby pump or hang huge quantities of washing on the hedge. They had seven children, the eldest of whom could not have been more than ten years old at that time. They were a very devout couple, and I think now it may have been this very quality of devoutness and passive acceptance of life's hardships that inflamed Miss Gillespie against them.

Pedalling back to the O'Hagan's place, she would hop to the ground and stand astride her bicycle, one foot on the road, the other on the pedal. 'Hi, there!' she would call to the children. 'Away in and tell yer da I want a word with him. A lot of words! Tell him to come on out here till I give him his character. Go on, ye wee Fenian brats!'

At this the children would run into the house and close the door, and Miss Gillespie's fury would increase. 'Are ye never away yet, O'Hagan? Take you and your snivellin' wife and your brood of whelps and brats and away you go—over the Border where ye belong. Away with the lot of ye—you've contaminated the landscape long enough, God knows. Away back to yer chapels and yer Popery and leave honest Christian folk to live in peace. This is a civilized, Protestant country—we want none of your kind here.'

She would keep this up for perhaps ten minutes, until hoarseness and shortage of breath forced her to cease. There was never any attempt made to stop her. Passers-by only laughed and teased her into stronger invective. The house presented a blank face to her abuse. We youngsters, crouching behind the hedge, whistled and jeered and threw pieces of clay and dried cow dung at her, but so intense was her absorption in the O'Hagans that she seemed not to notice anything else. When it was over she would remount her bicycle and, still muttering threats and imprecations, ride off up the road towards her own house. Shortly afterwards, the O'Hagans' front door would open and the children would come out to resume their playing, as if nothing had happened.

Some of the older people tried from time to time to break her of this habit (as they also tried to stop her from drinking). Their intentions were good, but their efforts were in vain. Miss Gillespie would not listen to reason. Her personal pride and integrity were as strong as her powers of hatred. She refused to accept instructions from anyone on how to conduct her life. Even the frequent appeals of the local Methodist minister were without effect. 'What business is it of yours how I behave myself?' she said to him once. 'You go on preachin' your wee sermons on Sundays and leave us stipend-payers to look after our own lives. What do you care, as long as the money keeps comin' in? Away and convert them heathen O'Hagans and let us good Christian folks alone!'

One week early in spring there was very heavy snow, and two or three other boys and I went to the door and asked Captain Gillespie if we could clean his path, hoping to earn a few coppers. We didn't get the money, but when we had done he invited us into the house for tea. It was a tidy little house, full of bits of ship's gear and bottled schooners. This was Captain Gillespie's hobby, and he explained the delicate process by which the apparently impossible feat of getting a four-masted ship through the narrow neck of a bottle is accomplished.

Miss Gillespie, who presided at the tea-table, appeared to be in a very irritable mood. Evidently she was annoyed with her brother for having invited us in. She had been baking in the afternoon, and we had big warm farls of soda-bread, oozing with melted butter, and tea which could have supported the original of any of the Captain's models. She herself ate and drank little, and, when she had finished, sat glaring and grunting at us while Captain Gillespie recounted one of his interminable tales of adventure in a clipper off Cape Horn.

While we were sitting there, a timid knock was heard at the front door. The Captain rose to answer it. We could hear a young, eager voice, and the Captain's deep rumbling replies.

Suddenly she looked at the door and shouted, making us jump. 'Who is it, Albert?'

The door opened and her brother came in, closing it after him. He looked rather uncomfortable.

'Er—it's one of the O'Hagan children. He says his father sent him to ask if you'd come down there right away.' He coughed nervously. 'Mrs. O'Hagan's going to have a baby. They—can't get the doctor. The road's snowed up.'

He stood there waiting, watching her from under his frowning, bushy eyebrows.

At first Miss Gillespie was unable to speak. Only her reddening face registered her rising anger. Then she said:

'Well, of all the impertinence! Of all the unbelievable impertinence! The likes of *them*, daring to send for me.'

'I think you'd better go, Bertha,' said her brother. 'The woman must be pretty ill.'

'Go? Here, go out and tell that brat to go home and tell his da I wouldn't lift a finger to help them, not if they were havin' triplets! The idea of it!' She was shaking like a jelly. Big tears began to roll down her cheeks. 'The very idea—them sendin' to *me* for help. Well, don't stand there with yer mouth open. Go and tell him what I said. Chase him out of here before I go out and beat the lugs off him!'

He shrugged his shoulders and went back to the waiting boy. Miss Gillespie seemed to have forgotten our existence. She sat with her hands in her lap and sobs shook her big body. The tears trickled over her fat cheeks and ran down the sides of her nose. 'The idea of it,' she kept saying, staring at the tablecloth in front of her. 'Just fancy, them sendin' for me!' Her voice was thick with tears.

We sat in a cloud of embarrassment, then, as if we had all had the idea at the same moment, rose and hurried outside. The Captain stood at the door, gazing after young O'Hagan as he walked slowly down the road. We thanked him for the tea and, once we were out in the roadway, shed our discomfort and began to laugh at the big woman sitting there crying over the tablecloth. We followed the O'Hagan boy and hung about outside the house, full of curiosity. We could hear the woman groaning and wailing inside. There were none of the children playing round the door.

We began to build a snowman by the roadside, and I climbed into a field and got an old bowler hat off a scarecrow to set on his head. The eldest boy came out and told us his father said not to make so much noise, because his mother was sick. We pelted him with snow-balls, and he had to run into the house again.

We got tired waiting, and were about to go back into the village when we saw Miss Gillespie cycling down the road. She was wobbling along the narrow lane between the banks of snow, and we expected at any moment to see her hit the side and tumble off. We waited on the verge of laughter. She did not fall, however, and when she reached us she hopped off and asked angrily what we were doing there. Her black straw hat sat on top of her head, secured by a long pin at each side. Her eyelids were red and swollen. You could hardly see her eyes.

'Away off with ye!' she cried. 'Away out of this, before I beat the ears off you with my own two hands.'

She pushed the bicycle at us, and we scampered off down the road, jeering and whistling.

Miss Gillespie made as if to mount her bicycle again, hesitated, and then, with a sudden impatient movement, placed it against the low wall at the front of the O'Hagan's house and marched up to the door. We waited no longer, but ran down to the village to tell what we had heard and seen. It was perhaps an hour later when Miss Gillespie came riding down the street, drew up outside Johnston's pub and went into the bar parlour. A few moments later Joe, Mr. Johnston's assistant, came out and wheeled her bicycle inside. It was not long before the word went round that shortly after her arrival Mrs. O'Hagan had given birth to another son.

She stayed later than usual in the pub that night, and then she came pedalling furiously up the hill past the house, puffing and panting, and did not as much as turn her head. Then, twenty yards farther up the road, she suddenly pulled up, made a precarious turn between the snow-banks, and came cycling back. She stopped outside the quiet house, where a dim yellow light shone from the kitchen window. She stood with one foot on the road and the other on the pedal, holding the bicycle up under her.

'Hello there, O'Hagan,' she called. 'Come out, O'Hagan. Come out here till I tell you what I think of ye. Are ye never away yet, you dirty Fenian dog? Why don't you clear out an' take your yelpin' pups along with ye? We don't want you here, among decent Christian people. Clear out, an' take your woman and her brood with ye!'

She began to cry and to shake the handlebars of her bicycle in impotent rage.

'D'you hear me, you dirty Mick?' she howled. 'Away back where you belong the lot of ye.' She paused, as though waiting for some reply, then began to sob and moan in great distress. 'Ah, God forgive me!' she wailed. 'God forgive me this night, that ever lent a hand to bring a Popish brat into the world!'

153

# Tolerance

## JIM PHELAN

'IDENTITY cards?' demanded the man by the bridge, and extended one hand a little way. He wore a dark uniform, a revolver holster swung ready and his brusque military speech had a tiny latent harshness which made his request the more peremptory. 'Identity cards?'

The tall man addressed came to a halt, obviously surprised. The girl by his side gazed curiously at the armed policeman.

'I don't quite get you,' the man commenced slowly, then added with a little laugh, 'Oh, sure, sure.' He turned smilingly to the girl. 'The identity cards, Linda,' he remarked. 'This is the border.'

He spoke with a slight American accent, had the easy manner of one to whom policemen, bell-hops, taxi-drivers, were valuable servants, knowledgeable persons often worthy of a tip. While his companion opened her handbag he turned to the policeman again.

'Forgot all about it, officer,' he announced with a grin. 'First time in Ireland since I was a kid. There was no border, no north and south Ireland, when I was around.'

The official smiled in reply and glanced about the vicinity of the little border bridge. Big and healthy-looking, with a red, good-humoured face, he had the genially apologetic manner often encountered among Customs men or border police in almost any country.

The girl passed the two documents. Glancing perfunctorily at them, the policeman noted that Mark O'Donnell and Linda O'Donnell resided normally in the United States, temporarily in North Ireland. Then he handed back the cards and stepped half a pace out of the way with a remark about the weather. The two pedestrians crossed.

'Funny,' commented the girl, as they strolled along the narrow dusty lane. 'I knew that in Ireland you had this foreign frontier business when you went up and down in a train, or drove a car on one of the main roads. But walking along *this*—'

She glanced in pleasure from side to side of the little country road.

155

Tall green hedges of hawthorn and sloe closed in on either side, while here and there the golden surface of a newly cut corn field showed up against the dark green of the pasture. On the opposite bank of the little river they had just crossed, an exactly similar picture of rural peace presented itself. 'Funny,' she repeated, with a head-shake of humorous mystification.

'I'd forgotten all about it,' her husband told her. 'The cop doesn't seem to take it very seriously, though. Still,' he mused, slowly and in a thoughtful tone, 'I suppose it is funny. Sometimes, anyway.'

They strolled for nearly a mile, enjoying the freshness of the after-harvest scents and the peaceful murmur of the countryside. Neither spoke much, only from time to time one or the other drew a long breath of enjoyment, attracting the other's attention with a glance. Then again they were halted by a barrier and a uniformed man's request for their papers.

'What—*another* border!' laughed Mrs. O'Donnell, and the tall young policeman laughed briefly in reply, after he had glanced at the papers, noted the well-dressed, nonchalant ease of the couple, and the girl's American speech. He handed back the two cards.

'Sure that's nothing, madam,' he grinned. 'If you kept on along this road you'd come to three or four more. It goes up and down a bit.' The three laughed together.

'Well, it's an ill wind and so on,' said O'Donnell quizzically, after a glance at the rustic peace of the district around. 'Gives employment anyway, yeah?' They left the policeman chuckling and walked slowly up the road.

'Come on—explain,' ordered Linda. 'What's all the wiggling frontier for? Is this some more of your Irish squabbling? Or—'

'Not guilty,' Mark cut in promptly. 'One side's supposed to be Ireland and the other England. Don't ask me why! It's a hangover from the old days, that's all. See?' he inquired hopefully at the end, to grimace when his wife grinned at the lame explanation.

'No,' came back Linda at once. 'That doesn't tell why it goes up and down so that—here,' she interrupted herself suddenly to demand, 'which side are we *on*?'

They laughed together as Mark cast a single swift helpless glance around him for the answer. Linda was still chuckling as they strolled towards the next 'border'.

In a tiny town, half a mile farther on, they slowed their pace, now and then halting in frank pleased curiosity to stare at the ancient houses, the country people, the donkey carts. Two churches, nearly opposite one another, held their attention for a moment, and Mark nodded to draw the girl's attention.

'There's part of your explanation,' he told her. 'One's Catholic, one's Protestant—folks used to scrap about it a lot at one time round here, and that would be why— Here,' he broke off, as an itinerant piper commenced to play in the street. 'This is better, and more to the point.'

They loitered in the streets, by the tiny stone Town Hall which had a market place beneath it. More than once, in their slow progress, the quaint and ancient town sights fetched a gasp of admiration from the girl.

'Good, eh?' questioned Mark, with a satisfied smile. 'So they weren't all lies I'd been telling you about Ireland?' He drew a long breath, and looked around the tiny main street with a pleasure that was almost naïve.

'This is a whole lot better than anything I'd expected—even after your boasting,' Linda told him at once. 'It's just lovely that everything's like you said. Everything might have changed.' For several minutes they strolled in the centre of the little town, listening to the unaccustomed speech, enjoying the dual thrill of being at once in a strange land and at home.

A heavy shower of rain sent them to shelter. Outside a bar, a street singer bawled a ballad of which they could not understand one word, but which brought the singer heavy largess from the strangers nevertheless. Inside they waved negation to the bar-tender's gesture towards a more private—and deserted—inner room, stood in the front bar among the farmers and labourers and loafers, keenly enjoying every second.

'Pardon me, sir,' said a voice, after a few minutes. 'I hope you don't mind my asking—do you and the lady come from England?'

The man's utterance differed radically from the rough, homely, attractive speech of the labourers and farmers at the bar. He had the indeterminately-cultured accent of waiters, theatre attendants, booking clerks, of almost any land. Seedy battered clothes rated him lower than the farm people present. Bleary eyes, unshaven chin and a shaking hand gave some indication of the reasons for the rating. 'From England, sir?' he questioned again.

'Well, no,' O'Donnell told him. 'We're Irish really. Or kind of.' With a quiet smile he noted his wife's glance around the people in the pub. 'Just come home,' he added. As Linda finished her whiskey he nodded to the barman and waved a finger to the other man's empty glass. The bar-tender brought three whiskeys.

'Good health, sir. Good health, madam,' said the newcomer heartily. He hastened to sample his drink. 'But you *have* been in England,' he resumed, as he replaced the glass on the bar. The O'Donnells agreed.

'Ah,' said the companion promptly, somehow with the air of one who has said it all before. 'Me, too. I've toured in—'

He stopped, looking from one to the other of the couple before him. 'Just a minute,' he went on, rubbing his hands slowly together. 'Now, what would you take *me* for?' He addressed himself mainly

157

to Linda, but glanced at her husband to include him in the question. 'Well?'

A tiny, grimly-humorous smile flickered around Mark O'Donnell's mouth, seeming to indicate that a prompt answer was on the tip of his tongue, but he said nothing. Linda surveyed the seedy figure.

'Wait a second,' she enjoined, smiling. 'You're—'

She ran her eyes over the battered clothes, the shapeless boots, the tragic attempt at respectability evidenced by a partly-clean collar and a grimy handkerchief sticking up at a jaunty angle from a breast pocket. Then she looked with new interest at the man's face, at his deep eyes, powerful even behind the bleariness, at the long-fingered hands that trembled a little as he reached for his whiskey.

'Yes,' she decided with finality. 'You're a musician. Hold it,' she instructed, lifting a forefinger as the man seemed about to speak. 'Violinist—no. Wood-wind?' She darted another quick glance at him. 'No. You're a pianist,' she announced, and smiled at the stranger. 'Okay?'

A new dignity seemed to imbue the shabby figure at the bar. He straightened himself, and glanced slowly from side to side in the manner of one surveying a mighty audience.

'*Right*,' he announced with emphasis. 'Right. Near enough,' he appended, after a split-second of hesitation. He paused, and turned to sip his drink. 'I'm an organist,' he stated in quiet pride. 'My name's Matt O'Cassidy.' A wholly ludicrous complacency was in his tone, as if he were stating that his name was Kreisler.

Thereafter for several minutes he alternated between boasting reminiscence—mainly of small towns in England—and vaguely apologetic references to his shabbiness. In the end, pathetically important, he inquired if the visitors would like to hear a recital.

They started. An organ recital, when mentioned in connection with the frowsy, drink-sodden wreck before them, appeared incongruous as a jazz band at a funeral. The organist straightened himself by the bar, seemed not to notice that O'Donnell was again paying for the drinks.

'Fortunately in position,' he told them, 'to give performance. The vicar here,' he went on in a slightly pompous tone, 'permits me to—er—maintain my practice, on the church organ. I mean the Protestant vicar,' he clarified. 'I can take you over to the church. That is, of course,' he concluded, with a debonair, man-of-the-worldly wave of the hand, 'if you have no objection.'

'We're Catholics,' the other man put in. 'But, of course, we don't object. We'd love to go. Yes, Linda?' he questioned.

'Sure,' said the girl promptly. 'I think it'd be lovely, to have an organ recital laid on for us, so to speak, in this darling little town. Let's.'

158

'It's okay, I take it? About our coming along?' her husband insisted, to O'Cassidy. 'We wouldn't want to offend anyone—'

'All right. *'S'all right*,' the other told him reassuringly, 'The vicar's a gentleman. Tolerant. Wide sympathy. Helpful,' he clarified. Then he leant on the bar and brooded for a moment.

'I'm a Catholic myself,' he told them inconsequentially, 'but—' He paused. 'Vicar's a gen'l'man,' he announced again, slurring his words in a way that paid tribute to the whiskey. 'Sorry t'say Father Kieran doesn' co-operate. No. Doesn' copperate,' he reiterated with some warmth. 'Own parish priest—and wouldn't let a man have even half-hour's practice now-then. No. The vicar, though—tolerant. Gen'l'man.' He accepted another whiskey, and talked, surprisingly well, of music and musicians, for some minutes.

Then, apparently reminded of his grievance, he paused suddenly in his flow of professional talk and brooded by the bar, frowning. A dubious side glance at his hearers reassured him that they were genuinely sympathetic, friendly and interested. Some of his dignity returned.

'No p'fessional 'gagements jus' present,' he explained. 'One reason and another. Small jobs now-then. Odd jobs.' A slightly lachrymose tone came into his voice. He leant confidentially towards the two strangers. 'Not t'put too fine a point on it—jobbing gardener. Yes. Job-gar'ner—while waiting p'fessional 'gagements.' His speech was becoming very slurred, and his two hearers exchanged glances.

'Well, who does Father Kieran employ?' O'Cassidy demanded rhetorically. 'Who zemploy, t'do his garden? Me—Catholic manna talent waiting p'fessional 'gagements? No. Oh, no.' He paused and leant still closer. ' *'Ploys Micky Timmins*,' he announced in a tone of horror.

Apparently the O'Donnells were supposed to be completely staggered by this last statement. O'Cassidy waited, to watch the effect.

'Micky Timmins,' he repeated. 'And him a Protestant—a *Protestant*. Drunk, too—no good's gar'ner. 'Ploys *him*. And won't even let man of genius have half-hour organ—maintain practice,' he finished, in a ludicrously aggrieved tone. 'No.'

'But, say,' put in the man beside him. 'That's right, isn't it? After all, it's not exactly——'

'Of course not,' interrupted the girl. 'That's very strict, everywhere, yes? No purely secular purpose—I think that's the phrase; a church must not be used for any purely secular purpose. Well, taking us into the church to hear you play would be— I don't see what else Father Kieran could do, do you?'

She turned to smile at her husband, but O'Cassidy appeared unsatisfied. His head sank lower, and he mumbled to himself for a moment. Then he squared up and looked around.

'Maybe,' he agreed half-heartedly. 'Maybe. But—own par'sh

priest. Man-o-genius, good p'fessional gar'ner. But 'ploys Micky Timmins—Pro'ssant—no good's gar'ner. And *no* p'fessional practice for man-o-genius. Not right. Not *ri'*.' He glared for a second. 'Vicar, though,' he added, cheering up, 'Gen'l'man.'

Mention of the vicar seemed to remind him. 'Let's go—church,' he suggested formally, with a dignified wave of his hand. 'P'mitted. P'fessional practice.' Squaring his shoulders, almost achieving a stride, he led the way.

The church was deserted, the organ was a good one, and after a few minutes of fuddled fumbling, O'Cassidy asserted his mastery of the instrument. Mastery it was, beyond any doubt, and two fairly-difficult classical compositions, played flawlessly without music, bore evidence that the man had not been emptily boasting. Whatever the rights of his employment feud with Micky Timmins, O'Cassidy was most certainly an organist.

Thereafter, for a few minutes, he played simple tunes, then Mendelssohn's *Spring Song*, an individual and delightful rendering. Incongruously there followed a string of cheap trashy melodies from second-rate films.

'I thought so,' Linda whispered to her husband. 'He is—or was— a cinema organist.'

Almost immediately her deduction was justified. O'Cassidy played a long chain of English sentimental songs, movie-house fashion. Now and then he rendered some threadbare classical piece, but displayed a tendency, on the slightest provocation, to drop into hackneyed film tunes like *Yours, South of the Border*, or *My Own*.

'No, no, *no*,' Linda interposed, after the third or fourth attempt. 'We know all that stuff—we work in Hollywood. Play *O'Donnell Aboo*.'

Shaken, the organist breathed whiskey fumes on the stops, fumbled a little in obvious unfamiliarity. Then, swaying slightly, he squared his shoulders and sat more erect.

An impromptu introduction flowed and echoed around the church, a mounting torrent of sound culminated in a harshly-proud screaming like the battle-call of a myriad trumpets, then into the building poured the opening bars of the Irish war song: 'Proudly the note of the trumpet is sounding.'

'This man,' whispered the girl, 'is a lot better than he knows. If only he'd stop trying to be clever!' Mark O'Donnell nodded agreement.

O'Cassidy played the song through, improvised for a moment, then turned, with the strained smile of the cinema organist, towards his audience of two.

'Enny ree-quests, please?' he inquired, with a near-simper totally incongruous on his unshaven face, and when seen above his battered clothes. 'Enny ree-quests, please?'

160

'Play *The Bold Fenian Men*,' called Linda immediately. In the almost empty church her American voice, demanding the Irish rebel song, was as strange in its own way as the player's artificiality.

O'Cassidy played. For half an hour they kept him busy, cutting in without mercy whenever he tried to play the second-rate movie tunes which apparently he regarded almost with veneration. At the end he rose and walked uncertainly towards them.

'I can do better than that—' he commenced.

'It was splendid,' Mrs. O'Donnell interrupted. 'Lovely. We're very grateful indeed. And we're honoured.' Her husband smiled and added a few words of praise. The organist glowed, and stretched himself anew as they moved to the door.

Outside the church, a tall grey-haired man in clerical garb came towards them along a path. O'Cassidy halted.

'Reverend Arthur Comyns,' he introduced the newcomer. 'The vicar here. Two—er—acquaintances of mine from America.' He displayed a slight tendency to shuffle his feet on the path. 'Been having a little practice, Mr. Comyns,' he explained, then turned to O'Donnell. 'The vicar,' he announced, as if mentioning the matter for the first time, 'kindly allows me to have little professional practice.'

O'Donnell and Mr. Comyns eyed one another, in perfect gravity but each with the same tiny mouth-corner twitching. It seemed fairly certain that the vicar had heard some at least of the recital.

The organist was obviously anxious to cut the interview short. The grey-haired clergyman, on the other hand, seemed equally keen to continue the talk with the strangers.

O'Donnell compromised. While Linda chatted with Mr. Comyns he drew slightly aside with O'Cassidy, to speak a few words of genuine praise and encouragement.

'Just try to remember that you're pretty good,' he enjoined. 'You're better than that phoney stuff you like. Try to remember it. And maybe you could keep out of the saloons a little. See?' Unostentatiously he conveyed a pound note to O'Cassidy's loose hand.

Matt's farewells were not protracted. With squared shoulders and springy stride, clutching in one hand the practical proof of the visitors' approval, he stepped out from the church gate—and crossed the road to the bar. The vicar looked after him dubiously.

'Something of an expert in his own way,' Mark O'Donnell commented. Mr. Comyns nodded abstractedly.

'When he doesn't try to be clever and modern-sophisticated,' Linda corrected. 'In improvisation he's—'

'He's nothing more nor less than a drunken, sponging waster,' broke in the vicar, almost in spite of himself it seemed. 'Father Kieran wouldn't allow him within a mile of his organ—and how right he is!'

The visitors looked at him in surprise. The eyes of the two men met, and they smiled together.

'Uh-huh,' grinned O'Donnell in agreement. 'Then why do—?'

'One must be tolerant,' said the vicar at last. 'Yes—tolerant.' He waited a second, but there was silence from the couple at his side. 'You don't know anything about this border?' he questioned suddenly.

'No—except that there seems to be an awful lot of it for such a small country,' laughed Linda, waiting eagerly for the vicar to continue.

'And that the man who drew the lines on the map seems to have been crazy,' put in her husband. 'Why, it wriggles like a snake with the colic.'

The vicar almost snorted. 'Not so crazy as it seems,' he stated, pursing his lips in irritation. 'Not by any means. Have you people never heard of gerrymandering?'

'Sure,' said O'Donnell promptly. 'Plenty of *that* in the States, way back. It means pulling a fast one in politics, doesn't it? For election time?'

'In theory,' said the vicar, his manner heavily didactic and impersonal, 'in theory it means wangling the electorate for your own ends. In practice, it means—places like *this*.' He waved a hand towards the little town. 'And it means tolerance.' He pronounced the last word as if it were synonymous with mayhem.

The strangers exchanged glances of mystification. O'Donnell turned to the clergyman with a puzzled headshake.

'Surely that's wrong, padre,' he said slowly. 'I should have thought all that fiddling and wangling around with a border meant the very opposite of tolerance. Doesn't it?'

The vicar did not answer at once. Indeed, he seemed to have forgotten the visitors. For a second he leant against a railing, a far-away look in his eyes, as if he were glimpsing some delectable scene of the past, or visioning some great future good fortune. He recalled himself with a jerk.

'Father Kieran and I are both old enough to remember it the other way,' he said inconsequentially. 'Hammer and tongs we used to fight—in the old days,' he added, still half-abstracted. Then he smiled boyishly at the pair before him. 'It looks as if it's coming to its end now,' he announced, eagerness in his voice. 'Yes. Its end.'

'That's right over my head, padre,' O'Donnell told him. 'Don't you *want* to be tolerant? I don't see what—'

'This place was gerrymandered,' snapped the vicar impatiently. 'The border wriggles about like a—whatever you said. That gives us, the Protestants, a majority here. And *that*—' he almost hissed the word—'means tolerance. Now do you see?'

Mark O'Donnell gaped in blank incomprehension, but Linda

turned smilingly to the vicar and nodded enthusiastic agreement.

'Of course,' she asserted. 'And how dreadful! Of course it's—how would you say, padre—if you've won at cards you can't very well boast about your own good play. You have to be polite about the other fellow's. Is that it?'

A guffaw, quickly checked, came from her side. 'Sure,' laughed O'Donnell. 'Sure. When you win with a very favourable handicap you have to be *specially* nice to the loser. Uh-huh?' He grinned broadly, straightened his face as the clergyman jerked around.

'Now you know,' said the vicar, still breathing hard. 'It's been torment, for years now, all smarming, and mock politeness, and—' He looked up angrily as the two visitors burst out laughing, then laughed heartily himself.

'Well, it has,' he persisted, and added, explosively, the single word, 'smarming!'

The three turned, to stroll together down the path towards the gate. The O'Donnells exchanged cheerful grins, turned and met an answering grin from the grey-haired man with the boyish face. They walked on slowly.

'—glad when it's all over and done with,' the vicar was saying as they neared the gate. 'When Father Kieran and I can argue hammer and tongs every time we meet.' He rubbed his hands. 'When Micky Timmins won't be allowed within a mile of the priest's garden—and when I can keep that drunken sponging waster O'Cassidy away from my church and my organ.'

# Pigeons

## MICHAEL McLAVERTY

OUR JOHNNY kept pigeons, three white ones and a brown one that could tumble in the air like a leaf. They were nice pigeons, but they dirtied the slates and cooed so early in the morning that my Daddy said that some day he would wring their bloody necks. That is a long while ago now, for we still have the pigeons, but Johnny is dead; he died for Ireland.

Whenever I think of our Johnny I always think of Saturday. Nearly every Saturday night he had something for me, maybe sweets, a toy train, a whistle, or glass marbles with rainbows inside them. I would be in bed when he'd come home; I always tried to keep awake, but my eyes wouldn't let me—they always closed tight when I wasn't thinking. We both slept together in the wee back room, and when Johnny came up to bed he always lit the gas, the gas that had no mantle. If he had something for me he would shake me and say: 'Frankie, Frankie, are you asleep?' My eyes would be very gluey and I would rub them with my fists until they would open in the gas-light. For a long while I would see gold needles sticking out of the flame, then they would melt away and the gas become like a pansy leaf with a blue heart. Johnny would be standing beside the bed and I would smile all blinky at him. Maybe he'd stick a sweet in my mouth, but if I hadn't said my prayers he'd lift me out on to the cold, cold floor. When I would be jumping in again in my shirt tails, he would play whack at me and laugh if he got me. Soon he would climb into bed and tell me about the ice-cream shops, and the bird-shop that had funny pigeons and rabbits and mice in the window. Some day he was going to bring me down the town and buy me a black and white mouse, and a custard bun full of ice-cream. But he'll never do it now because he died for Ireland.

On Saturdays, too, I watched for him at the back door when he was coming from work. He always came over the waste ground, because it was the shortest. His dungarees would be all shiny, but they hadn't a nice smell. I would pull them off him, and he would lift me on to his shoulder, and swing me round and round until my head

165

got light and the things in the kitchen went up and down. My Mammie said he had me spoilt. He always gave me pennies on Saturday, two pennies, and I bought a liquorice pipe with one penny and kept the other for Sunday. Then he would go into the cold scullery to wash his black hands and face; he would stand at the sink, scrubbing and scrubbing and singing *The Old Rusty Bridge by the Mill*, but if you went near him he'd squirt soap in your eye. After he had washed himself, we would get our Saturday dinner, the dinner with the sausages because it was pay day. Johnny used to give me a bit of his sausages, but if my Mammie saw me she'd slap me for taking the bite out of his mouth. It was a long, long wait before we went out to the yard to the pigeons.

The pigeon-shed was on the slates above the closet. There was a ladder up to it, but Johnny wouldn't let me climb for fear I'd break my neck. But I used to climb up when he wasn't looking. There was a great flutter and flapping of wings when Johnny would open the trap-door to let them out. They would fly out in a line, brownie first and the white ones last. We would lie on the waste ground at the back of our street watching them fly. They would fly round and round, rising higher and higher each time. Then they would fly so high we would blink our eyes and lose them in the blue sky. But Johnny always found them first. 'I can see them, Frankie,' he would say. 'Yonder they are. Look! Above the brickyard chimney.' He would put his arm around my neck, pointing with his outstretched hand. I would strain my eyes, and at last I would see them, their wings flashing in the sun as they turned towards home. They were great fliers. But brownie would get tired and he would tumble head over heels like you'd think he was going to fall. The white ones always flew down to him, and Johnny would go wild. 'He's a good tumbler, but he won't let the others fly high. I think I'll sell him.' He would look at me, plucking at the grass, afraid to look up. 'Ah, Frankie,' he would say, 'I won't sell him. Sure I'm only codding.' All day we would sit, if the weather was good, watching our pigeons flying, and brownie doing somersaults. When they were tired they would light on the blue slates, and Johnny would throw corn up to them. Saturday was a great day for us and for our pigeons, but it was on Saturday that Johnny died for Ireland.

We were lying, as usual, at the back, while the pigeons were let out for a fly round. It was a lovely sunny day. Every house had clothes out on the lines, and the clothes were fluttering in the breeze. Some of the neighbours were sitting at their backdoors, nursing babies or darning socks. They weren't nice neighbours for they told the rent man about the shed on the slates, and he made us pay a penny a week for it. But we didn't talk much to them, for we loved our pigeons, and on that lovely day we were splitting our sides laughing at the way brownie was tumbling, when a strange man in a black hat

166

and burberry coat came near us. Johnny jumped up and went to meet him. I saw them talking, with their heads bent towards the ground, and then the strange man went away. Johnny looked very sad and he didn't laugh at brownie any more. He gave me the things out of his pockets, a penknife, a key, and a little blue notebook with its edges all curled. 'Don't say anything to Mammie. Look after the pigeons, Frankie, until I come back. I won't be long.' He gave my hand a tight squeeze, then he walked away without turning round to wave at me.

All that day I lay out watching the pigeons, and when I got tired I opened the notebook. It had a smell of fags and there was fag-dust inside it. I could read what he had written down:

| | |
|---|---|
| Corn | 2s. 6d. |
| Club | 6d. |
| 3 Pkts. Woodbine | 6d. |
| Frankie | 2d. |

He had the same thing written down on a whole lot of pages; if he had been at school he would have got slapped for wasting the good paper. I put the notebook in my pocket when my Mammie called me for my tea. She asked me about Johnny and I told her he wouldn't be long until he was back. Then it got late. The pigeons flew off the slates and into the shed, and still Johnny didn't come back.

It came on night. My sisters were sent out to look for him. My Daddy came home from work. We were all in now, my two sisters and Mammie and Daddy, everyone except Johnny. Daddy took out his pipe with the tin lid, but he didn't light it. We were all quiet, but my mother's hands would move from her lap to her chin, and she was sighing. The kettle began humming and shuffling the lid about, and my Daddy lifted it off the fire and placed it on the warm hob. The clock on the mantelpiece chimed eleven and my sisters blessed themselves—it got a soul out of Purgatory when you did that. They forgot all about my bedtime and I was let stay up though my eyes felt full of sand. The rain was falling. We could hear it slapping in the yard and trindling down the grate. It was a blowy night for someone's back door was banging, making the dogs bark. The newspapers that lay on the scullery floor to keep it clean began to crackle up and down with the wind till you'd have thought there was a mouse under them. A bicycle bell rang in the street outside our kitchen window and it made Mammie jump. Then a motor rattled down, shaking the house and the vases on the shelf. My Daddy opened the scullery door and went into the yard. The gas blinked and a coughing smell of a chimney burning came into the kitchen. I'm sure it was Mrs. Ryan's. She always burned hers on a wet night. If the peelers caught her she'd be locked in jail, for you weren't allowed to burn your own chimney.

I wish Daddy would burn ours. It was nice to see him putting the bunch of lighted papers on the yardbrush and sticking them up the wide chimney. The chimney would roar, and if you went outside you'd see lines of sparks like hot wires coming out and the smoke bubbling over like lemonade in a bottle. But he wouldn't burn it tonight, because we were waiting on Johnny.

'Is there any sign of him?' said Mammie, when Daddy came in again.

'None yet; but he'll be all right; he'll be all right. We'll say the prayers, and he'll be in before we're finished.'

We were just ready to kneel when a knock came to the back door. It was a very dim knock and we all sat still, listening. 'That's him, now,' said Daddy, and I saw my mother's face brightening. Daddy went into the yard and I heard the stiff iron bar on the door opening and feet shuffling. 'Easy now: Easy now,' said someone. Then Daddy came in, his face as white as a sheet. He said something to Mammie. 'Mother of God it isn't true—it isn't!' she said. Daddy turned and sent me up to bed.

Up in the wee room I could see down into the yard. The light from the kitchen shone into it and I saw men with black hats and the rain falling on them like little needles, but I couldn't see our Johnny. I looked up at the shed on the slates, the rain was melting down its sides, and the wet felt was shining like new boots. When I looked into the yard again, Daddy was bending over something. I got frightened and went into my sisters' room. They were crying and I cried, too, while I sat shivering in my shirt and my teeth chattering. 'What's wrong?' I asked. But they only cried and said: 'Nothing, son. Nothing. Go to sleep, Frankie, like a good little boy.' My big sister put me into her bed, and put the clothes around me and stroked my head. Then she lay on the top of the bed beside me, and I could feel her breathing heavily on my back. Outside it was still blowy for the wind was kicking an empty salmon-tin which rattled along the street. For a long time I listened to the noises the wind made, and then I slept.

In the morning when I opened my eyes I wondered at finding myself in my sisters' room. It was very still: the blinds were down and the room was full of yellow light. I listened for the sound of plates, a brush scrubbing, or my big sister singing. But I heard nothing, neither inside the house nor outside it. I remembered about last night, my sisters crying because our Johnny didn't come home. I sat up in bed; I felt afraid because the house was strange, and I got out and went into the wee back room.

The door was open and there was yellow light in it, too, and the back of the bed had white cloth and I couldn't see over it. Then I saw my Mammie in the room sitting on a chair. She stretched out her arms and I ran across and knelt beside her, burying my face in her lap. She had on a smooth, black dress, and I could smell the camphor bags off it, the smell that kills the moths, the funny things with no blood and no bones that eet holes in your jersey. There were no holes in Mammie's dress. She rubbed my head with her hands and said: 'You're the only boy I have now.' I could hear her heart thumping very hard, and then she cried, and I cried and cried, with my head down on her lap. 'What's wrong, Mammie?' I asked, looking up at her wet eyes. 'Nothing, darling: nothing, pet. He died for Ireland.' I turned my head and looked at the bed. Johnny was lying on the white bed in a brown dress. His hands were pale and they were joined around his rosary beads, and a big crucifix between them. There was a big lump of wadding at the side of his head and wee pieces up his nose. I cried more and more, and then my Mammie made me put on my clothes, and go downstairs for my breakfast.

All that day my Mammie stayed in the room to talk to the people that came to see our Johnny. And all the women shook hands with Mammie and they all said the same thing: 'I'm sorry for your trouble, but he died for his country.' They knelt beside the white bed and prayed, and then sat for awhile looking at Johnny, and speaking in low whispers. My sisters brought them wine and biscuits and some of them cried when they were taking it, dabbing their eyes with their handkerchiefs or the tails of their shawls. Mrs. McCann came and she got wine, too, though she had told the rent man about the shed on the slates and we had to pay a penny a week. I was in the wee room when she came, and I saw her looking at the lighted candles and the flowers on the table, and up at the gas that had no mantle. But she couldn't see it because my big sister had put white paper over it, and she had done the same with the four brass knobs on the bed. She began to sniff and sniff and my Mammie opened the window without saying anything. The blind began to snuffle in and out, the lighted candles to waggle, and the flowers to smell. We could hear the pigeons cooing and flapping in the shed, and I could see at the back of my eyes, their necks fattening and their feathers bristling like a dog going to fight. It's well Daddy didn't hear them or he might have wrung their necks.

At night the kitchen was crammed with men and women, and many had to sit in the cold scullery. Mrs. Ryan, next door, lent us her chairs for the people to sit on. There was lemonade and biscuits and tea and porter. Some of the men, who drank black porter, gave me pennies, and they smoked and talked all night. The kitchen was full of smoke and it made your eyes sting. One man told my Daddy, he should be a proud man, because Johnny had died for the Republic. My Daddy blinked his eyes when he heard this, and he got up and went into the yard for a long time.

\*　　\*　　\*

The next day was the funeral. Black shiny horses with their mouths all suds, and silver buckles on their straps, came trotting into the street. All the wee lads were looking at themselves in the glossy backs of the cabs where you could see yourself all fat and funny like a dwarf. I didn't play because Johnny was dead and I had on a new, dark suit. Jack Byrne was out playing and he told me that we had only two cabs and that there were three cabs at his Daddy's funeral. There were crowds of peelers in the street, some of them talking to tall red-faced men with overcoats and walking sticks.

Three men along with my Daddy carried the yellow coffin down the stairs. There was a green, white and gold flag over it. But a thin policeman, with a black walking stick and black leggings, pulled the flag off the coffin when it went into the street. Then a girl snatched the flag out of the peeler's hands and he turned all pale. At the end of our street there were more peelers and every one wore a harp with a crown on his cap. Brother Gabriel used to fairly wallop us in school if we drew harps with crowns on them. One day we told him the peelers wore them on their caps. 'Huh!' he said. 'The police! The police! They don't love their country. They serve England. The England that chased our people to live in the damp bogs! The England that starved our ancestors till they had to eat grass and nettles by the roadside. And our poor priests had to say Mass out on the cold mountains! No, my dear boys, never draw a harp with a crown on it!' And then he got us to write in our books:

*Next to God I love thee*
*Dear Ireland, my native land!*

'It's a glorious thing,' he said, 'to die for Ireland, to die for Ireland!' His voice got very shaky when he said this and he turned his back and looked into the press. But Brother Gabriel is not in the school now; if he was he'd be good to me, because our Johnny died for Ireland.

The road to the cemetery was lined with people. Little boys that were at my school lifted a fringe of hair when the coffin passed. The trams were stopped in a big, long line—it was nice to see so many at one look. Outside the gates of the graveyard there was an armoured car with no one peeping his head out. Inside it was very still and warm with the sun shining. With my Daddy I walked behind the carried coffin and it smelt like the new seats in the chapel. The crowds of people were quiet. You could hear the cinders on the path squanching as we walked over them, and now and again the horses snorting.

I began to cry when I saw the deep hole in the ground and the big castles of red clay at the side of it. A priest, with a purple sash round his neck, shovelled a taste of clay on the coffin and it made a hard rattle that made me cry sore. Daddy had his head bowed and there were tears in his eyes, but they didn't run down his cheeks like mine did. The priest began to pray, and I knew I'd never see Johnny again, never, never, until I'd die and go to Heaven if I kept good and didn't say bad words and obeyed my Mammie and my Daddy. But I wouldn't like Daddy to tell me to give away the pigeons. When the prayers were over a tall man with no hat and a wee moustache stood beside the grave and began to talk. He talked about our Johnny being a soldier of the Republic, and, now and then, he pointed with his finger at the grave. As soon as he stopped talking we said the Rosary, and all the people went away. I got a ride back in a black cab with my Daddy and Uncle Pat and Uncle Joe. We stopped at The Bee Hive and they bought lemonade for me and porter for the cab driver. And then we went home.

*　　*　　*

I still have the pigeons and big Tom Duffy helps me to clean the shed and let them out to fly. Near night I give them plenty of corn so that they'll sleep long and not waken Daddy in the morning. When I see them fattening their necks and cooing I clod them off the slates.

Yesterday I was lying on the waste ground watching the pigeons and Daddy came walking towards me smoking his pipe with the tin lid. I tried to show him the pigeons flying through the clouds. He only looked at them for a minute and turned away without speaking, and now I'm hoping he won't wring their necks.

# The Kings Asleep in the Ground

## BRYAN MacMAHON

ONE DAY during a break in the half-hour allowed us for exercise round the top tier of A wing, Packy McSwiney of Bloody Foreland called for attention. Standing in front of the bearded naked men, he began to read in Gaelic from a scrap of blue notepaper.

I was squatting by the wall. The weak sunlight filtering through the long window in the roof was touching my tilted face. I did not bother to look up at Packy for I was tired, sick and cold.

For fifty-one days now we sentenced men had been on nudist strike for political treatment: it looked as if the strike would go on for ever.

I was tired, sick and cold. Tired of the prison sweats in the yard below who, in the subtlest ways, lost no opportunity of ragging us political prisoners. Sick to death of the clotted swab on my throat where Callaghan of Portumna had lanced a gland with a penknife. Sick to the heart of never being able to see a young woman sway away from me; sick to the soul of the thoughts poor food kept distilling in my head. Cold. Cold even in that mild April weather with the mark a Northern winter had set in my Southern blood.

Tired, sick and cold.

Packy, tall and gaunt, his eyes carrying the stare of the fanatic. A tuft of grey hair leaping north-west from the bare horseshoe of his upper brow to match the tuft between his goose-fleshed breasts.

'*A Cháirde*,' he began.

'Krrck!' someone said.

One or two of the men glared hard at McCarthy.

'*A Cháirde*,' Packy resumed, with a hint of menace in his voice, '*Dia Luain seo chughainn beidh. . . .*'

He went on to say that on the following Monday we Republican prisoners would have a debate in Gaelic on the clan system in ancient Ireland.

The hairy men nodded an indifferent assent. O'Brien, the warder, smiled and strolled away.

Finished reading, Packy crouched before me. 'You all right, Patcheen, boy?' he whispered.

Staring into the cleft where his navel had its hide, I nodded.

'Ye had a great clan, son. The O'Connors of Kerry fought against the Danes at Clontarf in the year 1014.'

Again I nodded. Within myself, I wailed: 'Oh, my God!' Then swiftly in my head, like the series of pictures that comes racing out of one of those little books a boy thumbs at the corners, I went over it all again. . . .

The 'bus; my toecapping the parcel of printed 'memos' past an empty seat until I drove it among the old woman's parcels. Then seven, eight, nine miles of easy riding. The stab of concern as a secondary schoolboy boarded the 'bus a mile or two this side of the border and sat on the empty seat in front of me. My qualm vanishing as I recalled that, lacking a fuse, gelignite is only so much brown sugar. My qualm of concern replaced by one of bitterness as I realized that, at most, I was only a year or two older than the lad in the monogrammed blazer.

Above the memory, Packy's voice droned on: 'Ye built Kyrie Eleison Abbey in O'Dorney, and Lislaughtin Abbey on the Shannon. Never forget that, Patcheen!'

The routine check at the border—the border Kerry-boy-me was going to smash so that Ireland would be united. The old woman grumbling as her parcels were turned over. I continued my staring at the loyalist weekly. Gradually the strain eased.

Then at the last minute with the 'bus on the move a big man had come leaping on to the footboard. Moving in, he took up a position facing the passengers. He was so tall that he had to stoop somewhat. His eyes fast on the old woman, he drew the glass slide and gave the driver an order. After a hundred yards or so the 'bus pulled off its direct route.

'Only for the foreigner setting father against son,' Packy was saying. 'ye'd be the last to yield to the dark invader.'

Halted outside the barracks, the 'bus was surrounded by uniformed men. A District Inspector jumped on board. He was followed by two constables.

'These yours?' the D.I. said to the old woman. He touched the parcels with his cane.

'Aye!'

'Come along!'

The old woman was hustled into the dayroom.

The tall man began to check our identity cards. Not a good mimic, I had been given a Southern name and a Dublin address. Emerging through the open upper quarter of the dayroom window, I could hear the old woman's voice. It had a note of hysteria in it. Yes, she was a

Nationalist—she believed that the partition of her country should be ended.

I stood up.

'Where are *you* going?' the big man asked.

'Into the dayroom!'

Inside, the police looked up as I said abruptly: 'I take responsibility!'

'*Claret was cheaper than paraffin oil, in the time of O'Connor of Carrigafoyle,*' Packy was proudly rhyming.

Five long, bitter years. In at nineteen, I'd be out at twenty-four. Five years of gold! What madness was in me then? What spell or rule was I under? Would I sell those years for a million quid? Not on your bloody life! And yet I had traded them for a single court-room statement. Compared with me, Don Quixote was a tower of wisdom. For had I not said: 'As a member of the Irish Republican Army, I deny the right of this tribunal. . . .'

Et cetera.

Packy put his mouth close to my ear. 'Drift with it, son!' he said. 'If you fight against it, you're done!'

Again I nodded. The navel opened as Packy rose and went away. Remembering that he had spent fifteen years behind walls I watched him go. He borrowed a pin from O'Brien, the warder, and pinned the notice to the whitewashed wall. The men kept shuffling along. No one bothered to stand and read the blue paper.

The bell rang.

Then it was beard after beard, red buttocks, varicose veins (like ivy coils), the remnant of one potbelly (now an old ballroom balloon) hammer-toe, lank shank and stallion flank, blue-glazed operation seam, brown mole, shaved poll, tender sole, ancient ulcer, not omitting one eye-shade. The last not an article of attire within the meaning of the act. Packy had given a ruling on that point.

* * *

The Governor had a spiky moustache which gleamed grey in his thin but choleric face. He wore a suit of dark material with a nondescript tie and white shirt. He was a decent-enough old skin within his limits.

For a while he puzzled over the blue notice. He turned it over and glanced at the back of it. He looked up at O'Brien, whose fleshy face was sweating.

'What does this say?'

'They're going to have a debate in Gaelic, sir.'

'On what subject?'

'On the clan system in ancient Ireland.'

'Will it be all right?'

'I couldn't say, sir.'

175

A pause. 'Limerick, eh, O'Brien?'

'Limerick, sir!'

'You're fairly fluent at this . . . Erse?'

'Middlin', sir.'

'You should be able to follow what they're saying?'

'If they kept to the Southern dialect, I'd make a fair fist of it. But the minute I start to take notes, they'll skeet to the Northern lingo. That's like chewin' rubber, sir!'

The Government pondered for a moment. 'Do your best, O'Brien. Make a report.'

'Very well, sir.'

That night the pipe in my cell was speaking like hell as Packy kept calling me up. I didn't answer. I pretended to be asleep.

\* \* \*

On the day of the debate instead of walking round the top tier we padded into the recreation hall. On the rostrum was a table on which stood a red plastic beaker. There were two chairs—one for Packy; he was formally proposed and seconded as chairman—the other for O'Brien, the warder. O'Brien sat a little to the rear of Packy's chair and had his arms folded across his chest. The other warders at the back of the hall were mostly Northerners. They were inclined to smile at O'Brien.

When we had taken our seats, Packy stood up fiercely stern, and hawked in his throat. All of a sudden he rounded on O'Brien: '*Bain díot do chaipín!*' he roared.

O'Brien jumped, then uncrossed his arms. The men laughed—the warder's right hand had been holding a pencil and his left hand a reporter's notebook. O'Brien took off his cap and placed it on the floor beside him. '*Tóg bog é!*' he advised Packy good-humouredly.

O'Brien's 'Take it easy!' made my mind revolt. How could a man take it easy when now on the river at home the kids would be baiting lines and drawing in pink trout? When now the hazels would begin to show form, now the primroses, now the stitchwort, now all the things that I so desperately loved.

The meeting came to order. McCarthy from Cork—he had a rich brown beard with a mad stab of red in it—was on his feet at once. Packy pounded him down. McCarthy crumpled up a grubby scrap of paper and sat down growling.

A thin man called O'Driscoll rose and began to enumerate the castles and conquests of his clan. He quoted at length from a poem in English on a raid of Algerian pirates on Baltimore, a town on the Southern coast.

Packy nodded his grudged approval of the use of English for the purpose of quotation.

Maguire of Fermanagh—he had a graveyard cough that pocked

176

mid-tier all night long—mentioned the quartering of guests and gallowglasses, the payment of horse-boys and dog-boys, and the spreading of green rushes on the dining-room floor of the Maguire castles.

The Professor quoted Latin. Packy didn't quite approve of his stressing the theme of disunity among the clans. '*Omnes erant Cesares*,' the Professor said sorrowfully. '*Nemo censum dabat.*' He then went on to mention Louis the Fat wrestling with feudal disorder.

O'Sullivan of Bere said that when Don Juan Del Aquila had basely made peace with the English at Kinsale, and so had stained the sword of His Catholic Majesty of Spain, the O'Sullivans had banged the Catholic garrisons out of Berehaven, seized the munitions and despatched the eldest son of the clan as a hostage to the King of Spain to indicate their lealty. This action had caused the Spanish King to conceive an abiding affection for the O'Sullivan clan.

But: 'Oh, my God!' I kept muttering. The bluebells and the stitchwort and the clumps of primroses at the end of the inchland where now for a certainty the sun was beating down with early-year ferocity. Oh, my God! the sandhills with the sea open and open and open.

Packy put in his spoke. He said that although his clan were feudatories of the O'Donnells, they claimed descent from Swaine, King of Norway, the ravager of the raven banner. The McSwineys were hereditary pipers, he said; the men had noses like eagles' beaks and the girls were handsome with fine foreheads and teeth.

McNamara of Tulla made reference to his predecessor, Fireball, who had fought fifty-seven duels and had not been scathed by a single ball.

O'Rourke of Mayo mentioned mortar made of bullocks' blood and powdered oystershells. He spoke of spiral staircases with the twist sinistral, thus designed to give swordsmen the advantage of the right-handed blow.

Again McCarthy tried to make a statement but Packy seemed resolved to keep him out. '*Suigh síos!*' he roared as McCarthy rose to his feet.

Fitzgerald, O'Reilly, O'Malley, O'Neill, all spoke. An intense man named Loftus raised a wan cheer by saying that although he was a descendant of Cromwellian adventurers, his mother was an O'Byrne of Wicklow.

The debate had now got into a certain rhythm. Long since O'Brien the warder had ceased to take notes. Now he seemed fully bored.

But, Oh my God! already Ballynanty Wood would be coming alive and the rabbits begin to go hoppity-hop. The valerian, too, would be in bloom on the Abbey walls. What was I doing here, naked in a foot-smelling shed, listening to gibberish about dead chieftains? Was it for this I had traded clean linen, cocoa with a head on it, kids playing at hopscotch, salmon in the final of playing, and, above all, the long laze of blue waves. Oh, my God! I muttered over and over again.

I woke out of a haze to find Packy McSwiney looking straight down at me. The rest had fallen silent. 'There's a lad here without a word out of him,' Packy said quietly, 'and the last High King of All Ireland was Roderick of his name! Well, Patcheen? What have you to say?'

As I shook my head violently, my eyes misted and my senses spun. Again I shook my head to clear my brain of darkness.

McCarthy must have been waiting for just such a distraction. So firmly did he rise that no one could gainsay him. He glanced at the piece of paper in his hand, then glared at the warder on the platform. O'Brien lost his flabby look at once.

'When we McCarthys,' the speaker began, '—we who fashioned the beauty that is Cormac's Chapel on the Rock of Cashel, under our chieftains Dermot O'Donnell Mór and Finghin—were pouring out our blood in an effort to dislodge the Normans from Munster, we were basely attacked by the calf-choking O'Briens. This was in 1169.'

O'Brien stiffened. 'What are you saying out of that ugly mouth?' he blurted in English.

There was a chorus of cries. Some of the men stood up and shook their fists at O'Brien.

'*Ná bac an Béarla!*'

'*Labhair Gaeilge!*'

'*Cuirtear amach é!*'

With the men's rising, the smell of foot-sweat grew stronger.

O'Brien was on his feet, too. 'I want to say . . .' he roared. But again the crowd of prisoners shouted him down.

Two of the warders moved forward into the hall. O'Brien snarled them away. They lounged against the wall.

'*Tá go maith!*' O'Brien said easily, then went on in Gaelic: 'I want to say that on no lesser an authority than that of Giraldus Cambrensis, Dermot McCarthy was the first Irish king to swear loyalty to King Henry II of England. This was in Waterford in 1161.'

'You sheevra!' McCarthy roared. 'When the Normans broke into our beloved Desmond, we Cartys beat them at Gallen Glen, and thereafter we played the devil in Desmond. We had three great castles—Ballycarbery, Castlelough and the Palace. What had the lickspittle O'Briens in their hungry Thomond?'

An old man with a grey beard came to his feet. 'My mother was an O'Brien of Thomond,' he said in a deep voice. 'She told me for a fact that the McCarthys were violators of churches, murderers of kinsmen and ravishers of consecrated virgins.'

This statement brought cheers and boos.

'There's your answer!' Warder O'Brien roared.

178

McCarthy pushed idle chairs aside. 'I'll take on a traitorous O'Brien any day of the week!'

The warder dragged at his tunic. A button flew and hit the wall. Packy thumped the table for order.

'If you're going to fight him, O'Brien,' he said, 'you'll have to strip! It'll be fair pegging while I'm chairman.'

O'Brien tore off his shoes, then dragged at his trousers-belt. One of the other warders hurried up.

'Don't be a fule, O'Brien!' he said.

'None of your affair!' O'Brien was stepping out of his pants and underpants.

'You'll get the knock for this!'

'Mind the damned door!' O'Brien tugged his shirt over his head.

Stripped, O'Brien was seen to be a powerful man, but a soft one. As he padded down the steps at the side of the platform his white body quivered. McCarthy with his mad beard and dark skin had already taken up a fighting attitude in the space between the front row of chairs and the stage. The other prisoners had resolved into two groups of partisans—one for Desmond, the other for Thomond. Dull and listless I sat aside.

O'Brien shuffled in what was the memory of a boxing adolescence. McCarthy came to meet him. For a moment or two there was soft tipping. Then the men came crashing together. McCarthy drove in with a rigid fist that raised a weal on O'Brien's stomach. But as he emerged from the close-in, O'Brien fisted him heavily into the mouth and drew blood. 'How'd you like that?' O'Brien said from between clenched teeth as he shuffled away. The blood came spilling over McCarthy's split lip.

Again the contestants drew closer to one another. The bystanders urged them to go in and kill. 'Desmond!' one crowd shouted, 'Thomond!' the other. There was a sense of madness in the hall.

I came slowly to my feet. I began to scream. My mouth set off of its own accord and I had no control over what it was saying. I screamed of bluebells and pink trout. I screamed of Kyrie Eleison Abbey. I screamed of the schoolboy with the monogram on his blazer. I screamed of the knife lancing my throat. I screamed the formula of non-recognition. I screamed the satin sheen of a woman's skin. I screamed Ireland free and united from the centre to the sea. In Gaelic and in English I kept screaming.

The fighting stopped. The men were all around me panting and urging me to put an end to my noise. But I wouldn't stop because I couldn't stop. My voice was careering away and dragging me in its wake. When at last Packy put his hands on my shoulders I stopped. There was an intense silence. One of the warders behind us came tearing through. 'The Governor!' he shouted.

Packy pushed me down, then beat O'Brien in a race for the

platform. There he slung O'Brien's clothes behind the curtain. 'Too late!' he yelled to O'Brien. 'Sit down!'

We all sat down. O'Brien sat in the middle of the men. I found McCarthy next to me. His head was lowered and he was spitting blood over his split lip. The spittle kept dangling from the stab of red on his beard. Now and again he drew his foot across the floor. He looked at me. 'It's a thing of nothing, Patcheen!' he said with an affectionate smile.

On the platform, Packy was himself once more. 'Poetry, Professor!' he said, with a glance at the door.

The Professor rose and began to declaim *The Dead at Clonmacnoise*:

> *In a quiet water'd land, a land of roses,*
> *Stands Saint Kieran's city fair;*
> *And the warriors of Erin in their famous generations*
> *Slumber there.*

Halfway through the second verse we saw the Governor's entrance into the hall mirrored in Packy's face. O'Brien crouched lower—the men nearest him leaned their elbows on the back of his chair.

The Professor's voice poured on. In it I found a strange healing.

> *Many and many a son of Conn the Hundred-fighter*
> *In the red earth lies at rest. . . .*

The Governor walked noiselessly by the wall. 'O'Brien?' I heard him whisper to one of the warders.

'The Irish lecture is over, sir.'

The Professor was now reciting *The Fort of Rathangan*:

> *The fort over against the oak-wood,*
> *Once it was Bruidge's, it was Cathal's,*
> *It was Aedh's, it was Ailill's,*
> *It was Conaing's, it was Cuiline's,*
> *And it was Maelduin's;*
> *The fort remains after each in his turn*
> *And the Kings asleep in the ground.*

I came slowly to the warmth and to the light and the beauty. Within myself, I kept repeating: 'And the Kings asleep in the ground.'

The little poem had ended. Advancingly shyly, the Governor coughed for attention. Packy held up his hand. The Professor shrugged and sat down. The Governor took up a position a little to one side of us.

'Mr. Chairman and gentlemen,' he said.

His eyes ran over our lines; I thought that his gaze rested overlong on the white shoulders of O'Brien.

'I have an announcement to make. The fact is, you see, I have received a message, a communication, that you have been granted political treatment. You may put on your own clothes as soon as you will. Thank you, Mr. Chairman and gentlemen.'

The Governor coughed and went away.

Packy slumped into his chair. He began to look steadily into the hollow of his hand.

We remained there wholly without movement. At last O'Brien came to his feet. Slowly he padded up the steps, pulled out his clothes from beneath the curtain and began to drag them on. As he did so, he glanced first at Packy, then at us. Thoughtfully he laced his shoes. He was struggling with the clip of his collar when the bell rang. Still we made no move. The Northern warders hung back. They looked at O'Brien. Suddenly we were all looking at O'Brien who now bulked big—bigger even than Packy.

O'Brien walked to the platform's edge. He ran his eyes over our faces. Of a sudden he snapped out in Gaelic:

'*Go réidh!*'

We readied ourselves. Stiffly.

'*Seasaig!*'

We stood. Proudly.

'*Iompaigí!*'

We turned. Rebelliously.

'*Siúlaigí!*'

We walked. Defiantly.

I walked with the rest. Then again it was beard after beard, red buttocks, varicose veins, pot belly, hammer toe, lank shank and stallion flank, shaved poll and ancient ulcer, all present and correct down to the single eye-shade with today's addition of split lip, one.

As McCarthy passed stiffly by, O'Brien winked at him. McCarthy returned the salute with a grin from his battered mouth. Inside in myself I was thronged with warmth and light and beauty. I had sloughed the treachery of April and had once again begun to be ruled by the Kings asleep in the ground.

# The Cry

## JOHN MONTAGUE

FINALLY HE rose to go to bed. His father had shuffled off a few minutes before and his mother was busy preparing a hot-water bottle, moving, frail as a ghost, through the tiny kitchen. Seeing her white hair, the mother-of-pearl rosary beads dangling from her apron pocket, the bunny rabbit slippers, he felt guilt at keeping her up so late. But he came home so seldom now that he was out of the rhythm of the household and tried to do only what pleased them. And sitting with their big Coronation mugs of cocoa, they had drunk in his presence so greedily that he felt compelled to talk and talk. Mostly of things they had never seen: of travelling in Europe, of what it was like to work on a big newspaper, of the great freedom of living in London. This last had troubled his father very much, centuries of republicanism stirring in his blood.

'What do you mean, son, freedom?'

'I mean, Father, nobody interferes with you. What you do is your own business, provided you cause no trouble.'

Seeing the perplexity in his father's face, he tried to explain in local terms. 'Nobody on *The Tocsin*, for instance, would dream of asking if you were Catholic or Protestant—at least not the way they do here. If they did ask, it would be because they were genuinely interested.'

'Then can you explain, son, why England has the reputation she has abroad? Didn't she interfere with freedom everywhere she went, from Africa to the North here?'

'That's not the real England, Father; that's the government and the ruling class. The real Englishman is not like that at all, he stands for individual liberty, live and let live. You should hear them in Hyde Park!'

'I must never have met a real Englishman then,' said his father, obstinately. His face had gone brick-red and his nostrils twitched, showing spikes of white hair. With his bald round head and bright eyes he looked like Chad, in the war-time cartoon, peering over a wall, but it was anger, not humorous resignation, he registered.

183

'Maybe,' said his mother timidly, 'they're all right when they're at home.'

And there the matter rested. His father had always been violently anti-English: he remembered him saying that he would be glad to live on bread and water for the rest of his life if he could see England brought to her knees. And the struggle there had been when he had first announced his intention of trying to break into newspaper work in London! Dublin would have been all right, or America where his father had spent ten years as a cook in a big hotel, before coming home to marry and settle in the little newsagency business. But England! Religious and political prejudice fused to create his father's image of it as the ultimate evil. And something in his father's harshness called out to him: during his adolescence, he had contacted the local branch of the I.R.A. and tried to join. They (rather he, a lean melancholy egg-packer called Sheridan who had the reputation of being a machine-gunner in the force) had told him to report for a meeting, but when the time came, he had funked it, saying that he had to go away.

And so, Peter changed the conversation. He spoke of shows he had seen, the big American musicals, the Bolshoi and Royal Ballets. But his father still seemed restless: once he saw him glance mournfully across at his mother and wondered what he had said wrong. Her eyes glinted with pleasure as he described a Charity (tactfully amended from Command) Performance, with all the stars arriving in their glittering gowns.

'Oh, that must have been lovely,' she said, with placid yearning.

It was only when he was climbing the stairs, that he realized what his father's glance had meant. 'Good night, now, son, and don't forget to say your prayers,' his mother called after him. That was it; because of his visit, they had not said the regular family rosary, waiting for him to remember and suggest it. How could he explain that he had never seen anyone in England say the rosary, except two Irish lads in his first digs in Camden Town, who had embarrassed everyone by kneeling down at their bedside and saying it aloud in Irish. English Catholics did not believe in loading themselves down with inessentials. But if he had begun to explain all that, they would have jumped to the conclusion that he had lost his faith completely. Religion and politics he should try to leave alone for the short time he was home.

\* \* \*

The room was on the top floor, that front bedroom in which he had always slept. The top sheet was turned down, with the same inviting neatness, the blue eiderdown was the same, even the yellow chamber pot beneath the bed. Over the fireplace was the familiar picture of Our Lady of Perpetual Succour, an angular Madonna cradling a solemn-faced child, a slipper dangling from his chubby foot. Opposite it, on the wall over the bed, was a Victorian sampler, worked by his grandmother as a young girl: THERE IS NO FUN LIKE WORK.

It was all so unchanged that it was almost terrifying, like being confronted with the ghost of his younger self. He heard his father moving in the next room, shifting and sighing. Taking off his clothes, Peter knelt down in his pyjamas for a few moments at the bedside; he hoped the old man would hear the murmur and guess what it was. Then he wandered round the room for something to read.

Spurning *The Wolfe Tone Annual* and *With God on the Amazon* on the dressing table, he discovered a soot-stained copy of *The Ulster Nationalist* which had obviously been taken from the grate to make room for the electric fire; this he carried triumphantly to bed.

The editorial spoke with dignified bitterness of the continued discrimination against Catholics in the North of Ireland in jobs and housing. Facts were given and in spite of the tedious familiarity of the subject Peter felt his anger rise at such pointless injustice. He turned the page quickly to the Court Proceedings:

## UNITED NATIONS FOR MOORHILL?

Moorhill Court was taken up on Wednesday with a lengthy hearing of a civil summons for alleged abusive language and assault.

Giving evidence, James MacKennie, Craigavon Terrace, said that Miss Phyllis Murphy had thrown a bucket of water over him as he was passing on his bicycle. Cross-examined witness admitted that he had spoken sharply to Miss Murphy but he had not threatened, as she said, 'to do her'. He admitted borrowing 5/- from Miss Murphy 'to cure a headache'. His solicitor, Mr. John Kennedy, said that his client was a veteran of the First World War and had a disability pension. It was true he had been in jail several times, but he was very well thought of in the community.

The defendant, Miss Phyllis Murphy, said that James MacKennie was a well known pest, and besides 'he had been coming over dirty talk'. She denied throwing water over him and said he had had been making so many 'old faces' that he had driven over the bucket of water. She denied saying she hoped 'that would make him laugh the other side of his Orange face'.

In giving his decision, the R.M. said it was a difficult case to disentangle but he felt both parties were to blame and he therefore bound them over to keep the peace for a year. It was a pity, now that people were trying to outlaw war, to find neighbours disagreeing; maybe he should ask the United Nations to come to Moorhill . . . (laughter in court).

Peter Douglas read on with delighted horror. For the first time since he had returned, he felt at ease; he threw the paper on the floor, and turned contentedly over to sleep. Somewhere downstairs, the cuckoo clock he had brought his mother was sounding.

\* \* \*

Some time later, he came suddenly awake to a sound of shouting. He listened carefully, but it could not have come from the next room. Perhaps it was his mother; no, it was too strong, a man's voice. It came from down in the street, but not directly underneath; he sat bolt upright in bed and turned his head towards the window. Yes, there it was again, clearer, and he sounded as if he were in pain.

'O, Jesus, sir, O Jesus, it hurts.'

Maybe somebody had been taken ill suddenly and they were carrying him to the ambulance? Or a fire: he remembered the night, years ago, when old Carolan had been carried out of his house by the firemen, screaming like a struck pig, rags of cloth still smouldering upon his legs. But who was the man in the street talking to, whom was he calling sir?

'O, Jesus, sir, don't touch me again.'

All across the town lights were beginning to come on; the shadowy figure of a woman, wrapped in a dressing-gown, appeared at the window directly opposite; only something unusual could sanction such loose behaviour in Moorhill. Maybe it was a fight? Then, with a cold rush of certainty, Peter Douglas knew what it was: it was someone being beaten up by the police.

'O, God, sir, don't hit me again.'

The voice was high and pleading. Then, there was a scuffle of feet and the sound of a blow, a sharp crack, like a stone on wood. Throwing back the bedclothes, Peter ran to the window and craned out his head. At the bottom of the street, he saw a knot of people. One of them was kneeling on the ground, his shape circled by the light of a torch held by one of the bulky cape-clad figures surrounding him. In the windows above, shadows moved, silent, watching.

'Come on to the barracks now and quit your shouting,' said an impatient voice.

'Oh no, sir, I can't, I'm nearly killed. Somebody help me, for God's sake, please.'

Again the voice was abject, but at a muttered order the torch was extinguished and the four figures closed in on the kneeling man. Was no one going to protest, none of those darkly brooding presences? Peter Douglas opened his mouth to shout, but he was forestalled. A door opened behind the men, letting out a shaft of light. He heard a sharp, educated voice:

'What in blazes do you thugs think you are doing? Leave the man alone.'

One of the four policemen turned, switching his torch directly into the face of the speaker.

'Keep your bloody nose out of it, will ye? Do you want to get a touch too?'

He heard further muttering and then a door slammed angrily. The four figures seized their victim, who now hung like a sack between them, and half-walked, half-ran him down the street towards the barracks. There were no further cries, only the drag of boots on the pavement, an occasional groan and (as the barrack door opened and shut behind them) a gathering silence. One by one the lights went out over the town. Peter Douglas was one of the last to leave, his eyes sore (he had left his glasses on the bedside table) from straining after any further movement. As he climbed into bed again, he heard the cuckoo clock, Cuckoo, Cuckoo, Cuckoo.

\* \* \*

When he came down to breakfast next morning, after a short and troubled sleep, he found his father waiting impatiently for him. Generally, he was in the shop by this time, but it was his mother's voice he heard, dealing with an early customer: 'Yes, Mrs. Wilson, nice weather indeed, for the time of year. . . .' And it was his father who prepared the meal, cornflakes, tea and toast, bacon sizzling fragrantly in the pan. It was clear he had something on his mind; Peter felt as suspiciously certain as a prisoner who finds his warder suddenly affable.

'You're pretty lively this morning, aren't you?' he said, digging into the cornflakes.

His father did not reply, fussing around the stove with plates and cloths until, triumphantly, he placed a full plate of bacon, eggs and sausages before his son.

'The old man can do it yet,' he said. Then he sat at the end of the table and watched his son eat, nervously, with an urban lack of zest.

'They don't seem to have much appetite in England, anyway,' he said, 'whatever else they have.' And then, without further preamble: 'Did you hear what happened last night?'

'I did,' said his son, briefly. 'Did you?'

'I only heard the tail-end of it, but I heard them all talking this morning.'

'What did they say?'

'They said the B-Specials beat up a young man called Ferguson, whom they accused of being in the I.R.A.'

'Was he?'

'Sure how would I know? Most people say not, a harmless lad that was courting his girl on the bridge, without minding anyone.'

'Then why did they attack him?'

'Why do you think? You know bloody well those boys don't need a reason for beating up one of our sort.'

'Maybe he had papers on him, or an explosive. After all, there's been a lot of trouble lately.'

In the preceding months, the I.R.A. campaign against the North had been revived. It was the same sad old story, barracks, customs huts blown up, and police patrols ambushed. Several men had been killed on both sides, and the police force had been augmented, even in relatively quiet areas like Moorhill, which though predominantly Catholic, was too far from the border for a raiding party to risk. A hut at the end of the town had gone on fire one night, but it turned out to be some children playing a prank.

'Damn the explosive he had with him, except,' his father smiled thinly, 'you count the girl. But those bloody B-Specials are so anxious to prove their importance, strutting around the town with their wee guns. Besides, they're shitting their britches with fear and mad to get their own back.'

'I see.' Peter forbore from pointing out that some of these motives were mutually exclusive, recognizing his father's mood only too well. He poured a last cup of tea.

'Well, what are you going to do about it?' said his father fiercely.

'What do you mean, what am I going to do?'

'You were talking last night about Englishmen and freedom. Well there's an example of your English freedom, and a fine sight it is. What are you going to do about it?'

'What do you want me to do? Look for a gun?' he said sardonically.

'You could do worse. But your sort would faint at the sight of one.'

Peter flared. 'Would we, indeed? Well, maybe we've seen too many, handled by the wrong people.'

'What the hell are you going to fight them with, then?' his father snorted. 'A pen-nib? A typewriter? A fat lot of use that would be against a Sten-gun.'

'It might be of more use than you think. Moral protest is always best, as Gandhi showed. But they did not teach you that in Ballykinlar.'

'Moral protest, me granny. How are you going to bring moral protest to bear on bucks like that? Force only recognizes greater force.'

Peter Douglas rose and, placing his back against the rail of the stove, looked down at his father. The dark-blue pouches under his eyes, gorged with blood, the right arm raised as though to thump the table in affirmation: he could have been cast in bronze as The Patriot. His own limp ease, the horn-rimmed glasses, the scarf tucked in neatly at the throat of his sports-shirt, the pointed black Italian shoes—everything represented a reaction against this old fire-eater who had dominated his childhood like a thundercloud. But now he felt no fear of him, only a calm certainty of his own position.

'You know well, Father, in your heart of hearts, that violence is the wrong way. Now you ask me what I can do. Well, in this specific case, I can do more than you or a whole regiment of the I.R.A. I can write an article in *The Tocsin* which will expose the whole thing. Good, decent—yes, English—people will read it and be ashamed of what is being done in their name. Questions will be asked, maybe in Parliament, if not this time, then the next. And gradually, if they are shown the enormity of what they are doing, the ruling classes of Ulster will come to their senses. One cannot hope to survive in the twentieth century on the strength of a few outdated shibboleths: prejudice always breeds violence.'

His father was silent, whether impressed or not, Peter could not say. Then, rising to clear away the breakfast things, he said:

'You'll do that then. You'll write the article.'

'I will.'

His father smiled, cunningly. 'Well, at least I got you to do something. You haven't completely lost your Ulster spirit yet.'

\* \* \*

Peter's first task was to collect the information. He began to move around the town, listening to conversations in shop and pub. At first he drew a blank; seeing him enter with his pale look, his city air, the men at the bar went silent or whispered among themselves. When they had established his identity ('O you're James Douglas's boy,' a double recognition of family and religion flooding across the face) they spoke again, angrily.

'Oh, the black boys gave him a good going over, like,' said one man with a knowing wink and nod. 'You don't get off lightly when you're in their hands.'

'Is he badly hurt?' asked Peter.

'Now I couldn't tell you that exactly, but the doctor was with him this morning. They say he has a broken arm, anyway.'

'I heerd he had two broken ribs and stetches in his head forby.'

'Oh, they gave him the stick all right.'

'You'll get no fair deal from the likes of them.'

'They're black as can be.'

But when Peter asked what was going to be done by way of protest, they looked at him bleakly, shaking their heads.

'Sure you know it's no bloody use,' said one, hopelessly.

'You'd be a marked man from that day out,' said another.

'Sure you know the black boys have it all sewn up,' said a third, joining the litany of defeat.

Their passivity only heightened Peter's resolution, the only thing troubling him being the lack of specific detail. Very few people seemed to know the boy who lived far out, in the Black Mountain district. And those who did did not always approve of him; they said he was very 'close' and used to hang around the juke-box in Higgins's Café. Yet they were all agreed on the wanton brutality of the beating, though the majority confessed to having been too far away to see much.

The source for the earlier part of the story was the girl, but she had run away when the struggle started and her father had forbidden her to leave the house. Since the man whom Peter had seen rebuking the police was the schoolmaster, he would not be home until evening and the nearest to an eye-witness he could find was the owner of the Dew Drop Inn. He and his wife slept in a room overlooking the street, exactly where the worst of the struggle had taken part. Yes they had struck him a lot, he told Peter, but he had heard one of them say: 'To be sure and hit him round the body, it leaves less mark.'

'There should be a boycott against them bucks,' concluded the publican, grimly.

In the Mountain Rest, however, Peter found the town clerk calmly drinking a large whiskey. Tall, with a drooping sandy moustache, he had served in an artillery regiment during the Normandy campaign and the boyish vigour with which he propounded atheism in a community highly given to religious hypocrisy had always amused Peter. The clerk thought that what had happened the previous night was a storm in a teacup. The boy had been looking for trouble and the only mistake was that the police had not acted promptly enough. 'The only thing to do with a gulderer like that is to hit him on the head with a mallet: that puts a stop to the squealing!'

No one spoke. Gulping down his lager, Peter left: it was time to start his article.

*　　*　　*

It is depressing to encounter violence again, its familiar pattern of fear and impotence. The first time I met it was in New York: a huddle of boys under a street lamp and then the single figure staggering backwards, hand to his side, while the others fled. My first impulse was to help but a firm hand held me back. By the time the ambulance arrived, the boy was dead.

That is the classic scene of urban violence; the spectator is absolved in the sheer *remoteness* of the action. It is not quite so scenic when it happens among people one knows. Recently I returned to the small town in the North of Ireland. . . .

Well, it was a beginning at least; a little academic in its irony, and the 'philosophical' lead-in would probably have to be scrapped; but still, a beginning. It would improve when he got down to the actual incident: should he begin with a description of the town to give the

190

background, or should he just plunge in? And there would have to be interviews with the police especially—not used to being taken up, they would probably condemn themselves out of their own mouths.

As Peter hesitated, he heard someone enter the bedroom where he was sitting, his Hermes propped on a suitcase in front of him. It was his mother; she had a brightly fringed shawl around her shoulders and she was carrying a hot-water bottle. This she inserted into the bed, with great ostentation.

'I thought I'd put it in early this evening, and have the bed warm for you. It was pretty sharp last night.'

Peter waited impatiently for her to leave, but as she delayed, rearranging the sheet several times, it became obvious that the hot-water bottle was only an excuse.

'I see you're writing,' she said at last.

'Yes.'

'Is it about last night?'

'More or less.'

'I suppose it was him put you up to it.' She always referred to his father in this semi-abstract way, as if he were not so much her husband as someone who had been wished on her years ago, a regrettable but unchanging feature of the household.

'More or less. But I would probably have done it myself in any case.'

'Do you think it's a sensible thing to do?'

'How do you mean, sensible? One can't let things like that pass without protest.'

She looked at him in silence for a few moments and then, placing her hands on her hips: 'You're much better out of it. You'll only make trouble for all of us.'

'That's not what Father thinks.'

'I don't care what he thinks. I've lived with that man, God knows, for over thirty years and I still don't understand him. I think he never grew up.' She offered the last sentence with a grimace of half amused resignation.

'But I agree with him in this case.'

'Oh, it's easy for you. You don't live here all the year round. That thing you're writing will create bad blood. I've seen too much fighting between neighbours in this town already.'

'But, Mother, you used to be a great rebel!' His father had often told, with great amusement, how she had been arrested for singing *The Soldiers' Song* on the beach at Warrenpoint; she had picked off the policeman's hat with her parasol and thrown it into the bathing pool. This incident was known in the family as Susie's fight for Irish Freedom.

'I've seen too much of it,' she said, flatly. 'My brothers fought for Irish Independence and where did it get them? They're both in

191

Australia now, couldn't get jobs in their own country. Look at you: when you want a job you have to go to England.'

'But I'm only writing an article, Mother, not taking up a gun.'

'It's all the same tune. Sour grapes and bad blood. It's me and him will have to live here if that thing appears, not you. Come down to your tea and leave that contraption alone.' She gestured towards the typewriter as if it were accursed.

Peter rose reluctantly. Despite her frail body, her china-pale complexion, her great doll's eyes, she had the will of a dragon. During the next few days, mysterious references to this article would crop up again and again in her conversation, references designed to make his father and himself feel uneasy, like guilty schoolboys.

'But surely you don't approve of what they did?' he said.

'Approve of them, of course I don't. They're a bad lot.' Muttering she disappeared into the kitchen, to reappear with an egg-whisk and a bowl of eggs. 'But we have to live with them,' she announced, driving the egg-whisk into the eggs like an electric drill. 'Why else did God put them there?'

*   *   *

One must distinguish between the Royal Ulster Constabulary and the familiar English 'bobby'. The Ulster police are the only ordinary police, in these islands, to carry revolvers; during times of Emergency, they are armed with Sten-guns. Add to that 12,000 B-Specials and you have all the elements of a police state —not in Spain or South Africa, but in the British Isles. Such measures are not, as is argued, preventive, but the symptoms of political disease.

Police! Peter Douglas never knew a moment when he had not feared and detested them. It was partly his father's example: walking with him through the town, as a child, or on the way out to the chapel, he would feel him stiffen when a black uniform came in sight. If a constable, new to the place, dared salute him, he would gaze through him with a contemptuous eye. It was also the uniform; the stifling black of the heavy serge, the great belt, above all the dark bulk of the holster riding the hip: the archetypal insignia of brutality and repression. There was one, in particular, who was known as 'the storm-trooper': a massive ex-commando, he strode around the town with a black police dog padding at his heels. He had long left the district, but for Peter Douglas, he had become the symbol of all the bitterness of his native province, patrolling for ever the lanes of Ulster, as dark and predatory as the beast at his side.

And then there were the Special police, young locals, issued with rifles and Sten-guns, and handsomely paid for night duty. The first time Peter had seen them he was about ten years old, cycling home one warm summer evening from his uncle's house in Altnagore.

There were about thirty, drilling before a tin-roofed Orange Lodge. Although he knew most of them, local Protestants whom he had met in shop or street, or in whose farmhouses he had been, they ignored him, gazing bleakly forward. Three nights later, they had stopped him and his father at a street corner and, pretending not to recognize them, held them up for nearly half an hour.

Darkly unjust these memories might be, Peter Douglas reflected as he walked down the street, but the events of the previous night seemed to bear them out. From Higgins's Café came a gush of light and music, the harsh sound of a pop record. Under the circle of a street light stood the diminutive figure of Joe Doom, the village idiot, eating from one of his tin cans. A group of children surrounded him, but they shrank back into the dark as Peter passed.

Outside the barracks itself, on a hillock at the end of the town, there appeared to be an unusual amount of activity. There was a Land-Rover, containing several police, drawn up in front, together with a long black car the wireless antennae and the dark glittering body of which unmistakably proclaimed a squad car. The barracks was a large building, painted in panels of white outlined with black; without the blue police sign over the door, it might have been a doctor's or a company director's house in some comfortable English suburb. But, surrounded on every side by great rolls of barbed wire and with a sandbag blockhouse, from the slit of which protruded a machine-gun, it looked like a fortress, the headquarters of the Gauleiter in an occupied town. As he came up the path, he saw a flash of movement in the blockhouse; he was being kept under cover.

'Is the Sergeant in?' Peter asked. And then, irritably: 'For God's sake, put that thing down. I live up the street.'

'What do ye want with him?' A young constable emerged, the Sten-gun dangling on his arm, insubstantial in its menace as a Meccano toy.

'I'd like to interview him. I'm a journalist and I work for a paper in England. I'd like to discuss the incident last night with him.'

'You're a journalist,' said the constable, with an intonation of flat incredulity. 'In England?'

'Yes, and I'd like to see the Sergeant, please.'

There was a moment's silence, while the policeman looked at him, his eyes pale blue and vacant in a dead-white face, emphasized by the black peak of the cap. Then he turned and motioned Peter to follow him into the day-room.

There were five men in the room, two local policemen whom he vaguely recognized, two rather sulky-looking B-Specials and a fifth, who by his bearing, tailored uniform with Sam Browne belt and polished leggings, seemed to be a superior officer. They looked surprised to see Peter.

'There's a man here, Sergeant,' said the Constable, addressing one of the local policemen, 'says he's a journalist. He works for some paper, in England.'

The Sergeant came forward, slowly. 'You're Mr. Douglas's son, aren't you?' he asked, with a mixture of civility and doubt.

'Yes, Sergeant, I am. I work for a paper in England and I'm home on a short holiday. I'd like to get a few facts from you about the incident last night.'

'Last night?' The Sergeant looked in vague desperation towards the well dressed officer.

'Which paper do you work for?' said the latter in a crisp voice. As he spoke, he came forward to face Peter as if by his presence hoping to subdue the intruder. It was the unmistakable voice of authority, British and chilling, as level in tone as a B.B.C. announcer's.

Peter explained, politely.

'Yes, I see,' said the officer, noncommittally. 'I think I know the paper.' Then, to the Sergeant: 'Don't you think we should bring Mr. Douglas into another room, Knowles?'

As Peter followed Sergeant Knowles into a large room at the back of the barracks, a thought struck him.

'That's the County Inspector, isn't it?'

'It is indeed,' said the Sergeant. He looked as if he wanted to say more but thought better of it, poking the fire for an instant in an aimless way, before leaving the room. So that was it: they were definitely troubled about the incident last night and the County Inspector had come down in person to investigate. He was on the right track after all.

The Chief Inspector entered the room briskly a few moments later. Planting himself luxuriously in front of the fire, he turned to Peter with a bright energetic smile. Thin hair brushed back above his ears, a long oval face with neatly divided moustache, lean-bridged nose and almost slanted eyes, he was decidedly handsome, a man born and used to command.

'Well, now, Mr. Douglas, it's not often we get one of you chaps knocking around this part of the country. Sorry I can't offer you a drink, but I doubt if the facilities of the barracks are supposed to rise to that.' He laughed briefly. 'You're a local man, I take it.'

'Yes,' said Peter. The bright offensiveness of the man's tone angered, but also cowed him, so that, almost against his will, he found himself volunteering further information. 'But I went to school in Laganbridge.'

'Oh,' said the Inspector with interest, sensing common ground. 'Went to school there myself. The Kings, I suppose.'

'No,' said Peter shortly. Then—incredulity merging into satisfaction at the unexpected trap into which the Inspector had fallen, deceived by the British sound of Douglas and the fact that *The Tocsin* was a London paper—he added, 'St. Kieran's.'

It was like confessing, Peter thought with a smile, to an unreconstructed Southerner that though one looked quite normal one really was a Negro. The Kings was one of the most famous Protestant schools in the North of Ireland, a Georgian nursery for cricketers, colonial administrators, gaitered bishops and even (as though to demonstrate its all-round ability) a distinguished literary critic. On the hill opposite, sheltering under the great bulk of the post-Emancipation cathedral, was the diocesan seminary of St. Kieran's where the sons of strong Catholic farmers, publicans and merchants studied, mainly for the priesthood.

'Oh.' The Chief Inspector paused, visibly taken aback. Then, with a gallant return to self-possession: 'Used to know your Bishop a bit. Nice old chap. Don't fancy his taste in sherry much, though.'

'His sherry?' echoed Peter in amazement.

'Myas.' They way he pronounced it, with a prefatory hum and a hissing follow through, it could have been anything from 'years' to 'my ears'. 'Gets his shipped direct from Spain; our boys see it through the Customs for him. Bit dry. Prefer Bristol Cream myself.'

If such a man though about Nationalists at all, it was probably as some obscure form of trouble-making minority; he did not mind contact with them providing it took place on the highest level, a Maharajah or a bishop, or some complaisant highly placed native official. And why should he change? Convinced of his tolerance, assured of his position within the framework of Queen and Country, he would probably end his days in honourable retirement with a minor decoration in the Honours List.

'I never met the Bishop,' Peter said curtly.

He might have saved his breath, the irony of his remark falling like a paper dart from that unruffled brow. The Inspector had already moved on.

'Well,' he said, 'about that little matter you mentioned. Don't think there's much in it for a fellow like you. Pretty small beer after all. Some young thug cheeked our boys and they took him in for a few hours to cool off. Released him in the morning. Routine affair.'

'After beating him up on the way,' Peter said, stubbornly.

'Oh, I wouldn't say that,' said the Inspector, judiciously. 'He did resist arrest after all, so they had to help him along a bit. May have got a few scratches, but that would be the height of it.'

'Enough to put him in a hospital bed.'

'Oh, you heard that, did you?' the Inspector said with interest. 'Well, well, it's wonderful how rumours get round, though I'm afraid you won't find much substance in that one. Chap kept complaining so we called the doctor. He couldn't find much wrong with him but just to be on the safe side he sent him down to the County for an X-ray. Released in a few hours, right as rain. Mother came to bring him home.'

'So you mean it was all nothing?' asked Peter, incredulously.

'Pretty well.'

'But the noise woke up the whole town.'

The Inspector laughed dryly. 'Yes, that was rather a nuisance. Chap was a bit of an exhibitionist. Roared like a bull, boys said, every time they laid a finger on him. Pretty cute trick when you come to think of it.'

'Trick?' Peter stared at the bland face opposite him. But he found neither deception nor doubt in the Inspector's level gaze.

'Yes, a trick. Can't be up to some of these fellows. Bit of a Teddy boy by all accounts, likes to show he's not afraid of the police. But I think he realizes he went a bit too far last night, made a fool of himself.' The Inspector rubbed his hands together in a gesture of satisfied dismissal. 'Well, there you are, there's the whole little story. Sorry I can't provide something more juicy for you. I know what you Johnnies like. Perhaps next time.'

Stunned, Peter followed him along the corridor and out through the door. He was half-way up Main Street before he realized that the I.R.A. had not even been mentioned.

\* \* \*

'So that's what he said to you,' said the schoolmaster admiringly. Peter had called on him on his way home and they had crossed the street to the nearest pub, the Dew Drop Inn.

'Yes. I'm afraid I was so taken aback I couldn't think of anything to say. I mean, it all sounded so plausible; maybe the man was telling the truth.'

'Still, that doesn't explain why he called upon me.'

'Oh, did he, indeed?' breathed Peter.

'Yes, when I drove in from school, there was His Nibs waiting in the parlour. Said he often heard my brother who works in the County Health Office speak of me and thought he should drop by. Then, cool as you please, mentioned the business last night and said I would be glad to hear it had all been a misunderstanding. They had given the boy a good talking to and sent him home. There was no further reason for me to be troubled *in any way*. Special Constable Robson was sorry for what he had said to me, but it was all in the heat of the moment and meant nothing.'

'So they *were* troubled. . . . And what did you say?'

'What could I say? I just smiled back and said I accepted Robson's apologies and was glad to hear the boy was all right. I work here you know and so—as he delicately pointed out—does my brother. Besides'—he blinked nervously and hunched his narrow raincoated shoulders forward—'I've been thinking the matter over and it seems to me we're not on very safe ground.'

196

'What do you mean? Surely a civilized man cannot let some one be beaten up under his eyes without protesting?'

'In an ordinary case, no. But the boy doesn't seem to have been badly hurt and we wouldn't be able to prove anything definite. We'd only be playing into their hands by showing ourselves as trouble-makers.'

Peter was silent for a moment, sipping his Tuborg. 'That's more or less what my mother says,' he said eventually, 'but not my father.'

'Your father, if you don't mind me saying so, is nearly as thick as an Orangeman in his own way. His kind of talk may be fair enough in Dail Eireann, but as you know yourself, it cuts very little ice here. After all, even if we did get a United Ireland we would still have to live with them so we'd better start now. And you must admit the police in the North have had a pretty rough time lately. If this was the 'twenties, there'd be a lot of dead Teagues around.'

'So you think I should drop the article I'm doing?'

'Oh, I don't know, that depends. Why don't you go and see the boy before deciding? After all, he was the one who was beaten up.'

The owner of the Dew Drop Inn peered hurriedly round the door. 'Come on, gentlemen, please,' he said. 'It's half an hour after the time already.' As they passed through the kitchen on their way out, a group of men were on their way in. They were the B-Specials Peter had seen at the barracks. 'Good night now, Mr. Concannon, good night, Mr. Douglas,' the owner said as he shepherded them through the door. Then he turned to greet his new customers.

\* \* \*

'That must be it,' said James Douglas, craning across the shoulder of the hackney cab driver. For ten minutes or so, ever since they had left the main road, they had been bumping along a narrow country lane. At first there were signs of habitation, but as they wound their way up the mountainside, first the houses and then the trees began to fall away, long stretches of melancholy bog opening up on either side. At last, just as the gravel surface of the lane began to merge into the muddy ruts of a cart track, they caught sight of a small cottage. Whitewashed, with a greening thatched roof, it stood on a mound, without any shelter or protection from the wind except a rough fence, hammered out of old tar-barrels. Against the wall, its front wheel almost blocking the half-door, was a battered racing bicycle, painted a bright red.

'That's it, right enough,' said the driver. 'Any bids?'

'It looks bleak all right,' said Peter.

'Hungry's the word,' said the driver cheerfully, as he applied the hand brake.

'Do you want me to come with you?' his father asked, looking at

197

Peter doubtfully. All the way to Black Mountain he had been humming to himself, in evident satisfaction, but the sight of the cottage seemed to have unnerved him.

'No,' said Peter shortly. 'I'll go myself.'

The swaying progress of the car up the lane had already attracted attention: a brown and white mongrel dog came racing down to greet it, and the startled face of a woman flashed briefly at one of the two small windows. As Peter descended from the car, his thin shoes sinking in the mud of the yard, the dog plunged towards him.

'Down, Flo, down.' A woman of about fifty, wearing a shapeless red jumper and a pair of thongless man's boots, appeared in the doorway. She stood, drying her hands in the corner of her discoloured apron, and waiting for Peter to speak.

'Does Michael Ferguson live here?'

A look of dismay, animal, uncomprehending, passed over the face. 'God protect us,' she muttered, 'more trouble.' Then, turning towards the door: 'He's in there, if you want him.'

After the light of the mountainside, the interior of the cottage seemed dim as a cave. A crumbling turf-fire threw a fitful smoky light over the hunched up figure of an old man who looked up as the intruder entered and then, with a noisy scraping of his stool, turned away. Beside the kettle in the ashes lay a sick chicken, its scrawny red head projecting from a cocoon of flannel. The other side of the room was taken by a cupboard and a bed upon which a young man was lying. There was a bandage around his forehead.

'Can't you rise, at laste, when someone comes to see you?' said the woman, gruffly.

The young man raised himself stiffly from the bed. He was about twenty, tall and rather well-built with broad shoulders. He wore an imitation leather jacket, heavy with metal buckles and clasps. It rode high above his waist, exposing a torn khaki shirt. This was stuffed loosely into a pair of threadbare jeans, supported by a studded leather belt with a horseshoe buckle. The outfit was completed by bright blue- and red-ribbed socks above the black heaviness of farm boots.

'Are you police?' His eyes, close-set in a face heavily blotched with acne, avoided Peter's; he could have been speaking to the dog which by now whined and twined around his legs.

Peter explained as best he could. In his nervousness, he found himself using words that, by the puzzled expression in their faces, he knew they could not understand, so he repeated his story several times. 'I want to help, you see,' he ended.

'I don't think I can do much for you, mister,' the boy said, at last.

'What do you mean, you can't do much for me? That's not the point at all. I want to do something for you. I want to write an article that will expose the way you have been treated by the police. You don't mean to say you haven't been beaten up?'

198

From the hearth behind came an unexpected sound as the old man swivelled on his stool. His eyes, small and red-rimmed as a turkey cock's, were bright with venom, and as he spoke a streak of spittle ran down the front of his collarless shirt.

'If he'd stayed home with his mother the way a dacent-rared boy should, not a hate would have happened him. But nothing for it nowadays but running off to the pictures and the music boxes. He deserved all he got, and not half good enough for him.'

The boy's face flushed, but he remained silent. Instead, his mother spoke for him.

'To tell the truth, sir, we'd as lief the matter was forgotten. It would be better for all of us, like.'

'That's right, sir. The way it is, I wouldn't make too much of it, sir.'

So there it was, plain as a pikestaff. The police had spoken not merely to the boy, but also to the mother. They were quite prepared for the boy's sake and the sake of his parents that the matter should be overlooked; in their magnanimity, they had probably provided transport, an impossible expense, otherwise, for people in their position. Whatever redress Peter could offer, whatever hope or help would mean nothing compared to their unspecified but real threats. He would never know the truth of the incident now: whether the boy had connections with the I.R.A., whether he had provoked the police; whether even, his—Peter's—interpretation of their silence was correct. Between their helplessness and his freedom lay an unbridgeable gulf and, with a despairing gesture, he turned to leave. The boy and his mother accompanied him; the former, despite half-hearted attempts to conceal it, had a distinct limp.

'I'm sorry I can't help you now, sir,' he said. His voice, though flat in tone, sounded almost kindly. As he bent his head under the door, Peter noticed that, above the bandage, his hair was plastered back in two oily swathes, like the wings of a duck.

As the Austin 10 lurched down the mountainside, Peter and his father were both silent. A storm cloud was gathering over the valley, dark as a shawl. Only the driver seemed in a jaunty mood, as he expanded on the history of the Fergusons for their benefit.

'He's not a bad lad that, you know,' he said reflectively, 'rough and all as he is. The two other boys, cute enough, sloped off to England. He was in Barnsley too, but he came back when the old man had the operation. There's many wouldn't do it.'

It was only when they had reached home that James Douglas spoke, climbing laboriously through the door his son was holding for him, onto the kerb.

'Are you still going to write that article?' he asked apprehensively, peering into Peter's face.

Peter looked at him for a moment, as though in calculation. 'I don't really know,' he said.

\* \* \*

. . . There is a way of dealing with such incidents of course, familiar to every colonial officer from Ulster to Rhodesia. The charge is dropped or minimized, the too zealous police or soldiers reprimanded, any public fuss avoided. Perhaps as the authorities claim, it is the best way in the end. But one is left wondering in how many small Ulster towns such things are happening, at this moment, *in your name.*

After his return, Peter had gone straight to his bedroom to continue the article, with little success. He could not even decide, staring blankly at the paragraph he had just written, whether to give it up or not: he could get a beginning and an end, but the whole thing did not cohere into the outcry, logical but passionate, for which he had been hoping. He rose to pace the room; finally, he found himself at the window, vacantly looking out down Main Street, as he had done on that first night.

It had been raining heavily for an hour or so, but now it was clearing. On the rim of the sky, just to the west of the town, a watery sun was breaking through grey clouds. Soft, almost a dawn light, it shone on the town, making the long line of the main street, from the Old Tower to the War Memorial and beyond to the railway station, seem washed and clear.

There it was, his home town, laid out before him, bright in every detail. He knew every corner of it, had gone to school in that low concrete building, run his sleigh down that hill, had even, later, brought his first girl down the darkness of that entry. He knew every house and nearly everybody in them. One did not like or dislike this place: such emotions were irrelevant, it was a part of one's life, and therefore inescapable. Yet all through his final year at school his only thought had been to escape; the narrowness of the life, the hidden bitterness of political feeling had suddenly seemed like the régime of a prison. The Irish were supposed to be a gay race, but there was something in these people, a harsh urge to reduce the human situation to its barest essentials, which frightened him. It was years before he had felt able to come back, sufficiently secure in his own beliefs to be able to survive the hostility their ways seemed to radiate.

But did that strength now give him the right to sit in judgement, particularly where an incident like this was concerned? Already, only two days afterwards, indignation had died down in the town. Was it fear or an effort to foster that good will which people like his mother thought was the only solution? Or mere passivity, the product of a commercial spirit which saw everyone as a potential customer?

200

Whatever destiny lay in these grey walls, they might surely be left to work out on their own, two peoples linked and locked for eternity.

As he looked over the town, sober with self-judgement, suddenly from out of a lane-way, as though propelled, shot a dwarf-like figure. His clothes were of various colours, and he wore a tattered cap pulled squarely over his ears. One foot was bare, the other encased in an elderly boot. Around his waist hung a bandolier of tin-cans. Peter recognized him almost at once: it was Joe Doom, the village idiot. He lived in a tiny house on his own, at the end of the town, begging pennies from passers-by, stewing scraps in his tin cans. The people teased him, fed him, tolerated him, with a charity older than state institutions, and in return, his antics, the gargles and lapses of logic which were his sole method of speech, amused them. Now he looked wildly around, at the sky, at the watery sun, at the light shining on the fronts of the houses. Then, as though focusing, he saw Peter at the window above him. Their eyes met for a moment and something like triumph entered Joe Doom's. He fumbled frantically behind his back, the line of cans shaking, and produced a piece of white cardboard. With a quick glance behind him towards the entry, as though for confirmation, he held it high above his head, so that Peter—or anyone else in the street who was watching—could read. In large crude letters, like strokes of charcoal, it spelt

Nosy Parker
Go home

# Victims

## VINCENT LAWRENCE

---

PEONY STOOD at the window and watched his breath film across the glass so that the boy coming up the hill appeared to float rather than walk. He raised his hand in front of his face, palm inwards, and spread his fingers, but it was almost a full minute before it began to shake. He let it fall to his side and looked out again, crouching a little so that he had a better view of the hills. They were clothed in a vibrant sweep of gorse and purple heather, and the land looked fresh and clean under the summer sun. He bent further and squinted through the leaves of the tree which grew beside the house, and the light winking through the foliage fell on his eyes like spattered silver and blinded him.

Behind him Waterman cleared his throat and said, 'Come away from the window. If you're seen there will be questions asked. We can't afford that.' He spoke quietly, but there was an implicit note of command in his tone, as if he were used to giving orders.

Peony turned his head and looked at him over his shoulder, but the light was still in his eyes and he could see nothing but a blur. He turned back to the window again.

'Five minutes to eleven,' Waterman said. He stood up and stretched. 'The boy should be back soon. There may be some news.' He was a large square man, with an open pored face that looked hard and unrelenting, yet his mouth was small and heart shaped and he wore his hair long and styled like a girl's.

Peony turned again from the window and sat down on the ground with his back and head silhouetted against the light. The room was large and bare, and it had a nondescript anonymity which the few pieces of furniture it contained did nothing to dispel. Some strings of withered onions hung from the ceiling, and the smoke-blackened fireplace had not been cleaned for a long time. Peony said, 'What would you do if I tried to escape? If I just walked out the door and didn't come back?' And he put his hands flat on the ground beside him as if he meant to suit action to words.

Waterman shrugged. He stretched again, and then began to roll a

203

cigarette. His movements were deliberate and rather ponderous, as if he had schooled himself not to rush too hastily at anything, as if the culmination of an action were to him something that must be delayed as long as possible in order to enhance the effect. When he had the cigarette lit, he drew in smoke slowly, and then meditatively blew it in a thin stream at the ceiling. 'You know it wouldn't do you any good,' he said. 'If the police didn't pick you up, we would. You're a marked man. Where would you go?'

'There are places.' Peony picked idly at the torn linoleum on the floor. 'I have some friends. They might help me.'

'You have no friends,' Waterman said. 'It's not a game, you know. Outside of this room you're a dead man. No more sun, no more summer.' He paused, then he added, 'No more nothing,' and surprisingly, he grinned.

'There was a time . . .' Peony broke off and tilted his head into a listening attitude. A door slammed somewhere below them and voices whispered furtively like the sighing of a wind. 'You helped me a lot at the beginning.' Peony spoke more quickly now. 'You told me I was one of your better pupils. You were proud of me. Do you remember . . . ?'

'I remember nothing,' Waterman interrupted him. 'People who live in the past are sentimental fools. Memory is like indulging oneself in a useless course of action which goes nowhere and does nothing. It's a refuge for the weak.'

'Supposing I said I was sorry,' Peony said. 'A man makes many mistakes in a lifetime. Why should one mistake be any more grievous than another? Nobody suffered.'

'But they could have. You put all of our lives in jeopardy. Do you think anyone would go out with you again? Would have confidence in your backing them up? Besides, you were recognized. The man knew you, he won't forget.'

'Then why not stand in judgement on him? As I see it, it's a straight choice between the two of us.'

'He's a respectable member of the community. You are not.'

'You mean I'm expendable?'

'Everyone is expendable. Let's just say that you're more expendable than others.'

There was a discreet knock at the door, and a woman came in carrying a tray. She was quite young, with a plain pinched face and faded blue eyes. Her mouth looked as if it would need a shoehorn to open it. She placed the tray on the rickety wooden table and left as quietly as she had entered. Only the strings of onions creaked softly in her wake as if mocking her silent departure.

'Have some tea,' Waterman said. 'You may as well be patient. There's nothing either you or I can do.'

Peony ignored him and turned again to the window. Beyond the line of hills he could see the curve of the bay, and in the distance the sea glistened impersonally under the sun like snail-track. The town was down there also, the slate-grey town where he had grown up and had spent the first seventeen years of his life. He had always thought of it as a mean place, a place which had drained away his youth and had given him nothing in return except the urge to get away. His father still lived there—he may even have been one of the ancient men who, earlier that morning, had sat outside the bank, in the sunbright square, staring with the disinterested inquisitiveness of the old at the few people who passed by. He was a man whom life seemed to have defeated at an early stage; even before his wife died, and for as far back as Peony could remember, he had been old and grey and dispirited. Peony had often sat and watched him, and wondered what thoughts went through his head. Perhaps he had merely retreated inside himself, into a world in which the harshness of reality had no place, and where silence reigned instead of hope. Peony, remembering, sighed and turned to face back into the room, and just then the door opened once more and the boy came in and stood quietly looking from one to the other of them.

He was a handsome boy, tall and lean, with long straight hair shaped in a pageboy cut. He wore a bright red sweater and wine coloured cord slacks, and the mere fact of his presence in the room gave it a touch of vividness which formerly it had lacked.

Waterman grunted and said, almost slyly, 'It took you one hour and thirty-five minutes. I was beginning to think that maybe you had run out on us.'

'I'm a stranger to the town,' the boy said slowly. 'I had to be careful. The Guards are out in force.'

'Getting in one another's way, I suppose,' Waterman said. 'Did you hear anything?'

The boy looked at Peony. 'They recognized him all right,' he said. 'The town was buzzing with his name. The house where he used to live was even pointed out to me.'

Waterman picked up a biscuit from the tray and looked at it moodily. He nibbled at it, and the crumbs fell like dust onto the front of his black reefer jacket. He said, 'I've got to make a phone call. We're not safe here but we can't move until it gets dark.' He seemed to be thinking aloud rather than talking to the others. He got up and began to prowl about the room.

'What time is it?' Peony said, and his question plainly exasperated Waterman, for he threw the half-eaten biscuit into the fireplace and said roughly, 'It's about twelve. Why?' he added, 'Are you thinking of going somewhere?'

'It gets dark very late at this time of year,' the boy said. 'Why can't we move now?'

'And risk being seen with Father Christmas here?' Waterman

stamped back to the table. 'They'll be coming up asking for his autograph. What do you suggest we do? Disguise him as a parcel of dynamite or as a Thompson sub-machine gun?'

As if reminded of something he went over to the boy's anorak, which was hanging on the back of a chair, and took the gun out and brought it back to the table. He handled it as carefully as a lover might handle his beloved. He put it on the table and stood regarding it. It was a large blue-black revolver, and the sun coming through the window glinted off it in brittle striations of reflected light. It brought a chill to the room, and Peony especially felt a quiver in his mind as he looked at it. He thought again of how they had walked the early morning streets of the city looking for a car. Waterman had been most careful in his choice, and he had finally settled on a Rover 2000, big and powerful and almost new. He had spent an agonising half hour sawing through the steel lock which ran from the steering wheel to the clutch pedal, and to Peony the minutes had crawled by like hours, while the slow stain of dawn brightened the sky in the east, and the drops of sweat from Waterman's face seemed to incapsulate time itself and to measure it out as sparingly as they fell from his brow.

At one stage a decrepit old man had come shuffling down the opposite side of the street rummaging in the dustbins which lined the fronts of the houses like battered sentries. His passage had been marked by a flock of ululating seagulls, the large dirty looking birds wheeling about his head and conveying a vague sense of threat. Waterman had slowly raised his head and watched the approach of the old man, and it was then that he had given the boy the gun. The tramp had stopped opposite them and had turned his toothless collapsed old face in their direction, but his interests lay elsewhere and he had soon moved on. For a long time afterwards Peony had wondered if the boy would in fact have used the gun. Now once more, as he looked at the gun resting on the table, he gazed at the boy and wondered.

There was a silence in the room, until Waterman suddenly said, 'I've got to go out for a while. There's no phone in the house. I shouldn't be gone for more than half an hour.' He walked to the door. 'You'd better be good,' he said threateningly over his shoulder, like a father admonishing his recalcitrant children, and then he was gone and the strings of onions moved once more in the draught from the slowly closing door.

Peony went back to his former position by the window, and when he looked up the boy was gazing expressionlessly at him, his eyes close and guarded and giving nothing away. 'Have some tea,' Peony said as if filling in the awkward pause which sometimes occurs after a guest has arrived and the conventional words of greeting have been said. 'It may be gone cold by now but it will probably be awhile before we get some more. The lady of the house is rather sparing with her hospitality.' He was talking simply to keep silence at bay, and the aimlessness of his words did nothing to break the sense of unease between them.

'You've been here before?' the boy said to show that he, too, was willing to pretend that their relationship was a casual one. 'I've never been in a farmhouse before. It smells funny.'

'Perhaps they keep animals in the cellar. I once knew a farmer who lived in a one roomed shack, and he brought the animals in to keep him warm during the winter. Can you imagine that?'

'No.' The boy moved to the table, but he did not sit down. He carefully avoided looking at the gun. He said, 'The tea has gone cold all right. If you want more maybe I can go and get you some.'

'Then you'd have to leave me alone, wouldn't you? I might not be here when you come back.'

'It wouldn't matter.'

'No, I suppose it wouldn't.' Peony looked up at the boy. 'Waterman would like to kill me, you know,' he said. 'He's probably outside the door now hoping that I'll try to break out. He regards killing as a vocation.'

'What do you expect me to do?' The boy spread his hands as if to show Peony that they were clean. 'We all live by the same set of rules. You must have known what you were getting yourself into. Tomorrow it may be my turn. How can you expect me to sympathise with you?'

'How indeed. I just thought you might care a little. You're very young.'

'What has that got to do with it? There are ten year olds up there throwing rocks and carrying rifles. Some of them have lived longer than their own fathers.'

'When I was ten I played with toy guns.'

'That's why you're so soft. No one will ever lean on us. I'll never take any rubbish from any man, as long as I live.'

'Perhaps you won't live very long.'

'There are always some who will survive, and those who die will be remembered. It's a fact of life.'

Peony shook his head. He said, 'A man can't live by hate alone. Something else is needed. Otherwise what will one do when the cause of the hatred is taken away?'

The boy looked at him almost patronizingly. 'One doesn't have to search for something to hate,' he said. 'There is evil and corruption everywhere. It's easy to make promises, but it's even easier to break them. The politicians talk of compromise, and the churchmen talk of loving one's neighbour. What happens when people don't wish to be loved? Or when compromise has to be all on one side? There's a limit to the extent that even a coward will allow himself to be pushed.'

'Yes, I suppose the issue is as simple as that, really. But so many people see so many alternatives. I think that nowadays there is a move away from simplicity, everything has to be clothed in pretence and justification. I envy you your certainty.'

'I know what I want, if that's what you mean. And I know that in this case there's only one way to get it. It has happened before. We're not the first, or the last. No one was born to be another man's door-mat.'

'But so many people seem not to care.'

'It only needs one. Once he gets up and says no, the rest will follow.'

'That's the kind of thinking that explains the emergence of a Mussolini or a Hitler.' Peony could not restrain an expression of tired despair. 'Who then is responsible for the tragedy that follows?' he said. 'It's usually the innocent who must pay the price.'

'No one is innocent,' the boy said. 'Even the weak make demands on the strong. They wish to be protected, they wish to be told that when darkness falls it will hide no terrors for them. You can't stand by and allow a bonfire to be lit, and then expect no accidents to happen. Everyone is to blame, and everyone must suffer.'

'And is there no place for love?' Peony said, almost tentatively.

'I've had sex,' the boy said brusquely. 'I'm not a virgin.' But for the first time he blushed and looked his age.

'I didn't mean that. I mean the emotion that is the opposite to hatred. I mean softness and warmth, and perhaps a realization of the beauty that really does exist in spite of all. I'm talking about companionship and laughter, I'm talking about the sort of wisdom that philosophers speak of, I'm—'

'Philosophers,' the boy said, interrupting him. 'I don't know what you're talking about. War should not be philosophized over, it should be fought, and fought well.' He was angry now, and he glared at Peony as he said, 'You talk too much. Why did you join the Organisation? I think Waterman is right about you: you're not to be trusted. You're not a fighter, you're a bloody poet.'

'Let me tell you something,' Peony said. 'There was a time when I thought and acted like you. When people spoke to me of the tragedy that was taking place up there, I asked them what tragedy they were talking about. I told them: Tragedy, it's no tragedy. What went before was tragic, now we're fighting back and it's a revolution. I recalled other instances to their minds, I talked about Algiers and Greece; I even quoted Marx at them. And I believed in what I was saying. I told them that man needed revolution, that it was in his blood. I put our own situation in its historical perspective; I cited names, dates and places. Gunmen like Waterman couldn't damp my enthusiasm, my idealism; they were merely instruments in the almighty good that was going to come out of all this.

'Then one day I had to cross the border to do a job. I had to assassinate someone, but I missed and killed a child. But let me tell you something else: it wasn't the death of the child that bothered me, it was the fact that I had missed the person that I was supposed to kill. Can you imagine that! I had taken one life, but I wasn't satisfied, I needed more. That night I made excuses to my friends in the Organisation, and they sympathized with me and told me better luck next time. No one mentioned the child. Do you accept that kind of outlook?'

Peony had not raised his head while he spoke, but he now looked up at the boy and said, 'You'll find little things like that coming along which will refuse to bolster up your idealism and your sense of justice. You asked me why I joined the Organisation. I'll tell you: I joined because a friend of mine whom I had a great regard for asked me to join. It was a question of identity, you see. I wanted to prove to myself that I was real, that I was a leader rather than a follower, and that life would not pass me by like an idle wind. Now I find that my dream has let me down, and I don't know why. I don't know why I allowed that man to wrest the gun away from me this morning, why I allowed him to tear the mask off my face. He was so close to me that I can still smell his after-shave lotion, can still see the minute veins radiating out from his nose like pencil lead under the skin. I could easily have knocked him down; I could have shot him; I could have done a hundred things, and I did nothing. I can't explain it to myself. How then can I possibly explain it to you, or to Waterman, or to anyone else for that matter? For some reason I didn't want to be there any more, I didn't want to be part of anything.'

When Peony stopped talking the boy was quiet for a moment, then he said doubtfully, 'Maybe you've just lost your nerve. If you were to go away for a while. . . .'

'It would have to be for a very long time.' Peony dredged up a smile like a rictus of pain. 'Some sicknesses take more than a lifetime to cure.'

Somewhere in the house a clock chimed, one single stroke which trembled in the still air and faded lingeringly like a note of music. I'm tired listening to you,' the boy said sullenly. 'You talk like an old man.'

'I'm twenty-eight years old,' Peony said. 'I have no wife, no children. I'm a victim of a certain set of circumstances which I drifted into like a piece of paper sailing aimlessly down a stream. I made a choice, and then my freedom of choice was taken away from me. I'm just trying to tell you that a time may come when you'll find yourself in the same situation as myself.'

'No,' the boy said. 'I did not have to join the Organisation, I was born into it. I come from a Republican family. My father died in gaol in 1958. All of my relatives suffered at some time or other for their country. You and I have nothing in common. You're only an outsider looking in.'

'Do you think that makes your position any better than mine?' Peony shook his head. 'You're a victim, just the same as me. There's no greatness, no glory. It's merely another dirty job, and it's not in any way heroic.'

'Who wants it to be heroic?' the boy cried. 'It's there, it has to be done. Isn't that reason enough?'

'You beg a lot of questions,' Peony said. His head drooped as if it were too heavy for his body. 'I'm tired,' he went on. 'I don't think I've ever been as tired before in my life.'

The boy stood up and leaned on the table. For the first time he looked at the gun. 'You disgust me,' he said. 'You can't take anything away from me, or give me anything. You've nothing to give to anyone.'

Behind them the door opened, and Waterman came in quietly and almost respectfully. He stopped for a moment as if sensing the tension in the room, then he said to the boy, 'What's he been saying to you?' and the solicitude in his voice was almost paternalistic. He looked from one to the other of them, but no one spoke.

After a moment Peony got up from where he was sitting on the floor, and, slowly and carefully, he began to advance towards the table. There was no particular expression on his face as he lifted the heavy tray and swung it at Waterman's head. The clang as it struck reverberated round the room, and Waterman stumbled and then fell over on his back. Dazedly he lifted his head and looked at Peony. There was a vivid red mark running the whole length of his face, from his right temple down to his chin. He transferred his gaze to the boy. 'Kill him,' he said viciously. 'Kill him now.'

Peony looked at the boy. 'I don't even know your name,' he said wonderingly. Behind him the sun suddenly found a gap in the tree, and it lit up the window in a blaze of brilliance. He turned towards the light, and the boy lifted the gun and, holding it in both hands, he shot Peony just behind the left ear. The blast blew away most of the side of his head, and bright drops of blood flickered through the reflected light like multicoloured rain.

Waterman got up off the floor and watched as the boy let the gun fall from his hands. There was blood in the boy's hair, and his face was stark white and covered in a glaze of sweat. Yet he looked more surprised than sick.

'You had to do it,' Waterman said, but the boy gave no sign that he had heard him. Carefully, almost in slow motion, he backed away and then turned and went out the door.

Waterman picked up the gun from the floor. There was a thin snake of smoke curling from the barrel, and the smell of cordite lay heavy in the room. Still carrying the gun he went towards the window and knelt down on one knee beside the body. He began to whisper an Act of Contrition into Peony's good ear, and all around him the light moved in shifting billows of colour.

# Incident

## J. J. COUGHLAN

623 POLSON dodged quickly behind the corner of the alley. Clang! went the steel bolt as it struck the sheet of galvanized iron in the roadway—the last remnant of the demolished street barricade which the sappers had removed in the morning. 'Bastard!' he croaked.

McDaid dived back into the cover of another alley one hundred yards further up the street on the fringes of the 'Warren'. 'Fuck it,' he grumbled to his five companions, 'missed the bastard.'

623 Polson was nineteen and McDaid was just seventeen.

Sergeant Williams slithered up behind Gunner Polson in his size thirteen brothel creepers. 'How many yobs up there, Polly?' he asked. 'I think there's four or five, Sarge,' replied the Gunner. 'Right then, Polly,' said the Sergeant, 'I want you to stay here and keep an eye on them. If you think they're going to make a rush, yell—O.K.?' ... 'Right Sarge,' said Gunner Polson. 'Come on lads,' shouted the Sergeant to the rest of the section. 'Up to top of street—that's where they'll have a go.'

623 Polson sneaked another look around the corner of the street and staggered back as a lump of concrete flashed by his face, clanging on the metal sheet. 'Fuck this for a lark,' he thought.

McDaid ducked back into his alley. 'Missed the bastard again,' he muttered.

Gunner Polson decided to risk a smoke—he could always hear the bleeders coming—they always cheered when they advanced—give him time to shout for the rest of the section—if the worst came to the worst there was always the S.L.R.—he snickered, 'that'll be the day.'

Bloody hell—how long more are these bloody Paddies goin' to keep this up? Two flamin' hours they'd been stuck here like a lot of spare pricks at a weddin'—he hadn't joined the army for this—never mind the bleedin' C.O. bummin' his chat on the telly to the reporter—they'd laughed like a lot of sick parrots in that lousy bloody billet of theirs the other evenin' when they were watchin' Joe Egg bein' interviewed ... 'this is just another facet of the job as far

213

as my chaps are concerned' . . . then Dusty Miller had thrown his
boot at the set and just missed the bleedin' thing. The lance jack
was goin' to stick him on a fizzer and all for it—but Dusty bloody
told him right out . . . 'listen Bom., we're airborne gunners—
specialists—not bleedin' riot police—it took them a lot of money to
train us—more even than it takes to train them Para Regiment
berks—we should be back in Sennelager doin' more practice jumps
with the 105's instead of pissin' around here lettin' a lot of gobshites
throw stones at us' . . . the rest of the Troop had backed up Dusty
and the lance jack had backed down—bit of a barrack-room lawyer
was old Dusty—but he was right and the lance jack knew it.

He pulled the IMCO lighter out of his pocket—only another five
hundred coupons and he could send away for that Kodak
'Instamatic 33' in the catalogue—he looked at the lighter. . . .
Blimey! the day he bought that—that time they were on border
patrol they'd stopped by the bridge for 'five' and he'd nipped across
the river to that little shop for twenty fags—the shopkeeper'd looked
at him queer like but he'd served him—then he saw the lighter—
only six bob . . . 'Give us that lighter too mister and a tube of petrol'
. . . then he'd run out right onto the big flat feet of the blue-uniformed
Paddy scuffer . . . 'Sorry skin,' he'd said and run like bleedin' hell
back to the patrol—he'd been wettin' himself all that day in case the
bobby'd reported him to the Irish authorities and they'd gone
moanin' to the C.O. about him—all the other lads in the Land-
Rover'd know it was him and Chalky White the Bombardier'd have
shopped him—he was that shit scared of losin' his tapes. But the
Paddy must have been a decent spud for a copper—he'd heard
nothin' about it. He sucked hungrily at the cigarette—didn't taste
as good on an empty belly—no soddin' dinner again today. 'Bastard!'

Two Saracens crammed with infantry rumbled by behind them—
he turned at their shouted obscenities, he gave them the 'up yer
pipe Jack' sign and yelled, 'Get some slipstream up yer arses,' that
always annoyed the bloody land army, that did. He risked another
look up into the 'Warren'—perhaps the Paddies'd gone home for
tea.

'Hi!' yelled McDaid at the other youths. 'Where yiz goin'?' . . .
'Och we're away for oor tay, Shewie,' shouted Kelly, 'it's time.'
'Come back, yiz wankers,' screamed McDaid . . . 'We're starvin','
complained Kelly, 'we'll be back after.' They trooped off into
the maze. McDaid bent down and picked up three of the fist-
sized stones they had dropped behind them—nothin' but a pack of
mobsters—they can't see any loot in the day's work an' they're away
home. He stepped into the street again and pegged three stones in
rapid succession at the corner behind which the soldier was lurking.
'Fuck ye, ye red-bereted bastard,' and retreated once more. He

sagged his small skinny frame against the rough brick wall of the alleyway, a look of blank despair on his narrow face—they were gettin' no place with this—nearly two years of it now—peggin' the same stones at the same people at the same times on the same days with the same results—if only he could get hold of a gun—like that one of Gerry McLaughlin's—the Thompson—what would he give to have one of them. . . . He'd run down that street and he'd riddle that British pig from his toenails to his murderer's beret—he'd frighten the rest of them murderin' bastards that much they'd run screamin' to the polis barracks like the cowards they were and never come out to kill the people anymore . . . but McLaughlin was lifted by the polis and the army and no one knew where he'd hid his gun—the polis had searched his house but they'd found nothin' . . . McLaughlin was wild brainy . . . but what use was it being wild brainy if he was up in Crumlin Road and the buckin' gun lyin' in hide someplace. He smiled when he thought of big Gerry—he was a case, always actin' the candy man . . . that night in Brolly's, the night he was elephants he'd had them all laughin' themselves sore about Father Brady . . .'Any damage I'm goin' to do,' he'd said, takin' them big gulps of stout an' smackin' his lips, 'is on the head of Father Brady.' Holy Jesus! . . . that's what he meant surely . . . he'd stuck the gun on the top of Father Brady's confession box—why else would he say that—Father Brady wasn't one of the boys—like the rest of the clergy he was always givin' out about them from the altar —he even gave Willy Devlin a wild skite across the face last year for throwin' a stone at Burns's windy—and Burns was a black-as-your-boot Orange bastard. He must have stuck the gun on the confessional in case he was lifted—Gerry was wild clever so he was— McDaid took to his heels and disappeared into the 'Warren'.

623 Polson yawned . . . blimey he was knackered . . . ten bloody hours' sleep in two days an' all this fartin' around . . . should never have joined the bleedin' army . . . the oul feller was right—he'd been a field gunner in the last lot—went all through Africa he did—lost three fingers off his right hand and a cob of his jaw too in the Mareth Line—spoke funny an' all after it—like one of them impressionists doin' a bloke with an impediment—poor oul bugger . . . wanted him to go to night school and study for them 'O' levels for that clerk's job in the Civil Service—balls to that—pen pushin' all his life— anyway his English was lousy . . . he'd always fancied the gunners, especially the paras—the jump money gave him nearly twenty-five nicker a week and he liked the proper soldierin'—but this bleedin' caper—bastard!

McDaid genuflected hastily and knelt in the pew. He dropped the holdall on the kneeler beside him—making a rapid sign of the cross he cupped his hands over his face and peered between his fingers in the direction of Father Brady's box—only oul Mary Logue was there waitin' for her turn to go in an' tell her weekly . . . 'two wee lies an' a wee curse only Father' . . . lyin' oul bastard . . . would she tell him all the times she'd slagged the neighbours . . . hypocrite like the buckin' rest of them—she'd gone in. He got quickly to his feet and barked his ankle against the wooden edge of the kneeler, 'Fu. . . .' He squeezed out of the bench and tiptoed past the altar—no need to genuflect now—the chapel was empty—oul Mary was in tellin' lies and the last penitent had just blessed herself at the font and had banged the side door on her way out—he was at the side of the box now—no need to worry about makin' noise, oul Mary was chitterin' away there twenty to the dozen—like one of them politicians—all talk an' no feelin'. He groped around on the top of the box behind the ornamental wooden carvings which embellished the roof of the confessional. . . . Buck it! . . . there was nothin' . . . an' he thought oul Gerry had some . . . ah . . . what was that . . . his middle finger had touched the loop of a piece of string—Gerry was a big feller— he nursed the tip of his finger round it and pulled—it was heavy an' big—it was comin', he could see it pokin' over the edge—it was a big paper parcel fastened with string—it must be the gun—he tugged until it overbalanced and he caught it in both hands as he would catch a wee baby falling out of its cot . . . this was it alright—he shoved the package into his holdall and slipped quietly out through the side door. He was just like big Gerry now—he was an I.R.A. man.

623 Polson yawned again and belched loudly, his stomach rumbled angrily—he looked at his watch—two and a half bleedin' hours now —Christ! Blimey, even the Paddies had to eat and sleep sometimes— the Sarge said they were crafty bleeders—did it on a rota basis to tire the lads out and crack their morale—Communist tactics. This tour in Northern Ireland wasn't doin' any of them any good, he was down to twelve stone and he couldn't grub proper either—eat it alright but it never tasted—must be all the smokin' on an empty gut . . . all the lads were doin' their tank about no sleep—it was like a dirty joke now—any berk mentioned sleep they all sniggered—what's that? . . . bleedin' officers weren't much cop either—up in the big barracks gettin pissed up every night and shaftin' them judies . . . bleedin' lousy country—no bugger wanted anythin' to do with them —the bleedin' Fenians spat at them and called them all the effin' pigs under the sun and the other Paddies weren't much better— always criticisin'—even the scuffers were a shower of gets—nice enough to your face but they'd nick you first chance they got for drunk drivin' or somethin'—they weren't so bleedin' friendly then— bastards. He sang the words of the song softly to himself. 'I'll sing you a song that's not very long—all coppers are bastards.' What

was it the Sarge called the Paddies—welly wearers—he started to chuckle . . . they never wore them here though—must be in England —true enough he'd seen the Wimpey chaps—they all wore wellies and they were all Paddies . . . blimey, that was a good un. . . . Pity about Mick McBride gettin' D.B. . . . he was the layer in two section from somewhere in Ireland—couple of the lads effed and blinded him because they got fourpenny ones with bricks—poor old Mick went on the piss and belted the T.S.M. and was doin' 112 days in Colchester—bastards. He put his hand in the side pocket of his Denison smock and pulled out his dog-end—fifth fag in an hour— his eyes were very gummy from lack of sleep.

McDaid arrived back in his alley—he was winded after the run— he had to take the long way around in case the boys wanted to know what he was doin' with the bag—they might think it was jelly an' want some—they might look in it an' pinch the gun themselves. He put down the holdall and lifted out the parcel—he fiddled with the knots but they baffled him—big Gerry used to go to sea—he lost patience and pulled madly at them till they broke—he cut his thumb. His hands shook uncontrollably as he unravelled the paper—what if it was jelly after all. . . . Boys a dear . . . it was the Thompson . . . oh you're a lovely wee thing . . . he caressed his small hands along the cold blued steel—McLaughlin had looked after her well . . . but how the buckin' hell did it work? He turned the heavy weapon over on its underside . . . there was a magazine still in the paper but where did you put it . . . that square hole there in front of the wooden handle— he pushed the magazine in . . . wrong end buck it . . . try the other— it went in and clicked . . . aah . . . now how did you cock it . . . there must be a knob or a handle someplace on it . . . there was a lot of yokes on it . . . which buckin' one? . . . try this—he pulled—it yielded and came back under pressure . . . another clickin' sort of noise—he was red up. He was an armed I.R.A. volunteer now—he held the weapon like he had seen Elliott Ness holding his in the *Untouchables*—an Irish hero at last.

623 Polson nearly nodded off on his feet—he jerked himself awake again—blimey—there'd be bleedin' murder if they caught him havin' a kip . . . he was starvin' an' all, he knew he wouldn't enjoy the rotten bleedin' grub anyway but it'd take that pain away . . . then maybe a couple of hours with his bracket down—please God. . . . The last time he'd prayed was for his mam to take him to New Brighton on August Bank Holiday when he was nine—when were they goin' to get relieved.

McDaid walked out of the alley and moved up the street.

623 Polson put his hand in his pocket—have another smoke— better have a shufti round the corner first—see if the yobs were

behavin' themselves—Jesus! there's a bleedin' nipper comin' up the middle of the road with a bondook . . . 'Sarge!'

'Steady lads,' shouted Sergeant Williams,' here they come now—Jones—Turpin—Smith—baton rounds—Now!' Christ, they don't half make a bloody racket.

'Sarge! Sarge! there's one with a gun—Sarge!' 623 Polson gripped his S.L.R. tightly.

McDaid heard the shouts—to him they were screams of fear—now see what that English bastard would do now that he was facing another armed man—what if he surrendered—should he kill him or take him prisoner and kick his arse right up the 'Warren' with his hands up—that'd show them Shewie McDaid was somebody after all—no—he'd shoot the bastard an' take his gun—he was halfway up the street.

623 Polson charged the S.L.R.—he didn't fumble and his movements were slick and purposeful—but his stomach was goin' mad—that kid wanted to kill him—why?

McDaid brought the Thompson up—his finger searching for the trigger—there . . . just squeeze it an' wave it like a fireman—he'd put the whole magazine into the dirty British pig.

623 Polson made his mind up—no use standin' here like a prick waitin' to get killed—go out in the street an' face him—the little bugger'd probably turn around and piss off into the 'Warren'—his throat was like rough concrete.

'Ye cunt ye,' screamed McDaid and pulled the trigger—every round in the magazine flew away harmlessly into the air and over the rooftops behind 623 Polson.

Gunner Polson stood in the centre of the street like a pig stunned by the slaughterman's hammer—the little bastard had opened up on him—he blinked his eyes—there was no pain and he wasn't on the deck yelling blue bloody murder either—he was standing on his own two booted feet with the S.L.R. pointing at the kid, a skinny pimply-faced get of sixteen—couldn't be more than eight stone—like that Charles Atlas advert of the geezer on the beach—before . . . but this little bleeder was starin' at him like a bloody lunatic an' he was goin' to have another go—he was levelling the Tommy at him again.

McDaid tugged madly at the trigger—nothing.

623 Polson fired the S.L.R. once—McDaid bounced across the street and hit the wall, he was still on his feet but his left kidney and half his stomach were shredded—Gunner Polson fired a second time . . . the kid was standin' there skrikin' . . . the bullet struck McDaid in the face and plastered the back of his head over the red brick behind him—it put a deep hole in the wall as well. 623 Polson started to dry retch, the pain of the spasms winded him and his inflamed eyes were scalded with tears.

As a direct result of the incident there was an outbreak of vicious street fighting on the perimeter of the 'Warren'—it lasted for two days and three nights until the combatants on both sides had exhausted themselves—one soldier and three rioters were shot dead and a further eleven soldiers and thirteen civilians were injured.

# Acknowledgements

FOR PERMISSION to reprint stories in this anthology, the following acknowledgements are due:

To the author and MacGibbon and Kee Ltd for *The Lake* by Patrick Boyle.

To the Executors of Daniel Corkery for *The Ember* by Daniel Corkery.

To the author and Constable and Co for *The Patriot Son* by Mary Lavin.

To the author and Faber and Faber Ltd for *An Aspect of the Rising* by Tom MacIntyre.

To the author and Jonathan Cape Ltd for *Pigeons* by Michael McLaverty.

To the author and MacGibbon and Kee Ltd for *The Cry* by John Montague.

To the author and Jonathan Cape Ltd for *The Mountain Tavern* by Liam O'Flaherty from 'The Short Stories of Liam O'Flaherty'.

To Sidgwick & Jackson Ltd for *Tolerance* by Jim Phelan from 'Bog Blossom Stories'.

To the author and Macmillan & Co for *The Kings Asleep in the Ground* by Bryan MacMahon

To the author and Jonathan Cape Ltd for *The Patriot* by Sean O'Faolain.

*Guests of the Nation* by Frank O'Connor from 'Stories of Frank O'Connor' (Hamish Hamilton Ltd) and *The Scoop* by James